THE NURSE

VALERIE KEOGH

Boldwood

First published in Great Britain in 2023 by Boldwood Books Ltd.

Copyright © Valerie Keogh, 2023

Cover Design by Head Design Ltd

Cover Photography: Shutterstock

Every effort has been made to obtain the necessary permissions with reference to copyright material, both illustrative and quoted. We apologise for any omissions in this respect and will be pleased to make the appropriate acknowledgements in any future edition.

A CIP catalogue record for this book is available from the British Library.

Paperback ISBN 978-1-80415-483-0

Large Print ISBN 978-1-80415-482-3

Hardback ISBN 978-1-80415-481-6

Ebook ISBN 978-1-80415-484-7

Kindle ISBN 978-1-80415-485-4

Audio CD ISBN 978-1-80415-476-2

MP3 CD ISBN 978-1-80415-477-9

Digital audio download ISBN 978-1-80415-478-6

Boldwood Books Ltd
23 Bowerdean Street
London SW6 3TN
www.boldwoodbooks.com

For Robert and Wendy with love.

PART I

1

I was ten when I made the decision to kill Jemma.

Her family – parents and an older sister – had moved from London to our small country village six months before. The first morning, Jemma had waltzed into our class completely unfazed by the wide eyes and audible whispers that followed her progress like sunflowers to her sun.

Our teacher, Miss Dryden, a tall willowy woman with steel grey hair and watery blue eyes, held a hand lightly on her shoulder and introduced her. 'I know you'll all be delighted to welcome Jemma to the class and help her to settle in.'

She was the first new girl to have joined our primary school class and she brought with her an air of city sophistication that easily dazzled us. Her clothes, hair, shoes, even her schoolbag were all a little bit exotic. To us girls who desperately wanted to grow up, she appeared to have reached heights we only aspired to.

It wasn't long before she became the girl everyone wanted to be friends with, not long before I, and others like me, discovered that the girls who surrounded her were arranged in a distinct hierarchy. There were the best friends, limited to four; a larger circle of girls who were allowed to join in the chat on occasion; a wider group who were allowed to peer in; and then a final group who were deemed unworthy of any access. For an individual or group to prevail, there needed, after all, to be another for them to lord it over. A group they could all be superior to.

I was in this latter group. I don't know why. Perhaps the pairing of the slight frame I'd inherited from my mother, with the overlarge nose and mouth inherited from my father, didn't present a beguiling appearance. Perhaps that was all it took... to look different.

Despite my appearance, school had been a happy place for me before her arrival. Inclusion was taken for granted. When it began to fade away, I was confused and bewildered.

The name calling started first, a mere week after Jemma's arrival. At first, I didn't understand, didn't know they were referring to me, when I heard one or more of her inner circle shouting *watch out here comes Jaws,* or, *have you been telling lies again, Pinocchio.* Each time they would fall around themselves with laughter, as if the sobriquets were amusing rather than mean... and painful... and confusing.

I wasn't the only victim. There were four other members of my unpopular group who received an equal share of this new unwanted attention. If only we marginalised group of five had gathered together, if we'd found strength in our common woes and learnt to fight back, but that never happened. Perhaps we were afraid of confrontation, or was it that we regarded each other with as much disdain as Jemma and her cohorts did. Whatever the reason, we stayed individually isolated in our roles as victim.

Over the following months, the bullies seemed to grow taller and bigger. I was the perfect victim, smaller and thinner than my tormentors, too easy to push around. They took more delight in their 'fun' with every passing day. When I didn't react, they'd close in, jostling me, grabbing my schoolbag, plucking at the sleeve of my coat.

That day, I didn't see whose hand had sent me flying. When I turned to challenge the act, I knew it was useless, so I picked myself up and walked away as quickly as I could. The stinging damage to my hands and knees brought tears to my eyes, but I refused to let them fall till I was a street away. On my own, over-whelmed by confusion, sadness, and frustration, one heaving sob started a free-for-all. I was barely able to see as I walked the short distance to my home.

My knees were skinned, the palms of both hands scratched and bloody. The band that kept my long thin hair back from my face had been lost. Tangled strands fell forward, catching in my tears and the bubble of snot that vibrated from one nostril with every pathetic hiccupping cry.

The back door was open, and I saw my apron-clad mother busily stirring something on the hob. 'Hi,' she said, without looking around, my noisy sobs lost in whatever was bubbling in the pot. It was silence that made her turn, one finely plucked eyebrow arching higher in a question she didn't need to ask when her eyes took in my dishevelled appearance.

She dropped the wooden spoon on the counter with a clatter that sent beads of sauce flying in a messy circle. Then I was in her arms and clasped to a bosom almost as flat as my own. 'Lissa! What happened?'

'One of the girls pushed me.'

Through my tears and pain, I saw my mother's horrified face and head shake of disbelief. 'No, darling, I'm sure it was an acci-dent.' She bathed my wounds as she muttered reassuring words, convincing herself, not me, that her version of my story was correct.

There was so much pain in her eyes that I couldn't help it, I relented. 'I remember now, I tripped and fell.'

I was rewarded by a warm comforting hug, by the relief on her face that she didn't have to confront something nasty, cruel and mean.

Young as I was, I knew she was emotionally fragile. If her world didn't run on happy lines, she'd retreat into herself, hiding away until the wave of whatever outrage had occurred, had receded. Once it had, she'd be back, full of loving smiles, ready to be the best mother a lonely, sad goblin of a child could want.

So it was better to lie. To keep the nastiness from seeping into our home.

Young as I was, I tried to protect her, but I couldn't stop the world turning...

2

As an only child, I was the sole focus of my parents' attention, and due to this nurturing, or perhaps my inherent nature, I was a bright child. I took delight in excelling, and before Jemma's arrival I was easily, and by a large margin, top of the class. My parents didn't hide their pride in me. 'We need to start putting money away for university,' my mother would say to my father as every monthly payday came around.

He was a big man, and tall, and he'd laugh, grab her around the waist and kiss her. If I was there, I'd try to squirm between them desperate for my share of his affection. Sometimes, if I tried hard enough, he'd swing me up in his arms and I'd hold on to the moment for as long as I could, lost in his love. Whether it was me or my mother he was hugging, he'd dismiss her concerns in the same way. 'Don't worry about that now.'

At ten, university was almost two lifetimes away. I was more concerned with what was happening the following day. Perhaps, I should have discussed my worries with my father, the name calling, pushing and shoving I was being increasingly subjected to. But when he was home, the conversation was always bright and bubbly, each of my parents outdoing each other with cheerfulness. Their mutual love spilling over and... sometimes... including me.

My father was a sales representative for a medical company. His territory covered the south-west of England including the cities of Bath and Bristol. The workload had meant he'd often had to spend a night or two away, but when the company had expanded four years before, that had changed. Now he was working away three to four nights a week and every second weekend. The absence was hard on my needy, emotionally fragile mother. If they rowed about it, if she begged him to get a different job, one that didn't entail so much time working away, I never knew. In all the years, I never remember hearing a raised voice or an unkind word. When my father was home, he was funny, charming, loving. The best, most indulgent, adoring, attentive husband. He'd take mother out for dinner; they'd go for long walks in the countryside and lunches in country pubs.

Occasionally, they'd bring me along.

Sometimes, I'd arrive home from school feeling incredibly sad, and they'd be in their bedroom with the door locked and I'd have to wait till they came out hours later. If I was feeling particularly sad, I'd sit on the floor outside their room, press my ear to the door and listen to their sounds of love – the laughter, whispers, grunts and groans – and I'd feel less lonely, less sad. Once, or maybe it was twice or three times, they didn't come out at all. I'd make myself some jam sandwiches for my tea, and watch TV with the volume turned way down so as not to disturb them.

My father didn't like it if I did.

When he was home, Mother would wear her best jewellery and prettiest clothes. Her hair would be washed every morning, make-up carefully applied and reapplied at intervals during the day. She dazzled: her eyes sparkled, her laugh was more joyous, her voice sweeter and she danced... around the kitchen as she cooked, in the garden as she pegged out clothes, with my father, with me, without either of us. To see her was to make you smile and your heart feel full.

When he went away again, she'd be distraught for a full day. Every time. She'd mope around the house dragging heavy feet along the floor. She'd refuse to eat or to cook anything for me, so I'd scavenge from the fridge eating the leftovers of the glut of food she'd cooked for him, or I'd slather butter onto stale bread and spoon jam on top. If she spoke to me at all, it was in dull monosyllables.

The following morning, she'd have pulled herself together and she'd spend the next couple of days until my father returned making it up to me. She'd indulge my every request, gather me to her for long cuddles that smothered and were of more benefit to her than me. She'd talk to me then. Long conversations about how she was feeling. Often, her remarks were prefaced with, 'You're too young to understand but...'

She didn't like to stay up late on her own, nor did she like to go to bed early. So those nights when my father was away, I'd stay up late to keep her company. If I fell asleep, she'd pinch my arm to wake me. The following day, or the days after, I would explain away the dark bruises that decorated my pale arms. 'I fell against the door handle...' Or the shelf, or the wall, whichever suited, depending on who asked. In school, seeing my marked arms, my tormentors added a new name... Pongo.

I wanted to correct them when I heard it, wanted to say it should have been Perdita, the mother of the *101 Dalmatians*, not Pongo, the father. I didn't of course, bizarrely relieved they'd chosen either of the heroic parents rather than the villainous Cruella.

Despite the bruises, and the days when I was so tired I struggled to keep my eyes open, those days with my mother were precious. They ended with my father's return, when he and she would form an almost exclusionary bubble and I'd be on the outside looking in, grateful for any teeny tiny bit of attention. Then he'd be gone again and there'd be that one horrendously long day of neglect, before more days of me and Mother.

Endless cycles of neglect when I'd be confused, sad, often achingly lonely, and cycles of indulgence when I'd almost be convinced my parents loved me.

Almost...

3

The day I decided I needed to kill Jemma, my father was away, and I was in the indulgence phase of my mother's care. After dinner we sat together on the sofa, my head resting against her shoulder, one of my hands clasped in hers.

In this phase of the cycle, my mother often listened to me, and I could voice my concerns without fear of them being dismissed. Only some of them: the bogeyman under the bed, the giant outside my bedroom window, the dragon in the wardrobe. I didn't bring up ones that might upset her: the constant bullying, my fear of not only being unloved but of being unlovable.

I waited till *Coronation Street* finished before turning to her. 'Am I ugly?'

She took her time, tilting her head while she looked at my face. It was the worry that my classmates were correct in their assessment of me that had forced the question. It was hanging between me and my mother, waiting to be dispelled by her as other fears had been in the past.

When her gaze lingered, the heat of her eyes boring through my meagre defences and turning my anxiety to horror, I wondered if my classmates were correct, and I *was* deserving of the awful names they called me. Perhaps I was the monster from under the bed, the bogeyman from the cupboard.

Finally, her expression softened, and she reached forward with one long slim finger to caress my cheek and tap my nose. 'You get your features from your father. He's a handsome man, you'll be beautiful when you're older.'

But in this, she was wrong. The large nose, appropriate to my father's square face, wasn't suitable for my thin heart-shaped one, and whereas the proportions improved as the years passed, my mouth remained unusually wide. Although ugly was possibly too strong a word, I was certainly closer to it than I was to its polar opposite.

* * *

Any reference to my big mouth... Jaws, Hippo, Crocodile... caused me to suck in my lower lip in a vain effort to make the aperture smaller. This too failed miserably when the lip became red and swollen. Nor did the application of ointment to cure this do me any favours.

They were careful, as bullies tended to be, and around teachers or anyone in authority their expressions were angelic butter-wouldn't-melt. They were careful, but not very clever, whereas I eventually became both. I'd inherited my short stature and slight physique from my mother, my intelligence, my craftiness, from my father.

Just how crafty he was, I didn't discover for years.

The expression *delayed gratification* was unknown to my ten-year-old self, but it perfectly encompassed my determination to wait till I was ready to put a carefully conceived plan into action. Putting up with their torment was easier when I knew a glorious end was in sight.

My plan was simple... I was going to cut off the head of the monster.

In the six months since Jemma's arrival, nobody had challenged the new status quo. The five members of that elite gang at the top were convinced they were invincible. They never expected any of us to hit back, and with all the noise they made trumpeting their superiority, they didn't hear the quiet mouse roaring from the cheap seats.

When I decided the time was right, it added to my satisfaction to adopt their means to get my end. Less than two weeks after I'd begun, I had Jemma isolated from her friends. My campaign was slow, quiet, and deliciously effective with a pointed word here, a nasty whisper there.

I sidled up to one. 'I heard Jemma call you fat, that's so unfair.' To another, I said, 'It's mean of Jemma to call you stupid.'

To yet another, 'Is it true you wet your bed sometimes?'

Her mouth fell open, then she looked around to see who was within hearing distance. 'Who told you that?'

Stupid girl, didn't she understand that by asking, she'd confirmed what I'd said? Not that I needed confirmation, I'd overheard her mother speaking to mine and had squirrelled the knowledge away for future use. 'I heard Jemma laughing about it to someone. Poor you, that's tough.'

And to the fourth member of the group, I went back to the insult that always worried girls of our age. 'I heard Jemma refer to you as the tubby one. She can be so mean, can't she?'

I saw the worry in their eyes. The words I said were bad enough, but what must have cut them to the quick was my fake expression of sympathy. How the mighty have fallen when their victim dares to pity them.

Of course, they shouldn't have listened to me. I was from the despised group, so far from the sun as to be in the dark but, catching them away from Jemma, they changed back to the girls they were before she arrived. Ordinary girls, with ordinary fears. It proved more than anything to me that Jemma had to go.

Their friendship, only wafer thin, quickly shattered under my deft whispering campaign. It was a good start to see Jemma without her satellites, to see her confused by their withdrawal. It wouldn't last though. I had no doubt she'd manage to lure them back or bring others from the outer group into her orbit. She was already showing a hint of the manipulative nasty woman she'd become. Really, the world would be better off without her, wouldn't it?

Wouldn't it?

I'd be doing the world a service if I stopped her from hurting anyone else. *As she'd hurt me.* It seemed I wasn't the forgiving sort.

There was a huge advantage to being small and slight, to being the kind of person eyes looked through as if I weren't there, nobody had any expectations or even noticed me. They didn't notice me in our local library, or comment on the hours I spent poring over books. The ones about serial killers. Looking for inspiration. Fascinating as they were to read, most of their methods were beyond me. I'd need to be cleverer. And careful. Much as I wanted to get rid of Jemma, I didn't want to pay for it by being locked away for years.

I went from books about serial killers to books on anatomy and physiology and found myself fascinated by what I read. Three books later, I knew two things... how to get rid of my nemesis and what I wanted to do when I finished school.

It seemed justice to use what had been done to me to get rid of the main instigator. Thanks to Jemma and her friends, I was considered by my teachers and my mother to be clumsy. Always tripping over my feet. My knees, and sometimes my elbows, continually scabbed.

Nobody would be surprised if I fell. It was sensible to use what I knew to put an end to being bullied and tormented.

To put an end to the vile Jemma, once and for all.

4

The concrete surface of the school playground was perfect for playing, and we passed our lunch breaks at hopscotch or skipping. I say we... but that's a lie. Girls like me were always excluded from these games. I wasn't the only one. The victims of Jemma's bullying sorority, we poor mishmash of rejects, hovered singly at the edges, looking in, never belonging.

After the success of my whispering campaign, Jemma no longer held pride of place in the middle of her group, but she hadn't dropped so low as to have joined our sad ranks.

The first part of my plan successfully completed, I needed to proceed with the second final one. With the certainty of my ten years, I never considered anything would go wrong.

The six-foot railing surrounding the playground was effective at keeping us curtailed within its boundaries, but its design allowed us to look out and others to look in. On the far side, a low, densely planted shrubbery lay between it and the footpath. The bushes were a magnet for rubbish blown along the street, and a dumping ground for empty cans and bottles.

Glass bottles: easily acquired, cheap, ubiquitous. It was my weapon of choice. The day before – one of those days when my mother was desperately missing my father, and barely noticed where I was or what I was doing – I went to our local supermarket's bottle recycling bins. I wanted to choose a bottle that could have been classified as pretty... or at least pretty enough to have appealed to a child. Nobody challenged me as I rummaged through the wine and beer bottles in my search for something suitable. It didn't take long to find the ideal candidate – a gin bottle, it had a nice shape, the glass attractively ridged. It was perfect. I wrapped it in my jacket, walked the mile to the school and planted it in the shrubbery. A few branches pulled around it hid it from passers-by.

There would be no opportunity for a second chance. If my plan failed, Jemma would soon gather her satellites close, and I would have to start again from the beginning. But I had no intention of failing.

* * *

When we were released into the playground that lunchtime, I sauntered across to the railing and hung around, at the same time keeping Jemma under observation. She was with one other girl and standing not too far from me. Alone would have been better, but I couldn't delay. The following day she might have lured two into her net, the day after, three or more.

I turned to stare through the railing, then with a double-take I'd practised several times in front of the mirror, I stared at the bottle, tilting my head from side to side as I admired it. I waited for several seconds before reaching through the bars to pick it up.

I raised it, looking at it with fake admiration, holding it up to the sun and letting it be seen by anyone who may have been staring in my direction. It was also allowing myself to be caught on the CCTV that covered this part of the schoolyard. The one they'd no doubt check through later to see exactly the progress of the disaster that was going to occur any moment.

Glass wasn't allowed in the playground, and the bottle would have been taken from me had the playground monitors been doing their job. They weren't, they rarely did, both women standing on the far side, heads together, gossiping.

'Isn't this pretty?' I said to nobody in particular as I walked in Jemma's direction. My words were loud enough to catch her attention and she turned to look at me.

I smiled at her and held the bottle out when I was within a few feet of where she stood. 'Look!' I said, waving it to show her. Then, in a carefully choreographed accident, I deliberately tripped and came down heavily. The neck of the bottle hit the concrete first and shattered into several pieces around me. I lay for a few seconds, winded from the fall despite the purposeful intention of it. A broken shard lay next to me. I moved my arm along it, not too deeply, but enough for blood to bubble along its length before getting to my feet, the heavy base of the bottle with its jagged ridge still held tightly in my hand.

Blood was trickling down my injured arm. I wondered, much later, if Jemma had rushed to help me... if she'd shown even a modicum of sympathy... would I have changed my mind? I'll never know because she didn't. Instead, she pointed at me, put her head back and howled, a long exaggerated laugh as if I was the funniest thing she'd ever seen.

The blood was dripping from my arm to the dirty white concrete of the playground. My face was a picture of misery. The cut to my arm stung causing genuine tears to leak from my eyes, snot from my big nose, the corners of my too-large mouth drooping downward.

I held my bloody limb out and moved towards Jemma with a

wail of anguish that stopped her laughter. She stood her ground and didn't back away as I was worried she might. There was no sympathy on her face and when the other girl made a move to come to my aid, Jemma glared at her, stopping her in her tracks. Luckily for me. It would have wrecked my plan.

My next step was easy. I stumbled again. It was a reflex action to put a hand out to stop myself falling – the hand holding the vicious remnant of the broken bottle. Jemma was too close, and too slow. My stumble brought me even closer, taking her down with me, the glass in my hand coming down on her neck. The weight of my falling body all that was required to make the cut deep enough to do lethal damage.

We fell together in a mess of limbs, hair, and blood. I screamed as I pushed down on the smooth bottom of the bottle I held with its vicious teeth embedded in Jemma's neck. The other girl stood back, her high-pitched shriek loud enough to stop all movement within the playground. It attracted the attention of the monitors who immediately looked about, meerkat-like, to identify the source of the noise. Precious minutes wasted as blood gushed from the artery in Jemma's neck. Oddly, she never screamed. In fact, as I pushed up from her dying body, she never as much as whimpered. What she did do, was to lock her eyes on mine, and I couldn't break away, not even when I was on my feet and staring down on her. Not even when the monitors arrived to see what was going on.

The older of the two arrived first, her face squeezed into lines of irritation at having had her chinwag interrupted. 'What's g—'

I've never seen anyone's face pale as quickly as hers did. She held a hand over her mouth and turned to her slower partner who was ambling across as if she had all day. 'Call an ambulance, quick!'

My eyes were still locked on Jemma's as I watched the monitor kneel in the puddle of blood that surrounded her. If she was wondering whether to remove the glass from Jemma's neck or not, I could have told her it was already too late. I'd seen the pumping blood slow to a sluggish ooze as her heart made a pathetic useless attempt to send what remained around her body.

Only when the second monitor returned, followed by as many members of staff as her screams had alerted, was I taken away. Only then, did I break eye contact with Jemma. And suddenly I felt bereft.

'Is she going to be okay?' I asked a teacher. The tremble in my voice wasn't forced. Of course, I knew she wasn't going to be. I'd done my job well. I was ten, the age of criminal responsibility, but I suddenly realised I hadn't been old enough to know that sometimes the things we want aren't necessarily the things we should get.

I was old enough to know that Jemma's eyes would haunt me forever.

5

I was taken to the head teacher's office where a first aider, who introduced herself as Miss Jeffries, cleaned and dressed my arm. She kept a soothing monologue going as she wiped the shallow jagged wound with something cold and wet that made me wince despite her reassuring words that it wouldn't hurt a bit. 'It's only a scratch, really,' she said, 'it'll heal up easily.' She dabbed my arm with dry gauze, tore open a bandage and applied it, pressing the edges down gently. 'I hope it doesn't hurt too much. Maybe your mum can give you something when you get home if it does.'

Miss Jeffries waited with me, chatting about nothing until the door opened and my mother hurried through, eyes wide, mouth trembling. 'Lissa!' She gathered me into her arms and squeezed me painfully. I didn't complain, she needed the reassurance of holding me.

'I'm okay,' I said into her hair.

She finally released me but kept her hands on my shoulders as she stepped back, her eyes raking me, stopping when they saw the bandage. 'You're hurt.'

I had the story rehearsed in my head, but I was careful it didn't sound that way, stuttering and stumbling over the words as I spoke. 'I found a p-pretty b-bottle; I was holding it when I t-tripped and fell.' I held up my bandaged arm. 'It broke and a p-piece cut me. When I s-stood up and saw the b-blood, I felt d-dizzy. N-next thing I remember is b-being on the g-ground on t-top of Jemma.' I looked from my mother's questioning blue eyes to the face of the first aider. 'She got c-cut too. I hope she's going to be okay.'

Miss Jeffries sucked her lips in before releasing them with a wet smacking sound. 'Don't worry about that for the minute.'

To my surprise, my mother nodded. 'I'm sure she's fine.'

The tight worried expression had lifted as soon as my mother saw I was all right. She was a woman who found it impossible to dissemble; had she known about Jemma, she wouldn't have been able to hide her shock from me as I was able to hide my thoughts from her. They hadn't told her about Jemma. It was possible they were still trying to save her. I'd read enough to have been able to tell them it was a lost cause.

I hoped we'd be allowed to leave. After all, I was injured. A child. My mother should insist. The execution of my plan had taken a lot out of me. Annoyingly too, I couldn't shake off the memory of Jemma's eyes fixed on mine. But when the door opened, and the head teacher, Mrs Mangan, came in accompanied by a man I didn't know, I knew it wasn't going to be that simple to escape. My uneasiness was obvious to my mother, but I guessed she saw it as a reaction to my injury when she put her arms about me again and held me close. I would have pulled away, I wasn't a baby, but it seemed the safer place to be.

Mrs Mangan, her normally pristine appearance marred by smudged mascara, glanced around. Her eyes landed on Miss

Jeffries who, with the merest tilt of a head, was dismissed from the room.

After a lingering inspection of me, Mrs Mangan addressed my mother. 'Mrs McColl,' she said, 'this is Detective Inspector Hynes. He'd like to have a word with Lissa about what happened.'

Still wrapped in my mother's arms, I peered at the man. He didn't look remotely like any detective I'd seen during afternoons spent watching TV with my mother. She had a fondness for the older series though and it was mostly *Columbo* or *Kojak* we watched. The detective who was looking at me with sharp eyes was neither scruffily dressed nor was he sucking on a lollipop.

'Why don't we all sit down?' Mrs Mangan said, walking around the desk with quick determination and taking her seat as if she was afraid the detective would usurp her position.

My mother shepherded me to one of the two chairs on the other side of the desk, taking the one beside me without once releasing her hold. It wasn't comfortable. It did, however, allow me to hide my face in her shoulder, a position I thought might come in handy should any of the questions become difficult. Not that I expected them to. There would have been little expectation that I could murder a classmate. I was finding it hard to believe myself.

Only by reminding myself that the end... freedom from Jemma's malign influence on my classmates and from their bullying... allowed me to justify what I had done.

From the shelter of my mother's arms, I watched the detective cross to where spare chairs were stacked one on top of the other in a corner of the office. He struggled to loosen the top one, the stack rattling noisily as he eventually yanked it free. I half-expected him to swing it around, straddle the seat, and rest his arms along the back of it. It's what *Kojak* would have done.

Columbo would have stayed on his feet, shuffling, looking as if he hadn't a clue. But that was on TV, this was real life... and I don't think any of them had a clue.

Hynes drew the chair closer to where I sat. Almost within touching distance. He leaned forward, rested his elbows on his knees and fixed his eyes on what he could see of my face.

'Hi, Lissa, my name is Aaron, I'm a policeman.'

It was my mother who answered, her face knotted in anxiety as it always was when faced with things she didn't understand. 'Why are the police involved?' Her eyes flicked from the officer to the head teacher as her arms tightened painfully around me. 'Can someone please explain?'

Mrs Mangan opened and shut her mouth before looking across at the detective. His nod was almost imperceptible, hers, in return, more emphatic. 'I'm afraid' – she angled her body to face our mother and daughter tableau vivant – 'Jemma's injury was more serious. She didn't make it.'

I wasn't sure I'd be able to portray the correct expression... the confused shock that would be the natural reaction for someone of my years. I was afraid relief and a certain measure of satisfaction at a job well done might leak into my face. For safety, I turned my face away and buried it in my mother's chest. When she spoke, I could feel the echo of her words reverberating through her body. 'Didn't make it?' I could feel her shocked confusion. 'Are you saying Jemma is dead?'

'Yes, I'm afraid so.'

It seemed a good time to speak. Lifting my head, I looked first at Mrs Mangan, then at the policeman, slightly taken aback to find his eyes fixed unblinkingly on me. 'But she just fell, she just cut herself like I did.' I raised my trophy arm again. 'How can she be dead?' The words were out before I thought to stutter or stumble, and I was immediately worried I sounded too calm. To make up for it, I wiped a hand across my eyes and nose and snuffled.

Hynes sat back on his seat and laced his fingers together. 'Your friend, Marie, has told us what happened.'

I wanted to argue with him. Marie wasn't my friend. She hadn't been Jemma's either... at least not in the first circle of friendship, not until recently. I wondered what Marie had said. She'd screamed... I remembered that.

The detective spoke gently. 'We'd like you to tell us, in your own words, what happened. Is that okay?'

My mother's grip tightened. 'Is this necessary? Lissa is a child. She's been injured. She should be at home, not being inter-rogated.'

Hynes unlaced his fingers and held his hands out. 'If Lissa is feeling up to it, it's better to get her story out while it's fresh in her mind. Better for her to talk about it too.'

My story. Did that imply he thought it was going to be fabri-cated, or was I overthinking things, letting the stress get to me.

'Well, it's up to Lissa,' my mother said.

Hynes nodded. 'Is it okay with you, Lissa? To tell me what happened?'

What happened... better. I'd rehearsed this moment carefully, had practised the words I would say. It was all going to plan except for one shocking truth... I'd never really expected to do it.

'I was in the p-playground,' I said, keeping my voice to a barely audible whisper. Hynes had to lean forward again to be able to hear. 'The sun was bright, and I saw something shining in the b-bushes the other side of the railing. I was able to reach it, it was a pretty bottle.' I stopped, allowed my lower lip to tremble and gave a noisy sniff. 'We're not supposed to have glass in the playground, but it was p-pink and had...' – I lifted both my hands and wriggled my fingers as I lowered them in the air – 'lines cut into the glass. I thought I could bring it home and Mum could put flowers in it.'

'Oh, darling,' my mother said. Her voice had thickened. I knew if I looked up, I'd see tears in her eyes.

'What happened then?' The detective's voice was encouraging. I wondered how fast it would change if he knew the truth.

'I walked over to show it to Marie and Jemma.'

'They're both friends of yours, are they?'

I could have lied, said we were besties, but Mrs Mangan would know the lie.

'No, but they were the nearest to me and I wanted to show off my p-pretty p-prize.'

'Right, and what happened then?'

'I fell.' Another hesitation for a bit of lip trembling. I lifted my arm. 'The b-bottle broke and cut me. I got up, then I saw the blood on my arm, and it must have made me weak because next I knew, I was lying on top of Jemma, so I hurried to get up.' I frowned as if puzzled by what I was remembering. 'Jemma didn't, I think she must have b-banged her head or something when she fell. Marie was screaming so loud that the playground monitors came rushing over. When the teachers came out, we were taken away.' I didn't mention Jemma's eyes. I didn't want to think about them. I saw the detective frown. Was he looking through me, seeing the blackness of my soul, the rot at my core?

'When you got up, after falling the first time, why did you hold on to the end of the broken bottle?'

A question I'd anticipated. 'D-Did I?' I took a shaky breath. 'I didn't know I had, why would I do that?'

'You don't remember falling on top of your friend with the glass in your hand?'

She wasn't my friend. I wanted to shriek the words; the desire so strong that once more I turned my face into my mother's chest.

'Lissa has said she doesn't remember, Inspector,' Mrs Mangan said. 'You can't badger the child.'

My mother had gone rigid. I didn't look up to see the shock on her face. I knew it would be there as the realisation sunk in. 'Are you saying that it was glass Lissa held that...' She didn't finish. I pictured her lips trembling. It was where I'd learnt my act from.

'It was a tragic accident, Mrs McColl. The glass caught Jemma across the neck. There was nothing they could do for her.'

A tragic accident. I slumped in relief within the cradling arms that held me. After some talk about signing a statement, words that floated over my head, we were allowed to leave.

At home, my mother took me straight to my room and, for the first time in many years, she helped me off with my clothes and into the childishly patterned pyjamas I had stuffed under my pillow that morning. A lifetime before. When I had been a child. Now... I didn't know what I was.

My father wasn't due to return for a couple of days, but Mother must have rung him and begged him to come home early because later that afternoon, to my delight, I heard his voice. I wanted to run down and tell him what had happened, explain that I hadn't... really hadn't... meant for my plan to work. He would take me on his knee, and I'd tell him about Jemma's eyes, how I could see them when I shut my own, ask if the memory would fade with time or haunt me forever. Of course, I couldn't do any such thing. Instead, I lay tucked under the duvet and listened to the low-pitched words that drifted up the stairway.

They looked in on me, minutes later, but I kept my eyes shut, my breathing slow and regular, even when, one after the other, they leaned down to press a kiss to my forehead. When they'd gone, leaving the door ajar so they could peek in on me later, I opened my eyes and sighed.

When night came, if the cloud cover was heavy, the velvety

blackness was absolute. That night, the sky was clear, twinkling with a million stars and strangely bright. I threw back the duvet and crossed to the window to look out.

A harvest moon, a big fat circle of light cut into the darkness, peered down on me. Usually, it would have fascinated me.

But usually, the moon didn't have Jemma's eyes.

Eyes that looked down on me and promised retribution.

6

It was agreed between my parents and the school that I'd take time off. Convinced I had to be traumatised by my part in Jemma's death, it was also decided that I should speak to a counsellor. These decisions were taken without my input. They looked upon me as a child, had no idea of my capabilities, of what I'd done. It was in my interest to play along, to be the innocent child they assumed I was. So, I attended the counselling sessions when I was told.

They were held in a room in a local medical centre. A large modern complex, it was a cold clinical place with icy white walls and cream plastic chairs. Luckily, my father had decided that the seriousness of the situation required that he stay at home, so both my parents brought me to the first session, holding my hands tightly as we entered the building. My mother had barely let me out of her sight since Jemma's death four days before and her constant reassurances were driving me crazy. It was hard for a woman as emotionally fragile as she was to understand that her only daughter was as unlike her as was possible.

Some attempt had been made to make the room I was brought

to less chilly. Chairs were upholstered in a garish floral pattern, matching curtains hanging from the one opaque glass window. An obviously fake green foliage plant sat in one corner. Light sliding through the window hit it and highlighted dust on the plastic leaves.

The counsellor, Mrs Barker, rose from behind a desk to greet us. A short stout woman, she had a kind expression and sharp eyes that made me instantly wary. Once introductions were made, she looked at my parents, then at me. 'You have a choice, Lissa. You can talk to me on your own, or have your parents stay with you.'

It was nice to be given the choice. I pulled my hands free from my parents' grip and took a step forward. 'I think I'd prefer to talk to you alone.' I heard my mother's gasp and turned. 'Honestly, Mum, I think it would be easier.'

'Of course, it would,' my father said. 'We'll pop across the road to the café and come back for you in an hour.' He gave my cheek a pat and looked at Mrs Barker. 'You won't allow her to leave without us?'

'Of course not,' she agreed.

My mother couldn't leave without grabbing me in a painfully tight hug. And then she was gone.

'Let's sit,' Mrs Barker said leading me to a corner of the room set out for a tête-à-tête. Two chairs, a low table holding a carafe of water and two glasses. It was probably designed to be a comfortable informal area, but I was immediately intimidated and wondered if it was too late to change my mind and beg my parents to return.

It was probably the usual reaction because Mrs Barker waved me to one chair and said, 'Don't be nervous, I really don't bite.'

There was no point in my telling her that it wasn't her bite I was worried about. There was something in her eyes that seemed to say she wasn't easily fooled. I sat on the edge of the chair she indicated.

She sat on the other, her two feet on the ground, hands crossed casually on her lap. 'Do you know why you're here?'

I'd done some research, knew I would be expected to talk, to open up my heart. Not my soul, though. Luckily, because that's where I'd locked all the bad stuff away. 'Because of what happened with Jemma.'

'Can you tell me about it?'

A predictable and boring question. I trotted out the same story I had told anyone who'd asked in the last few days... the GP my parents insisted on calling to see me, the social worker who came, the neighbour who visited, eyes wide with curiosity. As I had with them, I forced my voice to a lower register which I'd decided sounded sadder, and kept my eyes lowered to my clasped hands. At the end, I looked at her, wishing I was able to cry on demand. 'I keep thinking about it.'

That last sentence was probably the only honest thing I said to her that session, or any of the three that followed. What I couldn't tell her, of course, was what I couldn't stop thinking about... the look in Jemma's eyes as I watched her die. There was something sad, something beyond my ability to understand in those eyes. They haunted me.

* * *

The police, once they had their signed statement, took no further interest in me. An inquest ruled Jemma's death as a tragic accident and put no blame on the poor child who'd been tempted by a pretty glass bottle. The school was requested to make the playground safer and when I returned to my class almost three weeks later, the railing surrounding the playground had been sheeted with dark green metal.

It wasn't the only change. Before, I was either being bullied, or ignored and sidelined, rendered invisible. There were times... sad pathetic moments... when I welcomed the bullying, the interaction. Painful as it made me feel, it was good to be part of something.

After three weeks away, I could sense a subtle shift in my classmates' attitude towards me. I was no longer the mousy child who was so easy to target. I had gained a certain element of interest... even of notoriety... I had killed someone. It didn't matter to them that it had been ruled an accident, they were fascinated by it, and by me.

Ashling, who had once been Jemma's bosom buddy, waved to me when I entered the classroom. 'Come and sit with me.'

'There's space here,' Marie said, shuffling up on the bench. It was the nearest choice, but as I sat, I saw her smile of satisfaction and her victorious toss of hair. I had become a prize; the girl others wanted to be with. I imagined I heard Jemma's snort of derision.

That I didn't want to be part of my classmates' sad pathetic little cliques was beside the point. Seeing things from the inside was far preferable than seeing them from the outside. Jemma had the last laugh though because my newfound popularity didn't translate into invitations to their homes. My classmates may have been temporarily fascinated by me, but their parents were wary. They had no need to be. I wasn't so stupid as to be involved in anything controversial again. Why should I? My life was far more comfortable now that I was neither being bullied nor ignored, and I didn't care about the stupid parties and sleepovers my classmates went to in each other's homes. I hooked on a mask of sublime indifference and nobody... not one person... could have guessed how the exclusion hurt.

The final change was an end to the bullying culture. Without Jemma to lead the pack, the rest of the worst floundered. For a while, they looked to me as a potential replacement. That was never going to happen. I also wasn't interested in championing those who remained on the outskirts; they needed to fight their own battles and find their own way out of their grim little world. But when I saw Ashling laughing and nudging the girls around her after she'd 'accidentally' tripped up one of these sad creatures, I found it impossible to turn away. I watched as the victim stumbled, and almost fell, her face contorted in embarrassment.

I knew how she'd be feeling... not long ago, it would have been me lying there suffering an overwhelming, bewildering, painful sadness. It almost made me rush to her side. Instead, I turned to Ashling, looked her up and down, and sniffed. 'Seriously, that's so childish.' Without another word I walked away, shaking my head as if in disappointment.

'Lissa's right,' Marie said, and followed me. When I looked back, seconds later, Ashling was standing alone.

For the remainder of my time in primary school I kept out of trouble.

7

Despite the passing of years, Jemma's eyes continued to haunt me. I struggled to understand what she'd been trying to say those last few seconds as she lay dying. Maybe she'd been asking for my forgiveness... I like to think that was the answer, but I wasn't sure and perhaps that was why I couldn't shake her off. Or maybe haunting me was her retribution.

It should have been enough to stop me ever killing again but then needs must when the devil drives.

Mostly, I gave what happened in the playground little thought. Life had quickly returned to its usual routine: my father resumed his schedule of three to four nights a week and alternate weekends away, my mother to her cycle of neglect and indulgence.

And it would have probably continued that way, if life had a channel carved in stone to run along. But it doesn't, it changes course unexpectedly.

* * *

I was sitting at the desk in my bedroom working on an essay for my English class when the doorbell brought my head up with a grunt of irritation. My mother was at the supermarket. I hoped whoever it was would give up and go away. We didn't get many callers though, and curiosity dragged me from my desk to pull back the curtain and peer around the edge.

A police car was pulled up on the road outside. Surprised, but not yet worried, I moved to the other side of the window which gave a better view of the front door. Two uniformed officers stood on the step.

It had happened before. My mother had been caught speeding by a neighbourhood team with a speed scanner. The police weren't allowed to give fines, but they did call around to advise her to slow down.

It would be the same again. She'd be upset. Again.

Perhaps, if I went down, they'd be happy for me to pass on their message. Surely, they had more important things to do, so wouldn't want to return.

Convinced I knew why they were there, I had no worry about opening the door. 'Hi,' I said, smiling at the two grim-faced officers.

Although I was sixteen, I was small and slim and could have passed for younger. It was obviously what they thought too, as they hesitated before one said, quietly, 'Hello, is your mother in?'

'She's out at the supermarket.' I smiled and shook my head.

'Is it okay if we come in?'

Surprised, I laughed uncertainly. 'Is that really necessary? She might be a while and I have schoolwork to get done.'

'Can I ask how old you are, miss?'

I was tempted to be smart, to say they could ask but I wasn't obliged to answer, but there was something in their grim-set features that stopped the words. 'I'm sixteen.'

The officers looked at each other, the older nodding and repeating his question. 'Is it okay if we come in?'

Thanks to my mother, I'd watched more than my fair share of detective programmes on TV. 'Mum, is she okay?' She was a crazy driver, easily distracted. I imagined her car a mangled mess, her body twisted. 'Mum!'

My cry hadn't died when I saw her car pull into the driveway and I slumped against the wall in relief. She climbed out, hauled a carrier bag from the passenger seat, and stood with it hanging heavily from one hand as she glanced at the police car. Then she walked towards the door where the two officers stood, their expressions set into lines of uncomfortable determination.

The awful truth seemed to hit us at the same time. Mother dropped the bag of groceries as she raced forward shouting 'Mark', at the same time as I uttered a disbelieving, 'Daddy?' Mother grabbed the first officer, her hands pulling and clawing at his uniform until he grasped both of her hands in his and held them still. I stumbled away from them, back into the house, my mouth open in shock.

Stunned disbelief rendered me silent but Mother screeched... an ear-splitting litany of keening words, the pitch growing higher and higher. One of the officers tried to persuade her to move into the house and, when persuasion failed, resorted to lifting her bodily and carrying her through. He put her down beside the sofa. She stood rigidly, refusing to sit as she continued her keening, eyes wide, the fingers of one hand entwined in the other.

Then she stopped, her sudden silence almost as overwhelming as her keening. She flopped onto the sofa behind, and stared up at the officer who had carried her in. 'Tell me.'

'I'm so sorry,' he said. 'Your husband was found earlier today. In his car. A member of the public noticed he hadn't moved for several hours. When they failed to get his attention by knocking on the car window, they called emergency services. The paramedics who attended reported there was no sign of life and Mr McColl's body was cold. They estimate he died sometime late last night. There'll be a post-mortem, but their professional opinion was that he'd had either a massive heart attack or a stroke.'

I pictured my big happy, smiling father, in his car, dying alone. That he was dead was horrifying, that he had died alone, far from those he loved shattered me. One of the officers had gone into the kitchen. I could hear him opening and closing cupboard doors. Was he making tea? It seemed such an odd thing to do, but then what did I know? Maybe a cup of tea would make everything all right, reset the world, make the death of my father seem normal.

The other officer, he who had given my mother the bad news, was sitting in the chair opposite her. I thought he'd forgotten about me, but then he glanced my way and I could see the panic in his eyes. It drew me over and I sat on the sofa beside my mother. She was staring directly ahead, barely blinking. She didn't turn to look at me, to comfort me, or to share our grief.

The officer got to his feet and knelt in front of her, shaking her gently. I could have told him there was no point. I could have explained about the cycles of neglect and indulgence – how she'd found it so hard to cope with my father's absence that she'd struggle for one long day, turning inward and barely noticing the world around her, including me. I could have explained that it was only the thought of my father's impending return that made her resume living.

I reached for her hand, prised it away from the grip of the other, and held it. There was no life in it, no warmth. She'd gone away and this time she had no reason to return. My father had left her for good. I wanted to scream at her, to tell her that I was worth staying for, that I was still here. In desperation, I tugged on her hand, but her whole body swayed and her eyes remained fixed ahead.

'Do you have a doctor we can call?'

'Yes.' I released the hand I held, watched for a second in dismay as it immediately sought the other and her fingers were once more entwined as if I'd never parted them. I brushed tears from my eyes and went out to the hall table. An address book, filled with my mother's neat writing, was kept in the drawer. It held the details of everyone we knew. Flipping it open to the correct page, I handed it over without a word.

While the officer made the call, the other came through with a laden tray. He'd used the fine china tea service my mother kept for visitors. She'd have been horrified at the way he had the cups stacked together. I was tempted to reach out and separate them to keep her happy, then realised what a stupid thing it was to consider. My father was dead; nothing was going to make her happy again.

The officer had obviously emphasised the urgency of the situation because the GP arrived less than thirty minutes later, a concerned look in his eyes.

'Mrs McColl,' he said, dropping his bag on the floor and taking my recently vacated seat on the sofa beside her. 'You've had bad news. I'm sorry for your loss.' He reached for her hand, moved his fingers over her wrist. Checking her pulse. I wonder could he tell from feeling it that her heart was broken.

'She hasn't moved and has barely blinked since I told her the news,' the officer said quietly.

The doctor nodded. 'She's always been,' – he hesitated as if searching for an appropriate, politically correct word – 'a fragile woman. Mr McColl was her strength. His death is going to be hard for her to deal with.'

They encircled her, the doctor and the two officers, looking at

Mother with so much sadness that I wanted to scream, *what about me?* I was only sixteen. My father was dead. My mother had left me. The cycle of neglect and indulgence I had lived with for so long had finally been broken – unfortunately, it had stopped with the hand pointing firmly at neglect.

8

When all the doctor's attempts to get my mother to speak, move or react in any way failed, he made several phone calls, then took me into the hallway. 'I know this is hard on you, Lissa, but I'm worried about your mother, and I think the best thing to do, is for me to admit her so she can get specialist care.'

The burden of everything, my father's death, my mother's breakdown – even with my limited knowledge I could see this is what had happened – they pressed down on my shoulders, and I staggered under their weight. 'Specialist care?'

'A private psychiatric clinic. They have agreed to take her.' He looked back through the door to where she sat. 'I think it's the best place for her. The only issue would be the cost.'

'That won't be a problem. Get the best treatment for her. There's plenty of money.' I said it with such authority, he let out a sigh of relief. There was no point in my enlightening him. I had no idea how our finances stood and doubted if my mother did either. We'd always had enough for whatever we needed – and Mother needed this.

'Good, I think the sooner she's seen, the better.'

I left him to make more phone calls, and returned to sit beside Mother and hold her hand. The police officers could have told the doctor, had he asked, that I was too young to give consent for my mother to be admitted to a private clinic. At sixteen, I couldn't enter into a legally binding contract, but I didn't expect there to be a problem.

I squeezed my mother's hand and told her what was going to happen. 'You're going into a private clinic for a little while. Just to help you get better. But don't worry, I'll be fine.' I'd have liked to have had a reaction, some sign of regret for leaving me to cope with the horror of my father's death all alone. But there was nothing.

'Is there someone you can call to come stay with you?'

I looked around to where the two officers were sitting. I'd almost forgotten they were there. The question was gently put and filled with concern, but it hit me hard. Because there wasn't anyone. My parents had both been only children. My father's parents had passed away before I was born, my mother's a couple of years later.

I'd liked to have said I didn't need anyone, but that would have been a lie. Except, of the people I needed, one was dead, and the other had abandoned me. Grief for my loss was edged with conflicting emotions. Unreasonable anger towards my father – how dare he die and leave us? An aching sadness for my mother who adored him – and rage at her for retreating and leaving me to fend for myself. 'I can call the neighbours if I need someone,' I said. I could, but I wouldn't. 'I'm sixteen, I'll be fine alone.'

I could see the officer wanted to say something, could see his lips poised to speak but relaxed when an ambulance pulled up outside. I jumped to my feet. 'I need to pack some things for my mother.'

Ten minutes later, she was in the ambulance, a hastily packed bag on the floor beside her. 'I'll be in to see you as soon as they allow me,' I said to her, leaning down to kiss her cheek. 'You'll be better soon and be back home.' The lie was for her benefit if she heard it. I didn't believe she'd be home soon; I wasn't sure she'd be home, ever.

The doctor went with her. 'I'll give them your phone number and ask them to ring you as soon as she's settled.'

'Thank you.' And then they were gone.

One of the officers had made more tea and we sat, the three of us, having an uncomfortable tea party. I wanted them to go. Wanted to be on my own so I could howl. But my day of misery wasn't over yet.

'We obtained your details from your father's mobile.' The teacup rattled on the saucer as he reached to put it down. 'Do you recognise the name, Olivia Burton?'

The list of our acquaintances wasn't large. There wasn't an Olivia Burton among them. 'No, I don't, who is she?'

The two men exchanged glances and shifted in their seats. Although, they seemed to be of equal seniority, it was the same officer who had the larger speaking part. 'If I could get away without telling you what I'm about to say, believe me, I would.' He shrugged and sighed loudly. 'Unfortunately, that isn't possible.'

'I'm tougher than I look, officer.' It wasn't hard. With my short stature and slight physique, I might look like a frail child, but my looks were deceptive... I had killed after all. Not something I could share. 'Please, just tell me whatever it is.'

'Olivia Burton is... was... your father's other wife.'

9

My laughter rang out, startling the two police officers who reared back and then looked at me with an element of fear in their glances. Perhaps they were afraid they were going to have to recall the doctor. They needn't have worried. My laughter was part disbelief, part instant realisation that my mother and I had been fools, me for sixteen years, her for possibly all the twenty years she'd been married to my father.

My charming, handsome, funny, generous, kind, *bigamous* father.

Had my mother never been suspicious? I hadn't, but I was young, tougher than I looked, granted, but I hadn't seen much of the world, hadn't yet learned what people were capable of. All those lies my father must have told. The double life he led. It must have been exhausting. No wonder he died so young, the stress of it all.

'Are you okay?'

I wonder how many times over the coming weeks I'd be asked that particularly stupid question? It was, however, unfair to shoot the messenger. It did explain, of course, why the officers were keen to hang around. 'I'm fine.' A stupid answer to their stupid question. I was a long way from fine. 'Did this woman... Olivia Barton–'

'Burton,' he corrected me.

'Did she know?'

He rubbed a hand over his short hair before answering. 'No, she didn't know. They married four years ago; she kept her maiden name.'

Four years ago. 'My father worked away, a few days every week and alternate weekends, for as long as I can remember, far longer than four years.' They said nothing. What could they say? That it was possible there had been other women before Olivia. I got to my feet. 'Thank you.' I was dismissing them too soon. Dropping back onto the sofa, I wiped a hand over my forehead. I was in this alone and there were things I needed to do. A funeral I needed to arrange for my lying, cheating parent. 'Where is my father's body?'

As if afraid I wouldn't be able to retain the information, on top of all I had already received, the officer took out a notebook and pen and scribbled the information down. 'You just need to ring an undertaker; they'll collect your father's body and follow any instructions you give them.'

Any instructions... I'd obviously succeeded in convincing the officers that I was in control. I didn't have much choice, of course, my mother had abdicated all responsibility. There was some consolation that in her current state, she wouldn't know how dreadfully she'd been betrayed. 'Thank you, and for being kind.'

They seemed reluctant to leave and only did when I walked to the front door and pulled it open. 'I'll be fine,' I said. A lie I'd find myself repeating again and again over the coming days, and even when I was alone, I used it like a mantra. I would be fine. I had no choice.

* * *

Thanks to the address book and my mother's careful record in it of anyone important, it was easy to sort out some of the essentials. Next to the name of a solicitor, she'd written the word *will*. I rang and made an appointment to see him the following week.

Since my mother had organised the funeral of her parents when they'd passed away, she'd also recorded the name of an undertaker. I rang, gave them the details, and answered what questions I could.

'It'll be a cremation. I'll leave the choice of casket to you, the cheapest one you have please. We won't want any music at the crematorium either.' It was what my father deserved. The most basic of send-offs. Sorrow and anger were taking turns to rock me. His betrayal of my mother, of me, of our family. All those wonderful days out we'd spent, those dinners, the many indulgences. All inspired by his guilt, not love. Treachery and betrayal. If he were alive, I might have been tempted to kill him.

I'd never spent a night on my own or a night apart from my mother. I pulled the curtains to hide the creeping darkness, but it was the sad loneliness and weight of despair that sent me to my room. I crawled under the duvet and tried to capture the scent of yesterday.

I wondered what my mother was doing. Was she too lying in a bed trying to recapture a life that had vanished in a puff of smoke. Noxious smoke. But she didn't know that. Probably she was locked into a drug-induced sleep. Maybe when she woke, she'd remember she had a daughter.

Sleep wouldn't come and I lay there with my thoughts, wondering if I'd ever feel *fine*, if the lie would have to do. It was hunger that drove me from under the bedclothes less than an hour later. It seemed that one part of me was working as it should.

I had cooked for myself before, learnt to do basic stuff on those days over the years where my mother was on one of her neglectful days. There had been a lot of trial and error with burnt fingers, overcooked food and disastrous combinations. I stared into the fridge and was soon munching on some cheese and toast, minutes later throwing up into the kitchen sink. Hunger and devastating sorrow, it seemed, weren't compatible.

The night stretched before me, and after that the days ahead. What would I do? Anything I liked? Nothing at all? I wanted to train to be a nurse, that desire hadn't altered in all the years since I'd read those anatomy and physiology books. There was a part of me that felt I owed it to Jemma.

There was nothing to prevent me living alone. It was a terrifying thought. I liked my own company, but the word *alone* was intimidating. I had no belief in my mother returning. No belief she would come out of her self-imposed withdrawal. And young, inexperienced as I was, I knew it was for the best. My father's death had shattered her mind, his betrayal would have tortured it first.

In the morning I would make the necessary phone calls. Ring the school, explain my situation, tell them I'd be taking a few weeks off to bury my father. Ring the company my father worked for, explain he wouldn't be coming back. The car he had been found in belonged to them; I wondered if they'd already been informed by the police. Wondered too if they'd known about his two lives.

I'd have to investigate our financial situation too. My father kept the spare bedroom as an office. A room my mother and I were forbidden from entering. He used to joke about it. 'I keep secrets in there, if you found them, I'd have to kill you both!'

It seemed the joke was on us.

10

Bleary-eyed from a sleepless night, the next morning I sat to make those phone calls. Before I could start, the doorbell rang. It was our neighbour, Mrs Higgins, a florid-faced, buxom woman who wore clothes she made herself with enthusiasm and an absolute belief they were as good as any she'd have bought in boutiques in Bath. They weren't, but she had a caustic tongue, and nobody ever dared tell her the truth. That day she was wearing a dress with a neckline that gaped badly showing far more of her breasts than she'd have liked. Or maybe she knew. Maybe she didn't care.

'Hello,' I said and waited.

'I saw the ambulance.'

Her dress sense might have been woeful and her tongue caustic, but she was at heart a kind woman and on her face I saw only sympathy and a desire to be of help. Prurient curiosity would have made me angry; her kind sympathy made me cry. She didn't hesitate, taking me in her arms and holding me tight, then moving into the house with me held close.

'Tell me,' she said, sitting me down at the kitchen table and keeping hold of my hand. 'Your mum?'

I nodded, then shook my head. 'It's Dad, he's dead. When the police told Mum, she couldn't cope. Doctor Brennan said it was best that she go into a clinic.' I didn't have to elaborate. Mrs Higgins had lived next door for long enough, she'd seen my mother's highs and lows. 'You poor love. What a shock for you. You should have come around to me straight away. The police, honestly, they should never have left you alone. You're nowt but a child.' She squeezed my hand. 'I'm not having that. You move in with us till your mum is home, okay?'

I wanted to say no, that I was sixteen and quite capable of living on my own. I wanted to say I was tougher than I looked. I wanted to but didn't. I brushed the tears from my eyes and said, 'That is so kind of you, thank you, I'd like that very much.'

Caustic, badly dressed, with a heart of gold, Mrs Higgins was also a woman who didn't let grass grow under her large broad feet. She nodded to the fridge. 'Bring anything that might go off, there's no point in letting stuff go to waste. Then pack up whatever you need and come around when you're ready.' She jerked her thumb to the house on the other side. 'I'll let the Robinsons know so they won't be pestering you, okay?'

'Thank you, that would be kind of you.'

And with that she was gone.

My call to the school was short and to the point. It was the school secretary who answered. She was never particularly friendly, and I didn't feel the need to give more than the basic details. 'My father died suddenly. If you'd tell the head teacher, please, that I'll be taking a few weeks off to help my mother with the arrangements. Thanks so much,' I hung up without waiting for a reply.

I managed to keep a bowl of cereal and a glass of juice down. A hint of the normality that I knew would creep in day by day.

My father's office beckoned. It was locked. 'For security,' he'd say. 'I keep some information that my competitors would be delighted to get their hands on.' As if he were a spy and not simply a sales rep for a medical supplies company.

It was locked, but I knew where the key was kept. Under the plant pot that sat in a wall recess between the spare room and my parents' bedroom. Always in the same place. I suppose my father had so many secrets to hide, so many balls to keep in the air, that some things had to remain constant. Anyway, he'd have had no fear that either my mother or I would have taken it and gone into his precious office. We had too much respect for him. *What fools we were.*

I took the key, opened the door, and stood looking in for several minutes, sudden tears blurring my vision. Anger and sorrow were still grappling for dominion but here, where my father spent many hours, a masculine room that contrasted dramatically with the rather floral décor in the other rooms, one step inside, and it was sorrow that won over. The loss of the man I had so loved bent me double. His scent lingered in the air... the citrus cologne he always wore, the tweed jackets he favoured.

I sat on the leather office chair and rocked it gently as I looked around. He cleaned the room himself. Not often though and a fine layer of dust lay over the furniture. Thicker dust in the corners and at the edges of the laminate floor showed up his less than adequate skills. Even the far corners of his desk showed traces of neglect.

He had so much to hide, he couldn't risk my mother coming in and perhaps stumbling upon something incriminating. For the first time, I felt a glimmer of sadness for him. To have kept such a secret for so long. Then I thought of Jemma. Secrets... perhaps my father and I were more alike than either of us had ever known.

Pushing that thought aside, I pulled the chair closer to the desk and reached for the button to switch on his desktop computer. I made one guess at the password; when it failed, I stopped. It could be anything. Hoping I would come across it in a notebook, or scribbled on a Post-it, I looked through a pile of paperwork. A quick flick through and I gave up. It appeared to be work stuff and was of little interest to me. Instead, I reached for the first of the four drawers set under the desktop.

It was locked, so were the three underneath. A locked office, a locked desk. Such a level of security. How afraid of exposure he must have been. Did he never consider it would all come out after he died? Did he think he was immortal? Perhaps he expected to live longer than the forty-six years he'd had.

Frustrated, I aimed a kick at the lowest drawer. It didn't achieve anything; the desk was solid. There was a mug holding pens, I turned it out hoping it would be that easy and I'd find a key. Of course, it wasn't. There was a filing cabinet against the other wall. Six drawers. It too was locked. The final piece of furniture was a low bookshelf set under the window. Some books, the military biographies he liked. Mostly hardbacks given to him by my mother over the years. There was one from me too. I read the inscription, *to the best father ever, happy birthday, love Lissa,* and in a fit of anger, despair, grief, I tore the page out, then ripped it to pieces.

In the same fit of raw emotion, I rushed to the utility room and searched in the cupboard where a few tools were kept for convenience. Rarely used, they were neatly stored in an old shoebox. I took the lot back with me. It took a lot of banging and swearing with a hammer and screwdriver to remove the front of the top drawer. The rest were easier and soon all four were open. I tossed the tools to one side – the filing cabinet could wait for another day.

Clearing a space on the desk, I emptied the contents of the top drawer in a heap and started to go through it all, item by item.

The marriage certificate naming Olivia Burton as my father's wife shouldn't have come as a shock, but it did. As did her age. He hadn't gone for a younger model. He wasn't a complete cliché. Olivia was forty-five, six years older than my mother.

There was a photograph of her. Not a beauty, a more solid heftier woman than my mother. Had this been the attraction? Had my father wearied of the physical and emotional fragility of the woman he'd married? *The first woman he'd married.*

There were other photographs. All women, named and dated, going back years. The earliest was a mere two years after he'd married Mum. Girlfriends, lovers, mistresses? It appeared my charming father had cheated on his wife for almost all their married life.

I swept everything to the floor and reached for the contents of the second drawer. Neat files. Keeping his two homes emotionally separate, and fiscally together. They contained the details of our home, and the home he shared part-time with Olivia. He owned both... or rather the bank did. It took me only thirty minutes to go through everything and for the reality to hit me. He'd remortgaged our home four years before to fund the purchase of the second house. There were a couple of letters from the bank requesting he contact them regarding non-payment of the previous two months' mortgage repayments. Credit card statements, several of them, were all in the red. Maths was my strong point, and it was easy to do a quick calculation in my head. My father was in serious financial difficulty... scratch that, *we* were in serious financial difficulty.

I sat back in the chair, sending it rocking. Money had to come from somewhere. We were in arrears on the mortgage, all the credit cards were maxed out. The private clinic would want payment for my mother's care. I had to eat. All I could hope for was that my father had been sensible and had some form of life insurance. Plus, wouldn't there be a payout from his job? He'd been with the same company for as long as I could remember.

It seemed sensible to give them a call and find out where we stood. The police had probably contacted them about the car. They'd know my father had died. I wouldn't need to break that news.

I rummaged through the pile of papers I'd pushed aside and found the number of the company he'd worked for.

'Hello,' I said when the phone was answered by a cheery bright voice. 'It's Lissa McColl, Mark McColl's daughter. I wanted to check that the police had told you about his death.'

The long hesitation wasn't unexpected. The words that followed were. 'Miss McColl, I'm so sorry for your loss but, no, I'm afraid the police haven't been in touch.'

I was taken aback. 'He was an employee of the company, driving one of your cars. I suppose I just assumed they'd have informed you.'

This time a deep sigh filled the hesitation. 'I'm sorry, there isn't an easy way to tell you this so I'm just going to get it out. Your father hasn't worked here for several months.'

11

———

I put the phone down several minutes later, having learned more of the secrets my darling father had been hiding. The company had gone through a bad slump the previous year. Trying to claw their way back to profit, certain departments had been merged, and several employees were offered statutory redundancy. Perhaps they'd been given little choice but to accept. We'd never know because my father never told us. He accepted the redundancy and was given the car he was driving as a final thank you for his years of service.

The assistant had said the redundancy had been paid out the previous January. I hung up in the middle of her commiserations on the loss of my father and reached for the folder containing his bank statements. It took a few minutes to work back and find the deposit, running my finger down the column of figures and stopping at a larger sum. Larger but not large enough. This couldn't be right... it was only a little over thirteen thousand pounds.

A quick internet search taught me the difference between the statutory redundancy he'd been offered and an employer's redundancy scheme. Statutory redundancy was a miserable amount of money. It had been quickly swallowed by outstanding bills.

It was obvious from looking through the statement that my father hadn't managed to get another job. There was no money being paid into his account, just regular money leaving for the dinners, days out, the indulgences he kept providing, refusing to admit to himself... and certainly to us... that he couldn't afford them.

I'd have liked to have given up, to have shoved all the papers back into the broken drawers, willy-nilly. I wanted my carefree life back. The father I adored, not this pathetic lying, cheating failure. I wanted my mother – the neglectful or the indulgent one – either, both, any version of her as long as she came back and didn't leave me here all alone.

Foolish thoughts. That life was over. I sat and went through every statement, item by item. Years of them. Hoping to find the one thing that might make things... not better, but maybe bearable... evidence my father had paid into some form of insurance policy. Because he had to have done, hadn't he? He was a responsible adult, the father of a child, he'd have known he'd need to provide security in case the worst happened... the worst that did happen.

I relaxed when I found what I was looking for. A lying bigamous cheat he may have been, but he wasn't stupid. I changed my mind when I read through the final several months' statements. The premium hadn't been paid. A frantic search through the final drawer brought the policy to light and it was as I'd feared, if consecutive premiums are missed, the policy ends.

No insurance policy.

No money to pay my mother's medical bills. Perhaps she would be coming home soon. Doctor Brennan had promised someone from the clinic would ring to let me know how she was doing. That they hadn't didn't worry me unduly. It would take time to assess her and decide about treatment. Rather than ringing the clinic to speak to strangers, I rang the surgery and asked to speak to Dr Brennan. He was with a patient, and I was put on hold that lasted so long I was drifting off to sleep to the sound of 'Evergreen', jerking upright when the music stopped suddenly, and his deep voice rang down the line.

'Lissa, my apologies, I was planning to ring you later. How're you holding up?'

'My neighbour, Mrs Higgins, has been very kind. I'm going to stay with her for a few days until I get things sorted.'

'Good, I'm pleased to hear it, I really didn't like leaving you alone.'

I heard paper being shuffled before he spoke again.

'I've spoken to the consultant psychiatrist looking after your mother. I'm afraid it's not good news, Lissa. Your mother's mental state has always been fragile. Dr Ramirez considers she is in a withdrawn catatonic state. Putting it simply, your mother has a decreased response to all external stimuli. There's an absence of speech, she's refusing to eat independently and refusing to move. This means she requires twenty-four-hour care.'

'But they'll be able to make her better, yes?'

'They've started a course of benzodiazepines which may prove effective. Dr Ramirez also suggested that ECT might be of benefit.'

ECT... I'd seen *One Flew Over the Cuckoo's Nest*, I knew exactly what that was. Electroconvulsive therapy. My poor mother.

'It's very effective,' Dr Brennan insisted as if he'd read my mind. 'It had bad press in the past, but I know patients who have benefited from it. I think you need to trust that Dr Ramirez has your mother's best interests at heart.'

I didn't have much choice. 'When can I visit her?'

'Dr Ramirez suggested you wait for a few days. He knows your situation, that you have lost your father. He's very sympathetic.'

How sympathetic would he be when he knew there was no money to pay the bill? Perhaps staying away was the best option in the circumstances. I wasn't sure I could have faced seeing my mother staring into space. 'But I can ring, find out how she is?'

'Yes, of course. Here's the number for reception.' He reeled it off. 'And this is Dr Ramirez's direct line.'

I scribbled both down, thanked Dr Brennan for his help and hung up.

A withdrawn catatonic state. An internet search for the term didn't make me any wiser.

What was concerning was the twenty-four-hour care she needed. It didn't sound like she'd be coming home anytime soon.

I needed to find a way to pay for what sounded like a very expensive stay. I picked up the files on both houses. My mother only lived in one. The other... where my father's second wife lived... needed to be sold.

Whatever it took.

The end... as it always did... would justify the means.

12

Mrs Higgins was kind and comforting without smothering me. 'Here you go,' she said, opening the door into the spare bedroom. 'There's a TV here, so you can watch whatever you want, whenever you want.'

The room was spacious, the bed dressed in crisp white linen. She'd put a carafe of water and a glass on the bedside table. 'It's a lovely room, thank you. I'll try not to be any trouble.'

'As if you could,' she said, giving me a quick hug.

As if she'd let me. She was kind, she wasn't stupid. The TV looked like a recent addition, it made it clear that I was welcome to stay, but mostly in my room. It suited me. She and her husband had two children, both of whom were married and living abroad. The Higgins spent part of the year visiting them, months in Australia, and a strictly equal amount of time in Canada. If I was right, they should be heading off soon. I wondered if they'd allow me to stay in their home or if Mrs Higgins would drop a broad hint about moving on.

What I was going to do, I had no idea.

But there was one absolute certainty – whatever I had to do to secure my mother's care, I'd do it.

* * *

The following day, I met with the solicitor, Jason Brooks. A short, very handsome man, he rose to greet me with an outstretched hand. He held mine for several seconds, assessing me as he did so, then nodded as if satisfied with what he saw. 'Have a seat,' he said, leading me to a leather chair on the visitor side of the desk.

'Would you like something to drink? Tea or coffee, or there's mineral water, if you'd prefer.'

His manner was pleasant and friendly, and I found myself relaxing. 'No, thanks, I'm good.'

He sat on his side of the desk. 'I was so sorry to hear about your father.' His eyes flicked to a file on the desk, but he didn't move to pick it up. 'Your mother won't be joining us?'

Of course, he didn't know. So much had happened in such a short time that with everything swirling in a soup of emotion, it was hard to keep things straight in my head.

I'd lain awake for hours considering what I was going to tell people if they asked about my mother. That grief had driven her crazy... that she'd copped out of a life without my father... that she'd abandoned me. Sorrow washed over me again, tears of self-pity filling my eyes. Abandoned, it was such a lonely word. I pulled out a tissue, scrubbed at my eyes and reached into my core for some steel. 'The news of my father's sudden death affected her badly, Mr Brooks, she's receiving care.'

'I see.'

I wasn't sure he did. 'It's in a private clinic. It's going to be essential to free up some money to pay for it.' I looked pointedly at the file. 'My father's will?'

He rested a hand on it. 'Yes. It was rewritten almost four years ago.'

'After his bigamous marriage to Olivia Burton.' I was almost amused at the shock that widened the solicitor's eyes and made a perfect O of his lips.

He picked up the phone. 'Jenny, could you bring some coffee,' – he raised an eyebrow at me as if to ask if I wanted some. I didn't, but I nodded anyway – 'for both of us, please.' He hung up and gave me a wavering smile. 'Coffee helps to get my thoughts in order.'

When it arrived, he downed one cup quickly, refilled it and sat back. 'I knew there was an Olivia Burton in your father's life, but I wasn't aware of the details. He didn't volunteer the information and it's not my business to ask.'

I hadn't touched my coffee; I took a sip now. I hadn't thought to ask for sugar, and it was bitter and unpleasant. Or maybe it was my thoughts. I was imagining my bigamous father sitting in this very seat, talking about Olivia Burton. Imagined her sitting pretty in the house he'd paid for. Anger sliced through the sorrow and made my voice hard, the words coming out sharp and ragged. 'He remortgaged our house to buy the house she's living in. We're currently behind on the repayments. And there's worse, I'm afraid. I checked through bank statements last night; he hasn't paid the premium on his life insurance for several months.'

'No!' Brooks put his coffee down, the cup clattering noisily on the saucer.

'Something had to give. He only received a statutory payout when he was made redundant.'

Brooks ran a hand through his hair. He wasn't a fool; he knew statutory redundancy would have been a piss-poor payment. Especially for a man with two mortgages to maintain. 'Right, so we'd better have a look at his will.' He opened the file. 'It's a simple straightforward one. He left your home to your mother.' He raised his eyes from the document in front of him. 'She will either need to assume the mortgage or pay it off. This isn't something you can do, I'm afraid.'

'Being only sixteen has its drawbacks,' I said, trying for humour.

Brooks didn't look amused. I suppose I'd had longer to absorb my father's transgressions.

'I can contact the life insurance company and see if they would accept payment of the arrears at this stage, but I'd be lying if I told you there was a chance in hell.' He hesitated, staring down as if afraid to meet my eyes.

I didn't need to be a mind reader to know I was going to hear bad news. 'The other house?'

'Your father set up a trust granting Olivia Burton a life interest in it. When she dies, or if she remarries, the life interest ends.'

'So we can't sell it?'

'No.' He swallowed the remains of his coffee in a frantic, almost desperate gulp. 'It's worse, I'm afraid. If there's no money to pay the arrears on your mortgage, or to continue to pay the mortgage on the other house, it's your home that will need to be sold, and the mortgage on the other home either cleared from the available funds or be assumed by your mother.'

I laughed, a harsh disbelieving sound. 'You're joking, aren't you?' Although I knew he wasn't, knew that no matter how bad things had appeared, they'd just got substantially worse. 'So, my mother and I are made homeless, and that Burton woman carries on regardless?' I reached forward and slammed a hand down on the documents before him. Perhaps he was afraid I was going to grab them and rip them into pieces. I probably would have done had I thought it could do any good. 'Can we fight this trust? There must be a way.'

Colour flared in his cheeks. Not in anger, but embarrassment. 'Your father insisted the trust was locked down solid. I made sure it was.'

'So that's it?'

'I'm assuming Ms Burton is aware of your father's death.'

'Yes, the police were in contact with her.'

'She must have been shocked.'

Shocked? Probably. They'd been married for four years. I wondered if she was devastated at the lie she'd lived. She'd lost her husband, and the right to call him that. Shocked, devastated, falling apart – I didn't give a fuck about her. I shut my eyes. Not because I was reluctant to look at the solicitor, or because I was tearful. I shut them in case he saw them turn hard as I knew exactly what I needed to do.

The end… it would justify the means yet again. Olivia Burton's life interest in the house died with her. It made perfect sense that this should come as soon as I could arrange it.

After all, I had killed before. The second time was sure to be easier.

13

I left the solicitor's office with a headache pounding my skull. I must have looked wretched because Mrs Higgins took one look at me when she opened the door, and whisked me into the kitchen, pressing me down on a chair while she bustled around.

'I knew I shouldn't have let you go to the solicitor's alone,' she said, pressing the switch on the kettle. *Because tea was going to cure everything.* I swallowed the irritation. She was being kind and had volunteered to go with me that morning.

My reluctance was twofold. It was obvious she didn't really want to go, and I didn't want her to be privy to my father's will. It seemed essential that I keep our financial status a secret. More essential now in the face of what I intended to do.

I drank the tea she made me, answered the questions she asked as briefly as possible and made my escape.

The police officers who'd brought the news of my father's death had left me a number I could call if I had any questions. I had a few. Mrs Higgins had told me I could use their phone whenever I wanted. It sat on a table in the hallway and offered little if any privacy. It made more sense to go to my house to make the calls.

'I'm just going to check on a few things at home,' I said. 'I'll be an hour or so.'

'That's fine, dear, just come around the back, knock on the window and I'll let you in.'

She hadn't volunteered a key to the front door, and I hadn't liked to ask. Another day or two, and I'd thank her and move home permanently. By then, I'd have figured out a plan to ensure our financial security. There wasn't a choice.

It was strange to return to my home, to push open the door and hear the deafening silence. And then it wasn't silent... it was filled with echoes of my father's laugh, my mother's slightly off-key voice singing along with the radio, their voices entwining, separating, floating. I stood in the hallway and listened to them, straining to hear as the voices grew softer, desperate to cling onto them as they faded into a soft hiss, and then there was nothing. I cried when the weight of silence hung heavily around me again. I cried louder: for the charming, adoring father I'd loved, for the lying cheat of a man I'd never known, and who would never be able to explain what he'd done. I cried for my mother, for myself, for what I intended to do.

I sank to the floor, resting my head against the wall behind, letting the tears flow. When they stopped, I swore I wasn't going to cry again.

Our phone was kept in the kitchen. I pulled it over to the table, the cord stretching taut, and dialled the clinic to ask about my mother.

'Bartholomew Clinic, how may I help you?'

'Hi, my name is Lissa McColl, I'm enquiring about my mother, Cathy McColl.'

'Just hold, please, and I'll put you through to the nurse.'

I could have rung the consultant directly, but I wanted to know how my mother was doing, how she'd slept, if she'd said anything... if she'd mentioned me.

'Ms McColl, hello, my name is Barbara, I'm the nurse on duty on your mother's floor today.'

'How is she?' I crossed my fingers, praying the nurse would give me something better than *as well as can be expected*.

'She slept very well all night. This morning she was assisted to have a shower and has been sitting in the lounge with other residents since.'

I felt a lessening of the tension. This sounded good... almost normal. 'That sounds like she's making a great recovery. Do you think she'll be able to come home soon?'

Silence greeted my question. 'I'm sorry,' Barbara said, 'I was informed you were aware of your mother's condition.'

'That she was in a withdrawn catatonic state, yes. But it sounds like she's coming out of it.'

'I'm sorry, I seem to have given you a false impression. Your mother requires assistance with all activities of daily living. She was taken to the shower on a hoist, and then to the lounge in a wheelchair. Despite encouragement, she makes no attempt to move of her own accord and shows no reaction to anything or anybody. She's eating fairly well when assisted by a member of staff. She isn't speaking and still stares directly ahead.'

The nurse had painted a clear and shocking picture. 'I see, thank you. Will you tell her I love her, and I'll be in to see her in a few days. I've a lot to sort out first.' I wanted to visit my mother, to be able to meet her gaze and reassure her that I'd look after her for however long it took. I couldn't do that until I'd dealt with Olivia Burton.

'Yes, of course, and please ring any time.'

I dropped the handset back on its stand, folded my arms on the table, and rested my head. It was several minutes before I was able to straighten up. My second call was to the number the police officers had given me.

'Hello,' I said when it was answered. 'My name is Lissa McColl, my father, Mark McColl, was found dead in his car on 5th April. The officers who came to tell us were very kind and said if I had any questions, I could ring this number.'

'Of course, Ms McColl, just hold and I'll put you through to someone who can help.'

They had a strange taste in hold music or maybe they hoped the theme music from *Schindler's List* would imbue the person waiting with calm optimism... or make them cry. It took a second to clear the lump from my throat when the music was halted abruptly and a pleasant voice said, 'Ms McColl, I'm so sorry for your loss, how can we help you?'

'There's a couple of things. First, I was wondering if the post-mortem results were back yet?' It seemed suddenly important to know how my father had died, if he'd suffered, if he'd been there for a long time hoping for someone to come and help him. 'I believe the paramedics thought it might have been a heart attack or a stroke.'

'Okay, I'm bringing the report up now. No, it wasn't either. It appears your father died from a ruptured cerebral aneurysm.' He cleared his throat. 'That's when a blood vessel in the brain develops a weakness and bursts,' he explained. 'It would, according to the report I'm reading, have been very sudden, and very quick.'

'That's a relief.' And it was. I hadn't wanted the father I'd loved to have suffered. The other man, the lying, cheating, adulterous bigamist – him, I'd have liked to have died very very slowly. 'So does that mean his body will be released?'

'Yes, the inquest will simply be a formality. I see you've arranged an undertaker. We'll liaise with them if that's easier for you.'

It was. One less thing for me to worry about. 'Yes, thank you, that would be very helpful.'

He was also helpful in giving me advice about my father's car which was parked in the police station car park. It could stay there until I arranged to have it sold. It wasn't too old; it should bring a few thousand. Enough to keep me in funds for a while.

I hung up, satisfied with my work. Now I could turn my thoughts to a more pressing matter.

How I was going to get rid of Olivia Burton.

14

The best ideas come when you let your mind wander. I stayed in our bungalow until the light started to fade. Whatever I did, I had the advantage of surprise. An attack on Olivia should easily pass as a case of being in the wrong place at the wrong time.

I'd kept her photograph. It was in the back pocket of my jeans. I pulled it out and looked carefully at this woman whose life I needed to take. She looked hefty, was she also tall? I was barely five feet, and slight. But I was quick and clever. Sometimes, that was better.

The following day, hoping to catch a glimpse of Olivia, I made the weary complicated journey to the Gloucestershire town of Thornbury, twelve miles north of Bristol. It was a complicated journey – bus to Bath, a further bus to Bristol, then another to Thornbury where the bus took me to within ten minutes' walk of the house. It made sense to survey the area, see what my options were.

It would have been perfect if I could have laid my hands on

some quick-acting poison... ricin or sarin gas maybe. It would have made it all so much easier. Lacking this option, I was stuck with a messy, and much more difficult plan of attack. A variation of the one I'd used on Jemma years before.

A sharp knife. Knowing where to insert it. And every successful killer's weapon – the element of surprise.

I couldn't come up with a better plan and simply needed to find a way to implement it. There was no room for doubt, or second thoughts. Not even when, six years after killing Jemma, I could still remember those last moments. The strange sensation as her eyes locked on mine.

It had been necessary.

A means to an end.

This time, when death came, I'd make sure not to be staring into Olivia's eyes. I wasn't sure I could deal with being haunted by another. I didn't know this woman; her death would leave no absence in my life. This time would be different in another way... this time I knew the reality of death. The stakes were higher too, this wasn't only for me, this was for that woman staring fixedly into space in that private clinic. I was going to ensure her treatment continued, and if the worst happened, if she never recovered, I was going to make sure her life was comfortable.

She deserved it. It was easy to put the cycle of neglect I'd suffered out of my head, to simply focus on how indulgent she had been, and how much she had adored me. I had to – I had to have something to cling to. If this meant reinventing my past, well so be it.

I spent a couple of hours hanging around before Olivia Burton left her house and climbed into the Volvo parked in the driveway. The photograph didn't do her justice. In reality, she was certainly a bigger woman than my delicate mother, but she wasn't hefty, and only maybe three or four inches taller than my mother and me. I didn't think she'd cause me any trouble.

There was no option to change my mind. Olivia's death would be the solution to a problem.

* * *

Back in our bungalow, it took only a minute to find what I was looking for... a knife, sharp and long enough to be effective. The handle was solid, a firm weight in my hand. I waved and lunged with it, practising how I was going to drive it under Olivia's ribs and into her heart.

My mother kept a supply of sturdy shopping bags and the knife fit neatly along the bottom of the first one I pulled out, a canvas bag decorated with owls. There wasn't one with the grim reaper, anyway, owls were quick to pounce on a prey and this is what Olivia had become.

The following day, with the bag hung casually from my hand, I did the journey back to Thornbury. I'd timed it well, hitting the quiet spot that settled over the area between nearby schools releasing students and the start of rush hour. During my foray the day before, I'd checked for any CCTV cameras. There weren't any. There was no signal-controlled junction to cross, no shops, no businesses. I had debated wearing some form of disguise but decided that my small slight frame was sufficient to allow me to pass unnoticed.

The house was semi-detached, an ivy-clad fence separating it from its other half, a wall dividing it from the house on the other side. A wooden gate in need of repair hung open, the concrete driveway green with moss on the side sheltered by the wall. The air of neglect wasn't carried to the house. It was neat, with a bay window on both the ground and upper floors. The front door was glossy black, with two glass panels, a brass letter box and door-knob, a doorbell on the wall to one side.

Solid details. They helped me focus thoughts that were ducking and diving. What the hell was I doing? Murdering an unknown woman because my idiot lying cheat of a father had left us in dire straits? She'd committed no crime. *Or maybe she had – maybe she knew. Perhaps the life interest in the house had been her idea? Yes, that was it. She deserved to die for that.*

I didn't move, but perhaps a cloud had drifted across the sun because suddenly, I could see my reflection in the glass panels. My reflection – Jemma's eyes – and I would swear – *swear* – she winked at me.

A shiver slid over me – anticipation, fear, desperation – perhaps a combination of all, or maybe it was simple disbelief that I was really going to go ahead with this, that I was going to kill again. I'd thought this second time would be easier – it wasn't.

I checked the bag to ensure the knife handle was in the right place for me to grab. As with Jemma, there had been no time to practice, and if I was really going to go ahead with this there'd be no second chances. Only in that moment, did I realise my father would have had a key to the house. It would have been with the keys to the car. I could have asked for them, could have let myself in and dealt with Olivia in a different way.

Or would it always have come down to this? History repeating itself in my use of a sharp instrument. Perhaps it was better to stick to one weapon. Become an expert – in case I ever needed to kill again. Anyway, my tools of destruction were limited to what was easily acquired.

It was time. I reached forward and pressed my finger firmly to the doorbell. I heard it ring inside, a sad ding dong to announce the coming death. *Send not to know for whom the bell tolls, it tolls for thee.* Or for Olivia Burton in this case.

Luckily for me, the woman who answered the door wasn't aware her end was nigh. 'Hello,' she said, and waited expectantly.

I had time to register her pallor, the reddened eyes, the black shirt and trousers she wore. Grieving for her husband? I wondered if, like me, she was also in mourning for the death of truth. It wasn't something I could ask. It was better to get on with my plan, the words I'd practised in my head as I'd walked. 'Hi, I'm looking for Mrs Downs.' I blinked in feigned confusion. 'I thought she lived here.'

'No, I'm sorry, she doesn't.' Confusion faded her smile and corrugated her forehead.

'Oh, that's strange, this is the address I was given.' I lifted the bag I held, as if to look inside to check. My hand slipped in to close over the knife handle and I pulled it out in one smooth motion, lunging to drive it into her chest before she'd time to register what was happening, and long before she'd time to react and run from the grim reaper who'd darkened the sunny day.

Instinctively, she stepped away from the knife, backward into the hallway. As I'd anticipated. I followed, keeping the pressure up, driving the blade further in, angling it upward, ducking away from her pathetically reaching hands.

Once inside, I kicked the door shut behind, never taking my eyes from where the blood had begun to seep around the by now deeply embedded knife. If I was right, more blood was filling her chest cavity.

'I-I-I...' It was all she could manage in her disbelief and confusion, in the stark knowledge that there was no hope.

I wasn't sure if it would make any difference, but I refused to meet her eyes. It was possible that her death would haunt me regardless of whether I did or not. It seemed better not to take the risk.

Even when she dropped heavily to the floor, I kept the pressure on the knife. I didn't have to see her face, I could hear her breathing change, slowing, becoming a desperate gasp, growing quieter, and quieter. Slower and slower.

Only then did I release my grip and stand back. Her hands flailed uselessly as they sought to remove the knife. I could have told her that it wouldn't have done any good. The time for that had passed.

Blood was pooling from the stab wound, forming a crimson puddle on the cream carpet. Her hands had flopped uselessly to the floor, the movement of her ribcage barely discernible as each breath came slower and slower. Death was creeping over her.

I wasn't watching its arrival. Not this time. Oddly, although I knew she couldn't move, I was afraid to turn away from her, and stepped backwards into the kitchen. I washed the blood from my hands and wrists, checking further along my arm for any spatters. But there were none, and none on my clothes. Any pumping and spurting of blood had taken place inside Olivia's chest.

It seemed a good idea to make her killing part of a burglary. Back in the hallway, I kept my eyes averted as I edged around her dying body and went into the front room. It was a cosy room with a neat traditional three-piece suite, coffee table, dresser, and a bookshelf. It was to this latter I was drawn, my eyes glued to the photograph frames that sat between the rows of books.

Olivia and my father in each one. Smiling, staring into one another's eyes, his arm around her shoulder, her hand in his. I peered closely at my father's face looking for evidence that he'd been pretending, because he couldn't have been as content with this woman as he had with my mother, could he? Yet, in every photograph he looked happy – so damn happy I felt a rage envelop me and I smashed every frame to smithereens.

Upstairs, her handbag was sitting on the bed. I emptied it out and found her purse. There was an eye-opening amount of cash

inside; I took it out and shoved it into my jeans pocket. To rein-
force the burglary scenario, I pulled out more drawers and tossed
the contents on the floor. I would have liked to have ripped her
surprisingly sexy underwear to shreds and to have taken my
father's boxer shorts downstairs and soaked them in her blood.

Only the thought that the police might consider such acts
indicated something personal rather than a random burglary
stopped me. Something personal might have made them investigate her life more closely... and by extension mine. It also might
have made that too bright solicitor think that something wasn't
quite right. He might have wondered how convenient it was that
her life interest in the house was no longer a problem.

It was best to keep it to the burglary-gone-wrong scenario. I
filled my owl-patterned holdall with jewellery, a small bedside
clock, and some medication from the bathroom cabinet.

It was time to go, to leave the area before it became busy with
rush hour traffic.

I stopped halfway down the stairs and looked to where Olivia
lay on the hall floor. Blood had soaked into the carpet, making it
glisten in the sunlight filtering through the glass panels of the
front door. It would be impossible to get the stain out. We'd need
to replace it before putting the house on the market. It was good
to focus on the practicalities while my eyes watched for any signs
of life. There didn't appear to be any: strain as I might, I couldn't
see the slightest breath.

I moved closer, careful to stay outside the circle of body fluids,
the blood augmented by a pale yellow stain that spread out from
her hips. Her body was excreting everything and the noxious stink
made my nose twitch.

She was, I was relieved to say, very dead, and it was safe to
look at her face without fear that I'd catch her last moments. Her
eyes were open. So was her mouth. Had she died calling for help?

Perhaps she'd died calling for my father?

I wondered if he had died with her name on his lips... or my mother's... or even mine.

It was too late for regrets, but I suddenly wished I'd asked Olivia if she'd loved him, if she'd known he was lying, if she'd any inkling he had another wife living not many miles away. Most of all, I was sorry I hadn't asked her if he'd ever mentioned he had a daughter.

With a last look, I hefted the straps of the now heavy bag over my shoulder and opened the front door. I peered up and down the road. When I was sure it was empty, I stepped out, pulled the door shut quietly and kept my head down as I walked to the gate. A quick check each way and I was on the footpath and making my way home.

The swirling confusion of thoughts had gone – or perhaps not gone as such, more buried under a thick coat of numbness. When I'd killed Jemma, I'd believed I was too young to realise that sometimes the things we want, aren't the things we should get.

I was older now, and I knew I'd got exactly what I'd wanted.

The money to provide for my mother was the main aim but, and I was only admitting it to myself now as the numb fog was clearing, there was another reason – my father had been so keen on providing for Olivia after his death – now they could rot in hell together.

15

The Higgins's had a newspaper delivered. Three days after my visit to Olivia Burton, Mrs Higgins pointed out the headlines to me over breakfast.

GRIEVING WIDOW FOUND STABBED

'I don't know what the world is coming to!' she said, tutting loudly. 'The poor woman. She'd just lost her husband too. Shocking!'

I shook my head when she tried to hand it to me to read. 'I'm not sure I could read about anyone else's sadness.' I hadn't told Mrs Higgins about my father's bigamy. To my relief, it seemed to have escaped the attention of the press. It would be easier for me if it continued that way. Secrets – his and mine – were best kept hidden away.

'Yes,' Mrs Higgins said, folding the newspaper and putting it to one side. 'You certainly have had your full share recently, you poor thing.'

'I'm planning to go back to school next week. Try to get back into some routine.' I saw her lips tighten, knew that she was trying to find the right words to tell me her news. She'd been kind to me, I decided to make it easy for her. 'You've been lovely, and I really do appreciate it, but I'm going to go back home today.'

The look of relief on her face was almost comical. 'Are you sure it isn't too soon?' When I shook my head, she carried on, 'Well, it's probably just as well, we're planning a trip to Canada, leaving next week. I did have a word with Rachel, and she said you'd be welcome to go there, if you needed to.'

The Robinsons had three golden retrievers and five cats, all of whom were given free rein of the entire house. I'd rather move in with my mother. 'That's very kind of her, but I'm better getting on with my life. Hopefully Mum will be back home soon.'

'I do hope so for your sake,' Mrs Higgins said. She got to her feet. 'Let me give you some supplies to take with you.'

I hadn't planned on going till that afternoon. It seemed she had other ideas. An hour later, with my few belongings shoved into a borrowed holdall, and sufficient supplies to last me a couple of days hanging in an orange plastic bag from one hand, I headed home.

* * *

I'd sold the car the previous day. It brought less than I thought, but the four thousand I got for it plus the hundred I'd taken from Olivia's purse left me in funds for a while. Not enough to pay off the arrears on the mortgage, but the thousand I lodged would keep them sweet for the moment.

It also meant I had enough to pay for my mother's care... for a while anyway. I'd been afraid to visit for fear they'd ask for money, phoning every day instead, getting the same story each time.

Mum didn't seem to be improving. That afternoon, I'd visit and see for myself.

I put away my belongings and the supplies Mrs Higgins had given me, then sat and stared out the window. I wasn't sure what my next step was regarding the house in Thornbury. The sooner I could get it sold, the better. I'd know where our finances stood. I'd never had to consider where the money came from to pay for what I needed before. I asked, and mostly, I got.

Now, I was having to do a crash course.

I could hardly ring the solicitor and tell him that life interest he'd mentioned wasn't a problem any more. I'd have to wait till her next of kin contacted him. With no idea who this was, or how long it was going to take, it looked as if I was going to have to wait.

* * *

The Bartholomew Clinic was set in the middle of wooded grounds a mile outside the village of Monkton Combe, and four miles from Bathford. It entailed a two-bus journey, followed by a twenty-five-minute walk. Plenty of time for me to worry about what I might find when I got there.

An imposing gateway into the clinic's grounds opened into a winding driveway that took me five minutes to walk before reaching the surprisingly modern building that housed the clinic.

The administrator was pleased to see me. More pleased, if slightly surprised, when I told her I'd come to pay for my mother's care to date. 'Dr Brennan informed us of the circumstances,' she said. 'Since you're not of age to sign a contract, we have sent a letter to your mother's solicitor. It appears it may be some time before your father's estate is settled.'

'Yes, that's correct, but I do have some funds and I'd prefer not to let the bill accumulate.' I might be young, but I was old enough to know that money spoke. It seemed to be important that the clinic knew there would be money for my mother's care regardless of what happened. They would never know what I had done to ensure it.

The administrator's eyes widened when I took a roll of cash from my pocket and peeled off sufficient to pay for the first week's bill, an astronomical £900.

Whether it was money talking, or she was simply being kind, she escorted me to where my mother was sitting in a big lounge overlooking the gardens.

'I'll tell the nurse you're visiting,' she said, and left me alone with my mother.

My mother? It had only been a week. She'd sunken into herself, shoulders drooping forward, her chin resting on her chest, her thin hair in two curtains hiding her pasty face.

I knelt on the floor beside her chair. 'Mum?'

There was no reaction. Her eyes were open, fixed on her lap as if everything was written in the pattern of her dress... all her past, all her future.

I got to my feet and pulled a chair closer just as a nurse came through the door. She greeted me with a smile before turning to my mother and, keeping up a quiet monologue, she adjusted her position in the chair, then the chair itself, tilting it back a little. Her ministrations brought my mother's face up.

Her position may have changed but that was all. Now instead of looking into her lap, she was staring out of the floor-to-ceiling windows.

I moved my chair so I was almost directly in front of her, but there was no change in her expression, no light in her eyes, no upward curve on lips that were pressed in a tight line. I took her hand in mine. It was warm, limp, and when I squeezed it gently there was no response.

'Just talk to her,' the nurse said, 'tell her about your life, what you've been doing.'

She was probably surprised when I laughed. She'd have been a hell of a lot more surprised if I'd told her what I *had* been doing. A final adjustment of my mother's chair, and the nurse left.

With my mother's hand held in mine, I spent the next hour telling her the more mundane things I'd done recently. I spoke of how kind Mrs Higgins had been. About my visit to the solicitor and how everything was okay, that our finances were in good order and how Dad's life insurance would pay off the mortgage. All the lies that I hoped would settle any worries that were buzzing around her head. If I succeeded, there was no sign, her eyes remained as blank, her mouth as tight, her expression as dull and distant.

Perhaps I should have told her what I'd done. The shock of my father's death had locked her away, maybe another would drag her out. I could tell her the gruesome details, the feel of Olivia's warm blood gushing over my hand, her attempt to get away from me, how I'd waited and watched as she'd struggled for breath. I could tell her of the framed photographs, the ones depicting the happy couple... my mother's adoring husband, the love of her life hand in hand with his second wife... I could tell her how I'd smashed them all to smithereens.

But I couldn't tell her that, I couldn't tell her any of it.

I pressed my lips to her cheek, wishing she'd reach up to hold me in an embrace, that she'd look at me with love... that she'd look at me with any emotion at all. I stood, feeling hollow and walked from the room without looking back.

16

I didn't have to wait long to find out what was going to happen with the house in Thornbury. A week after Olivia Burton reluctantly departed this life, I was eating a late breakfast when the doorbell pealed and startled me out of the dark mood I had found myself in since I'd visited my mother. It had made me restless, prevented me from falling asleep or had woken me in the early hours.

It wouldn't be a neighbour at the door. Mrs Higgins had departed for Canada, and I'd let Rachel Robinson know that I wasn't in the mood for her company or that of her animals who she assured me, would be beneficial to my health.

'I could leave Billy here with you,' she'd said two days before, when I'd stupidly answered the summons of the doorbell instead of ignoring it. I'd looked down at the overweight dog, his tongue hanging out, a whiff of a distinctive doggy smell drifting towards me, and struggled to be polite. 'Thank you, but that's not necessary. I'm doing fine. And actually,' – a brainwave hit me – 'I'm allergic to dogs, and cats,' I added hurriedly.

She reared back as if I'd hit her. 'Really,' she said, the tone of her voice saying clearly that she didn't believe me. 'Well, in that case, I'll leave you to your own company.'

I hadn't seen her since. It wouldn't be her at the door.

I gulped down the last of my juice and got to my feet. It might even be someone interesting, someone to shake me out of the melancholy that was swamping me.

The person standing on the doorstep didn't look too promising. A craggy face was topped by a sunburnt bald head that was streaked with thin parallel lines of white hair. Stumpy legs stuck out from under a pair of creased cotton shorts and looked as if they struggled to support the grossly protuberant belly.

'Yes, can I help you?' I said, regretting having answered the door.

'Lissa McColl?'

Had he been better dressed, or at least not wearing shorts that showed off knobbly knees and the start of varicose veins, I might have thought he was a social worker coming to check on how the daughter of a dead father and broken mother was coping. Whoever he was, he knew my name and that made me nervous. 'Who's asking?' Rude, but necessary.

He held his hands up defensively. 'I'm sorry, I should have introduced myself first. My name is Alan... Alan Burton.'

It was a struggle to keep my expression locked in neutral. Of all the scenarios I might have predicted, this wasn't one of them. A brother or possibly a husband of the woman I had killed. Maybe Olivia too had been guilty of the crime of bigamy. Now wouldn't that be a laugh?

But I wasn't laughing when I stood back to allow him to enter. I tried to shake off the melancholy that was making my thought processes sluggish. Whoever this man was, it was essential to watch what I said. 'Come on through,' I said, shutting the front door and leading the way back into the kitchen. 'Have a seat. Would you like a cup of tea or coffee?'

'Tea would be good, thank you.'

Rather than sitting, he prowled around the kitchen, picking up and putting down the ornaments and mementos my mother had collected over the years: seashells from various beaches, a smooth stone from a river, a pottery elephant my father had bought her in Arundel because she'd admired it. This strange man picked up each and peered at it suspiciously.

'Here you go,' I said, putting a mug of tea on the table and positioning a jug of milk within reach. I waited till he'd sat and added milk to his tea before speaking again. 'Alan Burton, you are I assume related to Olivia.'

He took a miniscule sip of the hot tea before nodding. 'Yes, she's' – he shook his head and stuck out his lower lip – 'I can't get my head around saying *was* as yet. But yes, Olivia was my sister.'

I raced to find my place in the script. 'Was? I'm sorry, I don't understand.'

He sighed. 'Ah yes, I'm sorry, of course you don't know yet. I was speaking with her solicitor yesterday afternoon. I'm sure he'll contact you today and I'm sorry I rushed the gun it's just...' His already heavily lined face creased even further and I thought he was going to cry.

'Olivia is dead?'

'Yes.'

'I'm sorry for your loss. I never met her, of course, I didn't know she existed till recently.' I let my breath out in a trembling sigh. 'You're obviously aware that she was never legally married to my father.'

'Yes. Livvy rang me when she found out. She was distraught about his death and stunned to find out the lie they'd been living.

I met him a few times. Such a charming man, so full of life, funny and kind. Livvy adored him. I still can't believe it was all a lie.'

'It came as a shock to us too. My mother was particularly affected by it.' He didn't ask where she was, perhaps the solicitor had told him. 'It was obviously too much for Olivia too.'

He took a gulp of the tea and wiped a hand over his mouth. 'No, you don't understand! She didn't kill herself; she was murdered. A burglary. It was in the papers; I'm surprised you didn't see it.'

I held my hand over my mouth and widened my eyes. 'Oh no! That was her? A neighbour spoke about a woman being killed during a burglary recently, I didn't see the article though so never saw the name.' It was nice to be able to tell the truth for a change.

'It was a shock. I was her only living relative which is why I went to see the solicitor yesterday.'

To see what he was going to inherit. I guessed this was where the real shock lay for him. He'd have assumed the house was hers after the death of her husband. What a come down it must have been to discover he was to get diddly. There was nothing for me to say, so I waited.

'Mr Brooks told me Olivia had a life interest in the house which now reverts to your mother.' His smile was wolfish. 'And to you, of course.'

I didn't think a reply was necessary and merely nodded.

'I gathered from him that your mother isn't expected to make a full recovery though,' he said, assuming an expression of fake concern. 'That must be so hard on you. Only sixteen and to be alone in the world.'

I can't believe the very careful solicitor had been so free with information. It looked to me as if Alan Burton had gone to a great deal of trouble to find out the details of my situation. I just wasn't quite clear why. Not yet anyway. But I wasn't kept in ignorance for long.

He put his empty mug down. 'It's strange, but I feel we are related in a funny kind of way.'

'Really?' What was this strange, and increasingly creepy little man up to?

'Yes, it's like you're my niece.' He smiled in what I supposed he hoped was an avuncular manner.

I decided to play along, see where he was going with this. 'I don't have any relatives. An uncle might be nice.' When he grabbed my hand with his smooth clammy one, I had to stop myself pulling mine away with a snort of disgust.

'We could be good for each other,' he said, 'get ourselves through this bad period. Plus, I could help you with the finances. Save you whatever astronomical fees Brooks would charge.'

He looked at me expectantly. Did he expect me to jump up and throw my arms around him in gratitude at being rescued?

'I'm going to make more tea,' I said, getting to my feet abruptly. I took both mugs back and emptied the dregs into the sink. As the kettle came to a boil, I stared at the knives sticking from the block. The biggest was gone. Sitting in some police station as evidence. But there were a couple as sharp and almost as long. It would be easy to take one out, keep it concealed till I brought over the tea and used it to silence the toad-like man forever.

Two things stopped me. First – I'd killed two people and so far had managed to escape detection. I might not be so lucky next time, and prison was not on the list of places I wanted to visit. The second, and probably the more important deterrent – both my killings had been a means to an end. Killing Jemma had stopped the hideous bullying; killing Olivia had secured my mother's future. Alan Burton was a creepy little toad but if I killed him – if I started down that road of killing without real reason, of killing everyone who pissed me off, wouldn't that make me a monster?

Or was I fooling myself – was I already one? The thought made me shiver and I shut my eyes, blocking those tempting knives from view.

'Here you go,' I said, a minute later, putting a fresh mug of tea in front of him. I waited until he'd taken a mouthful before saying quietly, 'When you're finished, I want you to go away, and I never want to see you again. Okay?'

He sputtered and coughed, sending tea in a spray across the table. 'What?'

Perhaps my quiet restrained delivery had failed to get the message across. 'You heard me, you money-grabbing leech. Finish your tea, get out, and don't come back.'

He didn't wait, standing and backing from the kitchen with his mouth agape as if the sixteen-year-old pushover he'd assumed I was, had become rabid and turned on him, snapping and snarling.

So he escaped. Alive. But he'd made me face the truth about myself – maybe I wasn't a monster, but I had something monstrous buried inside.

Alan Burton was lucky she hadn't wriggled out to introduce herself to him.

17

Jason Brooks, our solicitor, contacted me later that day to break the sad news about Olivia. I didn't mention her brother had been to visit. Since I'd made my position clear, it was unlikely he'd tell the solicitor.

'Sometimes,' Brooks said once he'd finished, 'bad news can have pleasant repercussions and so it is in this case. With Ms Burton's demise, her life interest reverts to your father's estate.'

'Okay.' I was relieved to hear not the slightest suspicion in the solicitor's voice at this conveniently great news for me and my mother. I had to play it carefully though, maybe pretend to be a lot dimmer than I was. 'I'm not sure what that means for us though?'

'It simply means that the house Ms Burton lived in now belongs to your mother. It can be sold, I can handle the legalities for that, acting in her best interest. The money can be used to pay the arrears on the mortgage, your mother's clinic bill and provide for any care she might need in the future.'

I hung up. I'd done it. Made our life more secure.

* * *

My mother was unable to go to the funeral of her beloved husband. I had asked the undertakers to keep it simple... aka as cheap as possible. There was no hint of criticism, they were completely respectful and supportive all the way through.

Haycombe Crematorium is on the far side of Bath in Englishcombe. When the day of the funeral came, I searched Mother's wardrobe for something suitable for me to wear. She was my height and build, but I'd lost more weight and the black shirt and trousers I chose were too big. I hooked a belt around my waist. That was as much effort as I was willing to make for my lying, cheating father.

Jason Brooks had offered to pick me up, but I told him I'd prefer to make my own way. Perhaps he thought I was going to go by a limousine provided by the undertaker. They'd offered, but at a crazy price. The bus suited me just fine.

The celebrant did his best to say some kind words. He didn't get them from me. When he asked me, I told him about the bigamy, how my father had lied and cheated. He'd backed away from me as if bitten, an effect I increasingly had on people. They shouldn't ask if they can't handle the truth.

He must have spoken to someone more willing... Dr Brennan or Mr Brooks perhaps... because the kind words that he did say reminded me of the father I had loved, and they brought a lump to my throat.

If anyone was surprised by the poor turnout, nobody said. No neighbours came because I hadn't informed them it was taking place. I probably would have told the Higgins had they been around and not enjoying their stay in Canada.

My mind drifted during the short service. I stared out the window at the view over the valley below where a buzzard was circling, using thermals of rising air to climb higher and higher, wings barely flapping. I'd read somewhere that they can spot a moving target from over a mile away, then they launch a surprise attack before their prey is aware of their presence.

We had much in common. Neither Jemma nor Olivia had been aware I'd had them in my sights. I had hoped that in avoiding Olivia's eyes in that moment before her death I would escape being haunted by her as I had been by Jemma. It hadn't worked and now both women appeared in the oddest moments. Sometimes when I slept, more often when I was awake, like now. I shut my eyes to make them disappear and brought my attention back to the celebrant.

And then it was over, the curtain sliding across my father's coffin. Without music, the swish of the curtain and the whirr of the mechanics as the coffin was moved backward were audible.

I'd liked to have heard the crackle of flames, the sound of the cheap wooden coffin breaking, the sizzle as his body caught fire. Damn it, I'd liked to have lit the match.

* * *

Too fragile to cope, my mother never did recover. Luckily, the clinic had a long-term care facility, and she was moved to a private room there with a view over the grounds. It was impossible to know if she ever noticed. She might, and that was sufficient.

Because it was in a better area than our bungalow, the sale of the Thornbury house brought in sufficient equity to pay off the arrears and the outstanding mortgage on the bungalow. What remained would pay for the care home for a few years.

'It's not going to last forever,' Brooks said when he'd invited me to a meeting to discuss our situation. 'You're classed as a dependant so you are entitled to stay in the family home until you're eighteen but then, I'm afraid, the house will need to be sold.'

I'd already done some research so the news didn't come out of the blue. It didn't, however, make it any more palatable. 'I see.'

'Even the money from the sale of the bungalow won't last forever. When it runs out, the state will pay, but only a certain amount. It won't meet the full cost of the home she's in. The alternative would be to move her into a home where the fees *are* completely covered.'

Move her? Into somewhere affordable, where the care might not be as good, where she might have a small pokey room without a view, or where she might have to share? I shook my head. 'Absolutely not, they look after her well. My mother deserves the best. I don't want to move her.'

He nodded as if my answer was the one he expected. 'When the money runs out, you're going to need to pay the difference between what the state pays and what the clinic asks. It's called a top-up fee, and you're probably going to be looking at three or four hundred a month.'

Three or four hundred a month – I shrugged it off, young enough not to worry too much about the future.

Anyway, she was my mother. I'd have done anything for her.

I'd already proved that.

And if I needed to, I'd do it again.

PART II

18

When I'd read all those anatomy and physiology books prior to killing Jemma, I'd become fascinated by the workings of the human body. Studying how to kill someone possibly wasn't a good reason to think of nursing as a career, but I think it set a seed that germinated as I watched the nurses looking after my mother with such kindness and patience.

Maybe I decided to train to prove to myself that I was more than just a killer.

Unfortunately, it didn't take me long to realise I'd made a mistake and that nursing wasn't for me. Perhaps it was because my fascination with the human body lay more in how to kill it rather than how to save it.

With my mother's funds dwindling, I needed to be earning, so despite my misgivings I stuck with it, qualified and accepted a staff nurse's position in the Bath United. It was a job, it paid the bills, but I never learned to love it.

My fascination persisted with the human body, however, and I did enjoy parts of the job. I didn't take risks: I never went as far as to kill anyone, after all I had no reason to, despite how truly obnoxious some of the people I had to deal with were, but now and then I *experimented*.

'This should take the pain away,' I'd say to one of the patients in my care after I'd administered an injection for pain relief. And sometimes it was exactly as they'd been prescribed. But other times, it was sterile water. It never ceased to amaze me that one often worked as well as the other. I wasn't cruel though; I always monitored the situation and ensured the patient was cared for. Unless of course they were one of the truly obnoxious ones – I let them suffer.

Whereas I didn't actively hate the job, I wasn't interested in it enough to want to apply for promotion, so eight years later, I was still a staff nurse on the same surgical ward and answering to younger ward managers.

I became weary of it all and began to take regular sick days, or complained of backache that forced them to put me on restricted duties, mostly sitting down doing paperwork, and I stretched every coffee and lunch break to breaking point. Not mine, the ward manager's.

A few years younger than I, Pippa Jones became the ward manager when the previous incumbent moved to a more senior role.

I disliked her on sight.

With a new-broom-sweeping-clean mentality, Pippa called a meeting of the staff at the end of her first week and mentioned some changes to improve our practices that she planned to implement over the next couple of weeks. Every change she suggested, I raised a hand and informed her that we'd tried it before, and it hadn't worked.

There were halogen strip lights on the ceiling of her office, one positioned directly over her head. As the meeting went on, as I batted back each of her suggestions with aplomb, I could see beads of perspiration ping on her forehead.

She ignored my comments and went ahead with her pathetic attempt to change some of our practices and, as I'd warned her, none worked. After a few days of chaos, things quietly went back to the way they'd been done before she flew in on her broom.

I'd made her look bad though, and she wasn't the forgiving sort. She watched me, unaware I was watching her too, and because I'd been there so long, I was better at it. I had morals, of course, I would never hurt a patient in my care. But Pippa wasn't a patient and she'd stupidly prodded the monster inside that I'd managed to keep asleep for so long.

I might have killed her if a different opportunity hadn't presented itself.

We were often short-staffed on the ward, and multi-tasking was the norm, not the exception. One morning, after the handover from the night staff, I suggested, since we were once again short-staffed, that Pippa do the first medication round.

'It will free up the rest of us to concentrate on patient care,' I said, assuming my most dedicated nurse expression. I could almost feel the tension in the room as the other nurses, student nurses, and care assistants collectively held their breath.

Pippa had two choices... she could say no, she was too busy, or she could agree and bask in everyone's approval. I could see the dilemma in her eyes. She should have said no, of course she should, but her need to be liked won the day. 'Yes, good suggestion, I can do that.'

There were two sets of keys. I handed her one of them with a smile and left her to it. It wasn't her first time to take over the round. I'd checked up on her then, and she'd made no errors, but I lived in hope.

It was a frantic morning, and it was after midday before I had a chance to check up on her. I flicked through the medication records without much expectation, my eyes widening to see her initials on the sheet I was looking at. According to it, Adam Frazer had had his medication that morning. Slightly difficult since the man had died during the night. The night staff should have removed the paperwork and his medication. That morning's pills had been pressed from the cards and were nowhere to be seen.

There had been three admissions during the night, and Adam Frazer's bed had already been filled. Had Pippa given the medication to the new occupant in that bed?

Pulling out my mobile, I took a couple of photographs then headed to Pippa's office.

I knocked and pushed open the door without waiting for her say-so. She was sitting frowning at her computer screen and threw me an irritated glance before focusing on whatever she was doing. 'Is it important?' she asked. She hadn't bothered, in the privacy of her office, to hide her dislike of me. I didn't care; soon that dislike would be a stronger emotion, soon she'd hate me. And fear me perhaps.

'I think you might find it important. I know the NMC would.' The Nursing and Midwifery Council, the regulator for the nursing profession, keeps a register of all nurses. They also investigate any wrongdoings and would remove a nurse from the register if they were found guilty. The very mention of the NMC was enough to strike the fear of God into most nurses and had them evaluate and check everything they'd done or said in the previous days.

Pippa's eyes flickered.

I took out my mobile. 'I've something you need to see.'

The emotion that flitted across her face could have been irritation, it passed too quickly for me to be sure, and her face became an unreadable mask. 'If you must,' she said, sounding slightly bored.

'Right.' I held the screen towards her, showed her the signed medication sheet, flicking over to the drug cards with their telling gaps. 'There you go, have a look.' I kept my eyes fixed on her face, almost smiling to see her colour fade as the implications of them hit home.

'You gave Mr Frazer's medication to the new patient, didn't you?' I could almost see the cogs turning in her brain as she wondered if she could bluff it out or not.

'What do you want?'

I had to give her credit. There was no attempt to explain away her actions. Nor did she give any credence to my less than subtle hint that the NMC would be interested in knowing about it. She knew I wanted more than to have her suspended pending an investigation which would undoubtedly have ended with her either being struck off or having restricted duties for the foreseeable. Neither would be good for her career. No, she knew I wanted something more.

I perched on the side of her desk and looked down at her. 'Don't worry, it's nothing too awful, certainly nothing illegal. I simply want a quiet life, and by that I mean my choice of shifts, no criticism when I take a little longer for my breaks, no reporting to the HR department when I need a day's sick leave. Things like that.'

Her face was a picture and I struggled to keep from grinning like a naughty child. Really, I wasn't asking for much, but I knew, and she knew, it would undermine her authority to be seen to be giving me preferential treatment. Sadly, she didn't have a choice.

There was no reason to wait for an answer, I had all the negotiating advantages after all, so I stood. 'I'll leave it with you then, eh?'

I closed the door gently behind me and went off for my lunch break. I wasn't planning to rush back.

For the remainder of my time in the hospital, it amused me to push Pippa as far as I could. I took longer and longer breaks, took a sick day off each week, and generally did what I wanted. Luckily for Pippa, who had developed an obvious tremor when I was in her vicinity, this leeway didn't satisfy my creeping dissatisfaction. A month after our arrangement began, I handed in my notice and took a position with a private nursing agency.

19

Creeping dissatisfaction was one reason I decided to leave the hospital. The other reason, as it always was, was money. The care home where my mother languished had changed hands two years before. The change of ownership coincided with the last of her money and the necessity for the state to step in and provide for her care. Or at least, the sum they considered acceptable. That it wasn't sufficient to pay for the care where she was, was immaterial. The last of her savings paid the difference – the top-up fee – and her expenses for a year. After that, I had a choice, pay the sum myself or move her to a different home.

My thoughts on this hadn't changed over the years, rather they had become more rigid. My mother would stay where she was. Initially, the top-up fee was set at £100 and wasn't too burdensome. The following year, it jumped to £200. Still not too onerous. Unfortunately, when the home was taken over by a huge private care provider, this doubled to £400.

'There are cheaper homes,' Jason Brooks said when he rang me to discuss the matter.

There were. I'd looked at some of them. 'No, I'll cope, don't worry.' He no longer managed my mother's affairs, but he kept in touch, and was happy to offer me his advice. Luckily, free of charge. I think he thought of himself as a father figure. I suppose he was. But not like mine – the solicitor was honest.

I could have stayed in the hospital, applied for promotion, worked extra hours. More nights, more weekends. I could have; instead, I left and joined the nursing agency where the pay was better, and I could work what hours I wanted to make the income I needed.

I lived in a small studio apartment near the hospital. I'd learned to drive and used Mother's car for a few years, but when it started to give trouble, I decided to get rid of it. It was only a five-minute walk to the hospital, it seemed to make sense. I considered buying another car when I joined the agency, but they insisted there were plenty of nursing homes in and around Bath that I could get to by bus.

Some of the places required a bit of a walk. It didn't bother me; I liked the fresh air before and after being shut up for hours with sick or elderly people. The only day I had a problem with was on Sunday when the bus timetable ignored those who needed to be somewhere early. My solution to that dilemma was simple, I didn't work an early shift that day.

Some months, I had a surfeit of jobs to choose from, allowing me to be picky as to which shifts I took. Other months, I had to take what I was given. I didn't have the luxury to turn down work. The £400 a month I needed to pay the care home was a big chunk out of my salary, but it wasn't the only expenditure. There were all the little extras my mother required: the hairdressing, manicures, chiropody, toiletries and clothes.

The rent on my studio apartment in Bath, despite its small size, took most of what was left. It was convenient when I was working in the nearby hospital but now it made sense to move out of the city to find something cheaper. Not bigger though, I liked my accommodation to be small, cosy. Almost womblike.

Apart from accommodation, I lived frugally. The navy polyester tunics and trousers I wore for work were hard-wearing and rarely needed replacing. The remainder of my clothes came from charity shops. The only thing I spent money on was shoes. Comfortable laced ones for work, sturdier ones for walking.

With the decision to move from Bath made, I spent a couple of weeks searching for suitable accommodation. Since I wasn't interested in sharing with anyone, or renting a room in a multi-occupancy house, my options soon dwindled. Further, and further I went until, almost to my amusement, I ended up back where I'd started. In Bathford. The other end of the village from where I'd grown up.

I'd almost given up hope when I saw the advert on the noticeboard in my local Co-op. The tatty piece of paper with the corners curling and the telephone number barely legible probably put off a lot of people. It might have done me, except by that stage I was desperate. The information provided was basic:

Small studio apartment for rent. No children. No animals.

No indication as to cost. More annoyingly, no reference as to where it was.

The advert had obviously been there a long time. Unsurprising really. I took a photo and when I got outside, rang the number. It was answered almost immediately with a gruff curt, 'What?'

Charming! 'Hi. My name is Lissa McColl. I'm enquiring about your advert. For the apartment,' I added when the silence lingered.

'The apartment.' As if he'd no idea what I was talking about.

'The apartment,' I repeated. 'There was an advert on the noticeboard in my local Co-op. Near Bath United hospital.'

'Right.'

One word followed by a long silence. I thought he'd hung up when I heard him take a deep breath.

'When do you want to see it?'

'I don't want to waste your time.' Or mine. If it wasn't convenient for the bus, it wouldn't be of interest regardless of how cheap it was. 'It would help to know where it was.'

'Bathford.' He sounded surprised at my question. Maybe the advert had been written so long ago, he'd forgotten he hadn't put the location.

It was so unexpected that for a second, I was unaccustomedly lost for words. *Bathford!*

'Well,' he said, waiting for an answer to his original question.

'How about now?' I said, checking my watch. The buses were regular, I could be there in an hour.

'Now?'

'Midday?'

'Right.' The surprise was even more obvious this time. He reeled off the address. 'You know where it is?'

'Yes, I'll see you there at midday.' The address he'd given me was on the High Street in Bathford. I'd walked the length of it many a time while I lived there. It was unlikely to have changed much over the years. The bungalow where I'd lived was further out of the village, down a lane off Prospect Place. I hadn't been back since leaving. Our neighbour, Mrs Higgins, moved to Canada to live with her daughter after her husband died. She sent a Christmas card a few times; I didn't send one back and hadn't heard from her for a couple of years.

Bathford is three miles east of Bath. Once outside the horrendous traffic that clogged the city's streets, the bus trundled along at speed. Twenty-five minutes later, I climbed out and looked around. It had been almost eight years, I expected to feel a twinge of nostalgia, to find everything looking familiar. Instead, it could have been anywhere.

Luckily for me, since the High Street was about a mile long, I reached the address I'd been given after a ten-minute walk. The houses of the village were predominately of Bath stone, the creamy gold stone that made even the most meagre house look pretty. This though, wasn't meagre: Lily Cottage was a very pretty detached house. I found myself smiling at just how lovely it was, before frowning. Where was the small studio apartment?

Perhaps the advert had been misleading and it was a room in the house that was for rent. No matter how lovely, that wouldn't suit me.

There didn't seem any point in standing there, speculating, so I opened the small wrought-iron gate and walked the few steps to the front door. There was a doorbell and a brass knocker. I pressed the bell and when I couldn't hear it pealing within, I added a couple of raps on the knocker for good measure.

The door was pulled open so quickly that I hadn't time to take a step backward and found myself too close for comfort to the man who'd opened it. Although he must have been waiting for me to have responded so quickly, he looked startled as if I was an unexpected visitor and held the door as though he might need to slam it in my face.

'I'm Lissa McColl,' I hurried to say. 'I spoke to you earlier. About the apartment.'

There was no change in his expression. Perhaps he wasn't startled, and always looked oddly pop-eyed. He was a big man, tall and wide. When he remained silent and continued to stare, I shuffled back a step. 'Is it possible to see it?'

'Yes.' He looked me over, not bothering to hide his assessment, his gaze taking in my chunky shoes, my unfashionably baggy trousers, the shirt that didn't match. 'You'd better step inside.'

Perhaps he sensed my hesitation and sudden unease, because he stood back, opening the door wide.

I didn't know anything about this man, not even his name, and nobody knew I was there. I didn't think I was a stupid woman, yet, instead of running away, I found myself drawn into the house.

The line of a poem I'd learned as a child popped into my head. *'Will you walk into my parlour?' said a spider to a fly.*

It should have stopped me, should have had me turn on my heel and run away. Instead, I kept going until I was inside.

20

As soon as I was inside, the landlord pushed the door shut, folded his beefy arms, and looked down at me. 'You're little. It might suit.'

As a conversation opener, it failed dismally, my mind immediately flitting to coffins and graves, dark holes to hide a body. I might have turned and made an attempt to get away, if he hadn't suddenly smiled. 'It might suit you very well indeed.' He opened the drawer of a hall table and took out a set of keys. 'Come on, I'll show it to you.' But instead of leading the way further into the house or up the stairway behind, he waved to the door behind me. 'We need to go out again.'

Outside, instead of heading to the garden gate, he turned left and disappeared round the corner of the house. Feeling slightly bewildered, I followed.

A garage was set slightly further back. A wide pathway separated it from the house, a gate at the far end leading, I assumed, to a rear garden. Expecting to be brought through this, I was surprised when he stopped at a doorway set into the side of the garage. 'Here we are,' he said, pushing the door open and standing back.

Here we were indeed. The garage had been converted into a small studio apartment. There was no sign inside of the up and over door I had seen at the front. I guessed that had been left in situ to fool the authorities. Bathford was in a conservation area, there was no way he'd have had planning permission for the conversion of the garage into a separate dwelling.

Above the only entrance, a long narrow window ran the length of the wall. When the door was shut, it threw little light over the interior. The man, whose name I still didn't know, reached a hand along the wall, and pressed the light switch.

One end of the compact space was divided into two, a small surprisingly well-appointed kitchen on one side, and on the other a tiny bathroom with a shower, wash-hand basin and toilet. A single bed sat against the wall at the other end. The only other furniture was a single sofa, a narrow wardrobe, an even narrower bookshelf, a chest of drawers, and a small square table bracketed by two chairs.

'Well?' he asked, as I walked from one end to the other, peering into the bathroom as I passed.

I sat on the sofa. I wanted to smile, to shout, *yes, it's absolutely perfect*. Before I got too excited, I needed to know about the rent. 'It's a bit smaller than I'd hoped for.'

He shrugged. 'It's got everything you need.'

It had. I wanted it, but it had to be cheaper than where I was. 'I'll have to think about it,' I said getting to my feet. I reached the door, then turned. 'I never got your name.'

'Theo Bridges. It's very quiet here and I won't interfere with you at all. I work from home. I'm a scribbler and usually glued to the computer so you'll rarely even see me.'

I'd no idea what he meant by a *scribbler* and didn't care. I was more intent on getting this apartment at the right price. 'It's not bad, and as you say I am little.' I smiled. 'I suppose it might be tempting. How much is the rent?' I tried to neither look nor sound eager. When he named a figure almost half what I was currently paying, I had to swallow my whoop of excitement. 'I'll take it.'

He had turned away and his head swivelled back to look at me. I was glad it hadn't gone all the way around. I'd seen *The Exorcist*. It wasn't pretty. It wouldn't have stopped me renting the apartment though, it would simply have made me change the locks.

* * *

I'd already given notice to my current landlord, so I was able to move in less than two weeks later.

Theo promised to leave the key available and was true to his word. An envelope was stuck to the door with a strip of tape. I tore it open, knocked the key into my hand and opened the door.

It took me less than ten minutes to unpack. Theo had, as promised, provided a TV. I switched it onto a music channel, sank onto the sofa and let the sound fill the space.

I wished it could have filled the space in my head too. The one where the scary thoughts lived. Sometimes, I would swear I heard Jemma and Olivia howling their anger at having their lives taken from them.

Sometimes, I would swear they were asking for company.

21

When I joined the nursing agency, I had to do a full day of mandatory training.

A waste of a day. Worse, I had to pay for the pleasure. But since I couldn't work till the training was done, I zipped my mouth shut on my grumbles and resigned myself to hours of total boredom.

Thanks to the bus, I arrived early and was first into the room where the training was to be held. Uncomfortable chairs sat in rows before a dais holding a desk, whiteboard and flip chart. All the tools of the course-giver's trade. Weapons of mass boredom.

I had my choice of seats. The first seat of the third row seemed the best option. Near the door, it was convenient for a quick escape. Each seat held a notepad and pen, I picked them up, shoved them into my bag without looking and sat on a chair designed to ensure the occupant would never be comfortable enough to fall asleep.

It was going to be a very long day.

Windows along one wall gave a view over the office building next door. I was peering through the windows, watching as the workers arrived for their day when I had the distinct feeling I was no longer alone in the room.

I'd left the door open behind me. When I turned, there was a woman standing there, silently unmoving. I hadn't heard her footsteps on the corridor. It was as if she'd appeared from nowhere. More oddly, as she entered the room, I was sure I knew her from somewhere. When she came closer, I realised it wasn't her face, as such, it was something about her eyes.

'Hi,' I said.

'Hello.' She indicated the chair beside me with a tilt of her head. 'I may as well sit there, unless you're saving it for someone.'

'No, I'm not.'

The rows were well spaced apart and I didn't need to move to allow her past. It wasn't till she'd picked up her jotter and pen and sat, that I turned to her and said, 'You look familiar. Have we met before?' When she looked up from her examination of the standard jotter and logoed pen, I was startled once more by a sense of recognition when I met her eyes. There are things that take you back, a certain song, a sound, a scent, and usually you're propelled back in time by whatever it is to a pleasant memory. But this was different, I was filled with a creeping unease.

'I think I've seen you in the Bath United,' she said. 'I was there for a couple of years.'

'Oh, right, yes. I was there for eight.'

'Two was enough for me.' She smiled. 'I'm Carol Lyons.'

'Melissa McColl. Most people call me Lissa.' I returned the smile, but the unease lingered. It hadn't entirely vanished by the end of the long tiresome day and when she suggested we go for a drink as we left the building, I should have said no, should have made any excuse. I didn't though, I agreed and went along with her. I hoped if I spent more time with her, I'd figure out just why she seemed so familiar because I wasn't convinced it was from the Bath United.

I wasn't a drinker, nor was I keen on spending the little money I had to spare on drinking in the trendy bar she took us to.

She headed straight for a booth in the far corner with the air of someone who'd been there before. 'What'll you have?' she said and dropped her bag on the seat.

'Just a glass of tap water will be fine,' I said. 'I don't drink alcohol.' It was a convenient lie.

'Oh.' She looked taken aback but recovered quickly. 'After the day we've just had, I need one.'

So did I, but I'd wait till I got home. There was a couple of cans of cheap beer in the fridge, I'd be happy with one of them.

I had a chance to observe Carol as she stood at the bar waiting to be served. A tall woman, rather heavy around the belly and hips, her hair cut probably shorter than suited her, she wore loose colourful clothes in a light fabric that seemed to float around her as she moved. Expensive clothes. I didn't envy her then, just her freedom to spend money on things she liked. I had no yen for fancy clothes, what I wanted was to be able to travel. I'd never been outside the UK. I'd applied for a passport years before and that was as far as I'd got. Lack of funds, combined with my need to visit my mother at least twice a week locked me in place and probably would for years to come.

'Here you go,' Carol said, placing a glass of water on the table in front of me. She shuffled into the seat opposite and took a long drink from her glass. 'A G&T always hits the spot.'

The clink of ice in her glass, the slice of lemon that bobbed as she drank, made me regret my abstention. And my stupid unnecessary lie made it impossible for me to change my mind. I lifted my tap water and took a sip. 'I'm glad to be done with mandatory training for another year.'

'It comes around very quickly.'

Next, she'd be saying the years were flying by. 'Were you working in the Bath United till recently?'

'Yes, I finished there last week. Decided to try agency for a while, see if it suited me better.'

I took another sip of my water. It didn't taste good, I guessed it had been sitting in a jug in the fridge for a while. 'I finished last week too.'

'Yes, I followed you.'

I'd just taken a mouthful of water and my deep breath of shock had sent it flying into my windpipe making me cough and splutter. 'Sorry,' I said, slapping the flat of my hand against my sternum. 'It went down the wrong way.' It took a few seconds before I was recovered enough to be able to speak normally. 'What do you mean "you followed me?"'

She was swirling the ice around in her glass and looked at me in surprise. 'I was joking!'

Was she? She had a silly smile on her face, but it didn't reach those pale blue eyes.

We left as soon as she'd finished her drink. She was, she told me, parked in Charlotte Street car park. 'What about you?'

'I'm on the bus,' I said. 'I don't have a car.'

Her eyes widened in surprise. 'You're doing agency nursing and you don't drive!'

I wanted to point out that I hadn't said I didn't drive, merely that I didn't have a car which was a different thing entirely, but I didn't bother. 'The agency knows, they said it would be fine.' They hadn't actually; they said it would be awkward but that it was up to me to ensure I arrived for a job on time, regardless of how I got there.

'Right,' she said, obviously unconvinced. 'Well, I better be off. Fancy meeting again sometime, compare jobs, etc.?'

I noticed she didn't volunteer to give me a lift anywhere. For all she knew, we could live in the same area. A shiver ran through me at the thought that I might see her creeping around where I lived. Peeping in the window of my ground-floor apartment. Following me. I suddenly had to know where she lived.

'Yes, that's a good idea. Agency nursing might be a bit lonely.' I picked up my bag and pulled out my mobile. 'I'll take your number, then message you so you'll have mine.' When that was done, I dropped it back into my bag. 'Maybe we can meet on our days off. Are you far from Bath?'

'Larkhall. What about you?'

Larkhall was nowhere near my tiny place in Weston, and I found the tension slipping a little. 'I'm in Weston, near the hospital but I'm thinking of moving. The apartment I have is tiny and a bit expensive for what it is.'

'We'll meet up somewhere, maybe before or after a shift someday.'

And on that note, we left the pub and parted. I didn't really want to see her again. Friendship wasn't something I sought. Life was easier, suiting myself and nobody else. But I would meet her, that familiarity I had felt when I'd first seen her... I was sure it hadn't come from a random meeting in the staff canteen in the Bath United or passing in the corridors... it was something more and I needed to know what it was.

I also couldn't get her words out of my head, *I followed you.*

22

I'd only worked a few shifts for the agency before I moved to my new apartment in Bathford. There were several nursing homes within a few miles radius who were always crying out for staff, so as long as I could manage on the bus, I wouldn't bother with a car. When it came to winter, the chilly wait for a bus might change my mind. I hoped by then, I might have money to spare. I'd asked to do night shifts, to bring in even more money, and I'd signed an opt-out disclaimer with the agency that allowed me to work more than the recommended forty-eight hours. Most of the time I'd be working twelve-hour shifts. If I did five days, a sixty-hour week, I should be able to pay the top-up fee for my mother's care and be able to squirrel away enough to buy a decent car.

* * *

Two weeks after that mandatory training day, I was surprised to get a message from Carol.

Hope you're well. Fancy meeting for coffee?

I looked at it for a long time without responding. If there was a hidden meaning in the words, it was lost to me. I remembered the unease she'd triggered... that strange sense that I knew her from somewhere. But even as I thought I shouldn't, I was tapping out a reply to say I'd love to meet.

Living in Bathford, I was now on the same side of Bath as she, so I suggested meeting in the café in Alice Park. It was convenient for me, the bus stopped on the London Road immediately opposite, but it was in Larkhall, her patch of the woods, and I wondered if she'd suggest going elsewhere. To my surprise, she responded almost immediately.

Perfect, it's near me. How about tomorrow?

Tomorrow? Her eagerness to meet puzzled me. More... it worried me. Was I paranoid to think she must have a hidden agenda? A very well-hidden one, I couldn't see any reason for her interest in me. Unless she knew something about me – but I'd been careful in the Bath United. At least I thought I had.

Anyway, the following day didn't suit me, I was starting the first of three twelve-hour night shifts.

I'm working. How about on Tuesday?

Perfect. Midday in Alice Park?

I sent her a thumbs up, and dropped the phone on the table beside me.

* * *

If it hadn't been for the extra money, I would have avoided working nights. The shifts tended to be hours of boredom punctuated with brief spells of activity. It left too much time to think.

Depending on the home, I might have one or two care assistants working with me. They liked to watch TV or witter on about their boring insignificant lives. I avoided sitting with them and instead, made a vague excuse about reading patient files that I didn't care if they believed or not, and sat at the nurses' station. Usually, I'd read whatever book I'd brought with me, but on that first night the words on the page kept sliding out of focus. My thoughts insisted on drifting back to Carol, convinced as I was that she had to be up to something.

The nurses' station was well lit, but outside, along the corridors, subdued lighting created dark places where anything could be hidden.

Like the dark spaces in my head. But now, instead of Jemma and Olivia calling to me, it was Carol's voice I heard. But try as I might, I couldn't make out what she was trying to say.

Over the three nights, I alternated between being determined to cancel my meeting with her and my need to find out what, if anything, she was up to. It weighed on my mind, making me irritable. I could see the care staff looking at me and muttering to each other when they thought I couldn't see or hear. I could, but I didn't care much. I wasn't paid to be nice to them, and I never made the mistake of being irritable with the residents, the female residents especially. How could I be, when in each I saw shades of my mother? And as I tended to them, I was tending to her, and when they responded with a 'thank you' or a smile, or sometimes a pat on my cheek, I imagined my mother's voice, her hand, her love.

My imagination. It was all I had.

23

The quality of sleep after a night shift is different. Sleep comes with startling immediacy and departs in the same way. No matter how irritable, stressed or angry I might be, as soon as my tired head hit the pillow, I was gone and a few hours later wide awake. After the first night, I was asleep by eight forty-five and awake by eleven. The following day, I did a little better and slept till twelve. After my third and final night, when it didn't matter, I slept till two.

One night off, then I was back working four nights. Two in one home, and one each in two other homes. Not the best, but it was important to take the shifts when they were available because it was impossible to tell what might happen in the future. Plus being obliging went down well with the agency, and I hoped that would pay off eventually with the pick of the best shifts. Or better, work in a private home with one patient to care for.

By the Tuesday when I'd agreed to meet Carol for coffee, I was exhausted. I'd finished the last of the four nights that morning and had slept till ten thirty. Almost two hours sleep. It's no wonder that when I looked in the mirror, I laughed at the face I saw. I kept my hair short for convenience, trimming the ends when they started to feather over the Nehru collar of my uniform. My first grey hair had appeared when I was seventeen and now, at twenty-nine, there was only a hint remaining of the brown hair I'd once had. Between the grey hair and the pasty skin, I looked like a ghost.

I didn't eat well on nights either, and it showed. My cheeks were gaunt and my wide mouth and over-large nose were emphasised further as a result. Luckily, any hint of vanity had been hammered from me many years before.

It didn't take me long to decide what to wear since my wardrobe consisted of trousers, T-shirts and two shirts. I remembered Carol's upmarket, boutique clothes from the training day. I couldn't compete but neither did I want to look like I needed a handout. A pair of baggy white cotton trousers with a tight-fitting almost-white T-shirt was the best I could do. The black cat logo on the T was a little childish perhaps, but that couldn't be helped.

I threw my phone and purse inside the patchwork bag I'd bought for fifty pence in the sale box of a charity shop, locked up and headed off. I'd decided to walk. Alice Park was only two miles away, and it would be nice to breathe air not tainted by the super-heated air of nursing homes. It was a flat route; the day was sunny with a slight breeze, and I strode out feeling good despite my lack of sleep.

As I neared my destination, my footsteps slowed. I was still unsure of what to make of Carol, of her desire to promote a friendship between us. My earlier experience with my peers had left me with a reluctance to mix with them socially. Was I self-contained or anti-social? I wasn't quite sure. What I was sure of, however, was that there was more to Carol than was obvious.

Although I arrived at the café ten minutes to midday, she was there before me, at a table sheltered from the midday sun by the large canopy that covered most of the outdoor space. She looked as if she'd been there quite a while too, a book spread open on the table in front of her, an empty plate beside her holding crumbs of whatever she'd eaten.

'Hi,' I said, dropping my bag on a chair opposite. 'Did I get the time wrong?'

She dragged her focus from her book with what seemed to be extreme reluctance. Maybe I'd got the time wrong. Perhaps we'd arranged to meet at eleven. My fingers itched to reach for my mobile so I could check. Instead, I stood waiting for her to say something, the smile on my face feeling ridiculously forced.

'No, you're okay. It was such a nice day, I came early.' She shut the paperback and patted it. 'I was hoping to get it finished but never mind.'

I took my purse from my bag. 'Can I get you another coffee?'

'Thanks, a large cappuccino, please.'

'Okay, back in a sec.'

There was a queue at the counter. It gave me a chance to look at the menu displayed on the wall behind, and I cursed my polite offer when I saw the price of the coffee. I'd been so careful with money for the last few years, it didn't come easily with me to spend it on something so frivolous. Especially for someone else.

Service was incredibly slow and by the time it was my turn, I'd been staring at the selection of pastries for so long that my mouth was watering and I gave in to the temptation.

'Here you go,' I said. I balanced the tray against the edge of the table and offloaded Carol's coffee, my cake and mug of tea. Tea, I'd discovered, was a pound cheaper than coffee making my choice a no-brainer.

I sat and rested the empty tray against the side of my chair. I was going to be magnanimous and wave a careless hand when she offered me the money for her coffee, but when she didn't, when she simply stirred sugar into it and began to drink it as if it had been free, I felt a surge of irritation.

'How did your night shifts go?' she asked, putting her cup down.

'Fine.' I heard the bite in the word but if she did, there was no obvious sign. I looked around at the pretty setting, sat back in my chair and allowed my tense shoulders to relax. I might as well enjoy the money I'd spent. The almond Bakewell I'd chosen was fresh, crumbly and delicious. I ate the lot, and when it was gone, licked the pad of my finger to gather the remaining crumbs.

'Good?' Carol asked regarding me with a raised eyebrow.

'Very,' I replied. I pushed the plate away and lifted my mug of tea. 'This is a nice place. Do you live far away?'

'Five minutes' walk.' She pointed to a road visible through the branches of the trees that surrounded the café. 'Down that way.'

'Fuller Road?' It was a stab in the dark. There were a number of roads within a five-to-ten-minute walk away.

She hesitated, looking at me oddly. 'I didn't know you knew the area. No, not Fuller, a little further along Gloucester Road.' And then, obviously deciding it was silly to be so mysterious, she added, 'Swainswick Gardens.'

'I worked with the agency in the Larkhall Nursing Home, years ago,' I explained. 'That's not far from you, is it?'

She shook her head slowly. 'No, it isn't.' She lifted her coffee and sipped slowly, looking at me as if I'd just revealed some great secret. 'I didn't realise you'd done agency work before.'

How would she have done? She knew as much about me as I knew about her. 'While I was a student nurse, I worked every day I was free. My university fees were paid for, but I needed to earn money for everything else.'

'That can't have been easy.'

It had been an endlessly exhausting trudge. There had been

times when I wasn't sure I'd be able to continue, when I wanted time for myself, a day off from everything. Days when I wondered if moving Mother would be such a bad thing after all. Then I'd visit her and know I couldn't do it. 'It paid the bills, I can't complain.' I nodded in the direction of her home. 'Have you lived in this area long?'

'A few years.' She gave a shrug before smiling. 'I live with my parents. We used to live a few miles further out. When they wanted to move closer, I moved with them.'

And could afford expensive clothes as a result. Probably went on fancy holidays too. I hadn't seen her car; it was probably a BMW. I wondered how different my life would have been if my father hadn't died.

Would he have carried on living his dual life or would he have decided to give up one of his wives... and if so, which one? My mother had been destroyed by his death. But she was locked in a world where she was married to the love of her life – had he lived and chosen Olivia, how would my mother have coped? Would she have fallen apart as badly, and lived the remainder of her life locked in a hell where he endlessly abandoned her?

I felt a tap on my hand and looked up from my contemplation of what was left of my tea.

'Are you okay?'

I blinked. 'Of course, why wouldn't I be?'

Carol sat back, her eyes narrowed, a horizontal line crossing her forehead. 'Maybe because you've been staring into that empty cup for ages despite me asking you three times about where you grew up.'

Had she? I wiped a hand across my forehead.

'Maybe you've been working too hard,' Carol said quietly.

'I was working last night. Perhaps I should have stayed in bed this morning.'

'Last night?' She looked horrified. 'Why did you suggest meeting today?'

'It seemed like a good idea at the time.' I didn't want to say that her invitation to meet up had taken me by surprise. Didn't want to admit that she unsettled me, and I wanted to know more about her to see if I could understand why. Only then could I decide what to do about it, whether to see her as a threat and deal with her in some way. I hid a smile when I thought of the very sharp set of knives that had been supplied with my new apartment.

She'd asked me a question. Perhaps she was genuinely curious about me too. But I had secrets to hide so it seemed better to lie. 'I grew up in Bristol, but I've recently moved to Bathford.'

'Oh yes, you said you were thinking of moving from Weston. Bathford's handy enough for most of the hospitals and nursing homes we cover.' Carol spoke as if she were an expert on the agency's client base. She seemed to have conveniently forgotten that I'd worked with them before.

I regretted my decision to meet her. I could hardly ask her why she made my skin crawl. All I'd discovered was that she was local and had grown up a few miles away. Only then did I realise she'd not mentioned exactly where... Bathford was a few miles away, perhaps she'd lived there. I'd put her at my age, but I didn't remember her from school. Or at least, she hadn't been in my year. Would I have remembered her if she'd been in the year ahead or behind? I wasn't sure I would.

But perhaps she remembered me. There had been a lot of talk after Jemma's death. Whispers, sideways glances, pointing fingers.

Perhaps Carol had known Jemma, and what I'd done. Might she tell the agency? Have them look at me with suspicion? I couldn't afford to lose my job.

Carol was chattering away about something. I tuned in to what she was saying, surprised to discover she was talking with an unexpected amount of detail about the agency's private client base. Luckily for me, she was one of those people who liked to show off what they knew. It made it particularly satisfying to her, I suppose, since she was only with them a few weeks and I had, as I'd stupidly admitted, worked for them before.

She glanced around, then leaned closer, dropping her voice to a whisper. Conspiratorially... as if she was Jane Bond, working for MI6 and not a poxy nursing agency. 'I've been given shifts with a private patient living on Lansdown Road starting tomorrow. It's probably only going to be for a couple of days but still, I'm excited about it.'

Bully for you. 'That's great,' I said, trying to inject some sincerity into my words. It was exactly the type of job I'd have liked, what I'd been hoping for. A nice cushy position looking after one person. I wanted to ask how she'd swung it. Wanted to but didn't. There was a self-satisfied expression on her stupid face, I didn't want to see it grow more smug. So I swallowed my curiosity and tried to appear above it all.

Having shared her exciting news, she sat back. 'Maybe we could meet up again in a few weeks?'

I'd liked to have said, *when hell freezes over.* But I didn't. I needed to keep her close, to find out what, if anything, she knew about me, and why she bothered me so much. Anyway, if she had some pull in the agency, it would be a sensible step to be friendly. What was that expression...? keep your friends close and your enemies closer. It was appropriate. 'I'd like that,' I said.

24

When I returned from Alice Park, I sat down at my computer and emailed the agency. I wrote to tell them how very happy I was working with them, and how I was willing to be flexible not only with the shifts I worked but where I was sent. I finished the nause-atingly sycophantic drivel with the hope that I'd be working with them for many years to come, and pressed send.

I had a polite standard reply thanking me for my dedication.

A week later, I sent a follow-up email with a request to be given private home work if possible. I tried to think of a valid reason for wanting the change. There wasn't one, of course. Looking after one patient at home was likely to be easier, but it necessitated being super organised so that if assistance was required – if we needed help to transfer the patient, or to move their position, for instance – the care was arranged around the availability of staff. Not all nurses liked the responsibility. It didn't bother me.

Although the work would be easier, it wasn't the only reason I wanted it. I loved poking around other people's lives and being in a private home would give me so much more opportunity. Even in the nursing homes I liked to pry. I'd pick up the photographs the residents kept in their rooms and ask who they were. Most residents were happy to talk about their family. Sometimes, when they were asleep, I'd poke in their drawers, read letters and diaries, fascinated by the lives people lived.

I wondered if my fascination with these strangers' lives was because my own happy family life had been cut short. Perhaps I was searching for a sadder life than mine or my poor mother's. But if any of the residents had lived hard lives, it wasn't obvious. It was probable that they hadn't brought their secrets with them. Their secrets – perhaps that was what drove my curiosity. Secrets like the ones my father had kept. The ones I kept. Who could have thought, looking at my father, that he was a lying bigamous cheat. Who'd have guessed, looking at me, that I had killed twice, and was contemplating killing again?

I needed to be in private homes with access to all the detritus of the person's life. That's where I'd find the juicy stuff.

Unfortunately, the agency's reply to my second email was less than promising. They wanted me to know how *appreciated* I was, and they knew I would *understand* that they were unable to *facilitate* my request because work was allocated as it came in. It was, they said, given to whichever nurse was free.

Such crap!

It didn't help that the same day, I had a message from Carol.

The position with that poor man in Lansdown is lasting longer than I'd expected. Let's meet up soon and I'll tell you all about it.

It was an indication of how pissed off I was about her good luck, that I hoped the person she was looking after would die soon.

* * *

It was three weeks before I heard from Carol again. I had been tempted to send her a message to ask how work was going, but my recent shifts had been in one of the nursing homes we all dreaded being assigned to, and I was afraid she might know and gloat. I refused to give any credence to the thought that she might have a hand in my being assigned to the home, unwilling to believe she had that much power. Or maybe afraid she had.

Carol's message was short.

Coffee?

I stared at that one word for a long time before finally tapping out my reply.

If it suits, how about meeting for breakfast after I finish my run of night shifts on Wednesday?

Great idea! Where?

Manvers Café?

I was being extraordinarily nice, meeting there would allow her to park across the street in Manvers Street car park.

Perfect. See you then.

I tossed my phone aside and rested my head back. Maybe I should swallow my pride and ask her how she'd managed to get that position. Lansdown Road. It would be a big house. Grand. There'd be secrets there, I just knew it. Carol said she'd tell me all about it. I know what she meant though. She'd talk about the patient, his illness, the care she was giving, how wonderful she was. Whereas I'd want to know about the house, what was in the drawers, the wardrobes.

I'd want to know all the secrets of the man, his past, what he was hiding.

Because everyone hid things.

Didn't they?

And if I could find ones worse than my father's, maybe even worse than mine – maybe then, I'd feel more normal.

25

By the time Wednesday arrived I was exhausted. I'd worked four nights in one of the most difficult homes. Too many challenging residents and too few staff was always going to be a bad combination. I regretted my stupid idea to meet Carol and wondered if it wasn't too late to cry off. I was still wondering ten minutes later when I pushed open the door to the café.

Carol was already seated at a small table in the far corner of the large airy space. Was being early a power thing for her? It was our second meeting and once again, it looked as if she'd been there a while, the plate in front of her almost empty. She held a knife in her left hand, the fork in her right. It looked awkward and I wondered if she was defying convention because she thought it made her look eccentric, or if she simply did it to annoy. I immediately wanted to snatch the cutlery from her hands and switch them around, a bit like when you see a painting hanging slightly askew and you can't rest until you've straightened it.

To my surprise, she was in uniform. I took the seat opposite and dropped my bag onto the spare chair between us. 'I don't

know how you can eat that,' I said, waving to the sausages and
beans that remained on her plate.

'Easily.' She speared a fat sausage with her fork and bit off
almost half in one bite, proceeding to chew as she spoke. 'You not
getting anything?'

My gaze switched to the menu written on a whiteboard over
the till. It was typical heart-attack fare. No smashed avocado on
sourdough toast served here. I'd chosen the place for convenience
but hadn't been inside before and regretted my choice. 'I'll just get
a juice.'

The assistant behind the till couldn't have cared less, handing
over my order with a bored expression on her heavily made-up
face. I was tempted to ask if she did the eyeliner and heavy foun-
dation fresh every morning, or if she simply trowelled more on
top. Hard unfriendly eyes made me think twice. I took my juice
and sat as Carol was sliding a piece of toast around her now
empty plate. God forbid she should miss a drop of that artery-
clogging fat.

'How was your night?' she asked, giving the plate a final
polish.

I took a mouthful of juice before answering, my nose crinkling
at the taste. Despite what the menu had stated, it most definitely
wasn't freshly squeezed. Or at least not that year. 'It was manic. I
didn't get a wink's sleep.'

Carol pushed her plate away and picked up her mug. 'It was a
waking night, you aren't supposed to sleep, you know.'

Why had I agreed to meet her? I didn't even like the sanctimo-
nious smug cow. 'You never sleep, I suppose?'

'Not if it's supposed to be a waking night, I don't. You could get
into serious trouble if you're caught.' She leaned closer and
dropped her voice to a barely audible whisper as if the café was
packed with people desperate to know what we two were talking

about. There was only one other person in the café, a heavy, scruffy-looking man who was shovelling beans at speed into his mouth as if he was afraid someone was going to try to take them away. I wondered what his story was. He'd probably be more interesting to talk to than the woman sitting opposite. I sipped some more of the orange liquid in my glass and tuned back in to what she was saying.

'There was a nurse fired from the agency last year for doing exactly that,' she said.

She spoke in the kind of voice some people assumed to tell the worst kind of news. *I'm sorry, your mother/father/aunt/uncle* – delete as necessary – *has passed away.* She probably put on a matching expression too – the downturned mouth, the sad eyes – and I just bet she added the hand wringing.

'The family of the woman she was supposed to be looking after had put hidden cameras up when the woman claimed she'd been left alone for hours. There's a rumour they sued the agency for thousands.'

She leaned even closer, almost within kissing distance. I'd have liked to have spat in her eye. 'Shocking,' I said, although it wasn't.

'The nurse was struck off the register.'

That was slightly more worrying. I needed my job, or rather the money it brought in. 'I'm talking about sleeping for minutes, not hours.' I was sounding defensive, and it annoyed me. 'Anyway,' I said, determined to change the subject, 'how's it going in Lansdown Road? I thought the job was only going to be for a couple of days.'

'It was. He had a chest infection and was very poorly but was supposed to make a full recovery from that.' She put on her sad face again. 'He'd been diagnosed with cancer a few years ago and had initially responded to chemo but after the chest infection, he started to deteriorate. The wife has been told he has months, maybe only weeks.'

'Hard,' I said, because I couldn't think of anything more suitable to say. 'Is it a good set up?'

'Yes, it is. He's a big man though and it takes two to sit him out of bed. I liaise with the agency, and they send a care assistant to help me. The wife is determined to look after him at home. She's nice, but fussy about his care, wants everything done exactly as she wants.' Carol shrugged again. 'It's okay with me, it's what we're paid for after all.'

I had to press my lips together to stop myself giving her a mouthful. She was the kind of nurse who would happily double as a servant if that's what the punter wanted. The kind of nurse who would put on a martyred face and insist it was a vocation, not a job. Such crap is what kept nurses' salaries so appallingly low.

'I was supposed to be off today but the nurse doing the other shifts asked me to change a day so...' Carol shrugged. 'I'd nothing else planned for the day. I don't start till nine thirty, so I was still able to meet you.' Her mobile was sitting on the table, it buzzed as a call came through and she reached to answer it. 'Hi.'

As she listened to whoever was speaking, I saw her usually genial expression harden and her fingers press the phone tighter to her cheek, as if she wanted to absorb the words, not just hear them. 'And what am I supposed to do?'

This was followed by some grunts. Whether they were of agreement or not, it was impossible to tell. I was getting bored listening to half a conversation and would have knocked back the end of the orange stuff and left her to it, if she hadn't finished the call and put the phone down with a decidedly grumpy snap.

I really hoped the man had died, that the job she was so happy about was over. I didn't mind sacrificing the man – it sounded as if he wasn't long for this world anyway and he might as well make himself useful. I adopted her sad expression. 'Not bad news, I hope.'

Her lips had narrowed to two thin lines. They barely moved when she muttered a brief, 'Yes.' Then with a loud, long-suffering sigh, she explained. 'That was the agency. The care assistant that was booked to come and help me get Mr Wallace out of bed this morning has had an accident and can't come. They've tried, but they can't find anyone else.'

It wasn't unheard of that we were left high and dry this way. 'What did they suggest you do then?'

'Tell Mrs Wallace there's been a problem and leave him in bed for the day.'

'Can't you ask the night nurse to stay and help you?'

'No, she leaves at seven. Mrs Wallace gives him his breakfast, then sits with him until I arrive. Then she goes to play golf.' She raised her eyes to the ceiling dismissively. 'She likes to have Mr Wallace sitting out by the time she returns.'

Twenty-four-hour nursing care was expensive. It appeared Mrs Wallace was cutting corners where she could. 'The same in the evening, is it?'

Carol was lost in thought. Probably anticipating Mrs Wallace's reaction. 'Yes,' she said, finally. 'I finish at six, she gives him his evening meal and stays with him till the night nurse arrives at ten.' She lifted her tea, took a sip, and put it down with a grimace. 'She's not going to be happy with him being left in bed all day.'

'It doesn't look as if you've much choice.' If I sounded a little bored, it was because I was. Bored, tired and sorry I hadn't gone straight home rather than wasting my time coming to meet Carol.

'It's not fair. He doesn't have much time left; he should be getting all the care he needs.'

'Are you getting him out of bed for his sake or the wife's?' My question was reasonable. So often, as nurses, we were forced to do things for the family's sake rather than the patient's welfare. I saw the question annoyed Carol and hid my smile.

'Keeping Mrs Wallace happy, keeps *him* happy. Annoying her will stress him.'

And stress Carol. I drained the last of that awful juice and put my glass down. 'Right, I'd better let you get on with your day. I'm off to my bed.'

'Unless...'

I was gathering up my bag and jacket and wondering if I should wait for a bus or walk the three miles to Bathford, when I was conscious of a speculative light in Carol's eyes.

She reached across and grabbed hold of the strap of my bag. 'Unless you came and helped me. Ten minutes max, then you can buzz off. The care assistant that comes in the afternoon is different so will turn up okay. I just need to get Mr Wallace up.'

I laughed, thinking she was joking. When I saw she was serious, my laughter stopped abruptly. 'The agency would never allow it. I've just done a twelve-hour shift.'

'They wouldn't need to know.'

'Ah,' I said, looking at her with sudden understanding. 'You mean you want me to work for nothing, is that it?'

She looked taken aback. 'It's ten minutes to help a friend, that's all.' Her mouth tightened. 'I suppose, *I* could pay you. It would be worth it.'

It was so tempting to say okay, that I'd do it for a full hour's pay. I was almost that petty, but only almost. 'Right, ten minutes of my time. You can have it for free.'

Lansdown Road, where the Wallaces lived, was a long road, rising from Bath and twisting and turning for miles. I'd been along the first stretch of it once, years before, when some idiot manager in the hospital had arranged a night out in the Charlcombe Inn. The Wallaces lived closer to the city, on one of the nicer parts a little past St Stephen's Church.

Carol parked on the road outside a beautiful three-storey detached house. 'Here we are,' she said, as if perhaps I was wondering why she'd stopped.

I stepped out, looked back down the road we'd travelled and admired the view over the chimney pots to the green fields on the other side of the city. Carol, probably conscious of my ten-minute time frame, was already hurrying towards the stone steps that led up to the front door.

She needn't have worried. Now that I'd seen the house, my weariness had taken a back seat to my curiosity, and I wasn't in a rush to leave. I peered down at the ground-floor windows as I climbed the broad steps. 'Servants' quarters on the ground floor, are they?'

'Probably in the past,' Carol said. She fiddled with the bunch of keys she held before slotting a Yale key into the lock. 'The kitchen is down there, and a big living room that opens out into the garden, that's all I've seen. There's no staff, apart from a cleaner who comes in two afternoons a week. Mrs Wallace does the cooking herself.'

I was amused by the way she'd said that, as if Mrs Wallace cooking for herself and her husband was such an extraordinary thing. Carol was incredibly servile. It wasn't my nature.

The front door opened into a large hallway. The wooden floor was covered with a selection of fine rugs in jewel colours. A stairway, with elaborately carved newel posts, curved from it to the upper floors. On this floor, closed doors were tantalising me. I desperately wanted to look behind each one, see what secrets lay there.

A house like this, there had to be secrets.

26

Carol looked up the stairway, then grabbed my arm. 'Listen, I don't want Mrs Wallace getting the wrong idea.' She pulled me towards a door. 'Would you wait in here until she's gone. She's always ready to leave for her golf as soon as I arrive, so I'll give you a shout in a minute or two.'

It seemed unnecessarily cloak and daggerish to me. I was about to say so when it hit me what was really concerning Carol. She didn't want Mrs Wallace to get the idea that the agency didn't have sufficient staff and perhaps take her business elsewhere. Carol didn't want to lose her coveted job. 'Fine,' I said. It wasn't as if she was giving me much choice, her grip on my arm was vice-like and she was edging me towards the door as she spoke. Then before I could object, she opened it and shoved me, none too gently, inside.

I wouldn't have minded so much had it been a room I could explore but the silly cow had shoved me into a cloakroom. One small window gave sufficient light, but apart from the pockets of the few coats that were hanging there, there was nothing else of interest, and nothing in any of the pockets apart from grotty paper tissues.

Carol was correct though. Within a couple of minutes, I heard footsteps on the wooden treads of the stairway, then a loud clunk as the front door was shut. I waited till I heard the second set of descending footsteps before I opened the door and peered around its edge.

'Thanks,' Carol said with a grin. 'I told you it wouldn't be long.'

I was tempted to point out that it was three or four minutes out of the ten I'd promised her, but I'd already decided she had no sense of the ridiculous and would probably have taken me seriously. I didn't want her to change her mind and decide to leave the poor old soul in bed for the day. Not when I'd come this far. Not when I had the chance of seeing more than the inside of a cloakroom.

'We'd best get a move on; the clock is ticking.' As if realising I wasn't joking, she turned and ran up the stairs. I followed at a more sedate pace, my eyes flicking over the paintings that lined the walls. I'd noticed the beautiful ornaments on the tables in the hallway too. I wondered about the hours when there was no nurse. It suddenly struck me as strange. There didn't seem to be any shortage of money, or maybe all the money they had was here, in these... things.

'The night staff nurse ensures he's sitting upright for breakfast,' Carol explained as she pushed open the bedroom door. 'Mr Wallace has difficulty swallowing so Mrs Wallace prepares special easy-to-swallow meals and feeds him with a teaspoon. It takes about an hour, but she says it gives her quality time with him. It's the same in the evening. I make sure he's back in bed and sitting up before I leave at six, and she'll give him his evening meal. Then the night nurse comes back at ten.'

The bedroom we entered was massive, probably three times the size of my entire home. Double bay windows gave a stunning view over the rooftops and gardens of the valley that fell away behind the house. The wooden floor was bare, the rugs that had once covered it rolled up and resting slumped against the wall like they'd had the life beaten out of them. The heavy carved wardrobe and a matching chest of drawers were beautiful and too big for most modern homes.

Maybe there had once been a matching four-poster bed. Certainly there would have been something more elegant than the hospital bed that stood in the middle of the room, positioned deliberately to allow access from all sides. It looked as incongruous as the ugly hoist that was waiting to be used to transfer Mr Wallace from his bed to the nearby chair.

The man in the bed was obviously ill. I thought the doctors had been very optimistic with their 'months, maybe weeks'. I'd looked after many terminally ill people by then and I'd have guessed days, if not hours. But who was I to question the doctor?

Mr Wallace said a weak 'hello' when he saw Carol. She bustled around him, keeping up a stream of sickly platitudes. If I'd been dying, they were the last things I'd have wanted to hear. If I'd been dying, I'd have gathered up every ounce of energy and told her to fuck off.

There were framed photographs on top of the dresser. As Carol bustled around getting organised, I strolled across and had a look. Lots of photos of the happy couple. A few included older people I assumed to be relatives of one or the other. No photographs of anyone younger. 'They don't have children?' I asked.

Carol was preparing the chair, moving its position, plumping cushions. Faffing. She stopped and looked at me, squinting in the sun that poured through the windows. She kept her voice low as she answered me. 'No, they don't have any. They're only married a few years. She was married before. Widowed young, I believe, but there were no children from that marriage either. It's tough, they should have had many years together.'

I arranged my features into a suitably sympathetic expression. 'So, he's not that old?'

'He's seventy, she's younger, maybe late fifties, sixty at the most.' She pointed towards a door to the back of the room. 'I just need to get a few things, and then we're good to go.'

Considering the ten minutes I'd volunteered had long since passed, it was just as well.

From curiosity, I trailed after Carol, my eyes widening at the large, surprisingly modern en suite bathroom. I guessed that sometime in the past it had been converted from a smaller bedroom. From the free-standing roll-top bath in the corner, to the super-sized shower cubicle with the largest waterfall shower-head I'd ever seen, it was obvious that no expense had been spared. Carol waved a hand in front of a sensor and water gushed from the wall-mounted spout into a heavy, curved glass basin positioned on a marble counter.

'Nice,' I said. It was an understatement, but I wasn't willing to allow her to see how impressed I was, how envious that she was working in such surroundings. 'Can we get on though? It's been a lot longer than ten minutes.'

Carol couldn't afford to be offended by my tone, but I could see by her tight mouth that she wasn't impressed with me. Tough, I was working for free which didn't sit easily with me. I was also shattered and needed to get to my bed.

Back in the bedroom, Carol repositioned the reclining chair, pressed the locks on its castors, and drew the hoist over to the bed. 'Mr Wallace, we're going to get you out of bed now, okay?'

I'd have loved if he'd said he didn't want to get up, that he wanted to be left in peace to die in the comfort of his bed, not to be put into a chair and forced to look out at a world he was never going to be able to join again. But he was past being able to make that decision. Carol was working for his wife, and *she* wanted him out of the bed and in that chair.

He was a tall man. Not heavy, at least not any more, but his length made transferring him safely from bed to chair an awkward manoeuvre. Using a hoist to transfer was designed to be a two-person procedure. Like most nurses, I'd often been forced by circumstances to act alone, but I would have struggled with Wallace's gangly unwieldy frame.

It took time to slide the sling under him and position his limbs to ensure they'd be safe during the transfer. He groaned as the boom of the hoist raised him from the bed and my mouth tightened to see him in such discomfort purely to satisfy the wife's wishes.

When he was safely deposited in the chair, Carol turned to me with a smile. 'Thank you.' The castors rumbled noisily on the wooden floor as she pushed the chair across to the window and the world beyond, the one he'd soon be leaving, then she moved a smaller chair closer to sit beside him. 'Do you mind seeing yourself out?' she said. 'He's often a little restless for a few minutes after being moved and I don't like to leave him.'

Of course, he was restless! The poor man had been dragged from the comfort of his bed for no reason. 'No problem.' I picked up my bag. 'I hope the rest of the day goes well.'

Shutting the door softly behind me, I headed down the stairs. Several doors opened from the large hallway. It seemed a shame not to make the most of the opportunity I'd been given and investigate a little.

I opened the front door, then shut it with an unnecessarily loud bang. With a glance up the stairs, I crossed the hallway, opened one of the two doors facing me, slipped inside, and shut the door softly behind me.

The room was huge with tall bay windows overlooking the garden to the front. A group of three sofas was set around a stone fireplace. Three cushions sat on each, flat against the back, all with a trendy neat dent in the top. A grand piano stood against one wall, sheet music on the stand above the keys. Unlike the sofas which looked as if nobody ever sat on them, these were dog-eared and obviously used. Mrs Wallace possibly. I'd never learned to play, but I'd like to have sat and run my fingers along the keys, played lady of the manor for a while. It was tempting but would have brought Carol down, and despite grinning at what she might say, at the look of horror on her face at my deception, I wasn't finished exploring.

Shelves to each side of the fireplace were filled with all kinds of tat – high class and expensive, but tat nonetheless – and I felt for whoever had to lift and clean each piece. It was obvious it was done, there wasn't a speck of dust anywhere.

I crossed the room to a huge sideboard that almost stretched the length of the wall. Almost half of its surface held alcohol: most in bottles, some in finely carved glass carafes. Alongside, an ornate silver tray held delicate wine glasses and goblets. The other half of the surface was crammed almost to overflow with framed photographs. I picked up one to peer closer at Mrs Wallace. She was tall, slim, conventionally attractive with perfect features and hair cut in an asymmetrical bob.

There were older photographs: men and women with a vague resemblance to each other, uncles and aunts, perhaps even cousins. There were some of Mr Wallace as a younger man too. I picked up one for a closer look, my initial twinge of sorrow changing to a jolt of shock in an instant. I carried the frame to the window for a better look but in the light that filtered through the net curtains, the resemblance between Mr Wallace and my father was even more striking. Both were movie-star handsome. Both had that heavily Brylcreemed hairstyle that was the fashion of the day.

I'd kept no photographs of my father, unwilling to have a constant reminder of a man who'd cheated us so badly. There was one in Mother's room in the nursing home. I doubt if she even noticed it. It was one taken a year before he'd died, one taken while he shared his life with his other wife.

This photograph, in its ornate silver frame, resembled my father as a younger man. The one before he'd learned how to cause pain. And I wanted it. There were so many frames on top of the sideboard, would anyone miss one? Surely not if I carefully moved the surrounding frames to cover the gap.

It was tucked into my bag before I debated the wisdom of stealing from a dying man. If I had, I'd have shrugged it off. He wasn't going to care. I stood back with the purloined frame safe in my possession and regarded the remainder of the display. There was a second, almost identical frame further back. I could put a photograph of my mother in it. I was almost tempted by the old *in for a penny in for a pound* maxim. But I wasn't stupid, if someone missed one small frame, they might consider it was mislaid, if they missed two, they'd think *theft*.

With the frame in my bag, and a final glance over the display, I opened the door, listened for a moment, and slipped back into the hallway. I should have left then, I really shouldn't have tempted fate, but it was impossible to resist exploring further.

The next door opened into a rather dark dining room. It had an air of abandonment about it, and I wouldn't have been surprised to see cobwebs stretching from the chandelier to the corners of the table. But when I switched on the light, setting the chandelier aglow, it was obvious the same care that had been given to the other room had been given here. It was clean and surprisingly devoid of anything personal. For someone intent on finding secrets, it was extremely disappointing.

Back in the entrance hall, I glanced towards the front door, then towards the door in the furthest corner of the hallway. One look behind it and I'd go home, that's what I told myself as I crossed to it and pushed it open. Unfortunately, it opened into a short corridor. It lured me on, as did the descending staircase at the end. If I encountered anyone at the bottom, that incredibly efficient cleaning person for instance, I'd simply claim I was looking for the toilet.

The stairway led down to another small corridor. Light shone from under the door facing me and before I could stop myself, I'd grabbed the handle and pushed. It opened into a large, bright open-plan kitchen-cum-living room with a stretch of glass doors overlooking the garden and that lovely view.

There was nothing exciting to be found in any of the cupboards apart from the usual plethora of stuff most people kept. There was a drawer stuffed with recipes torn from magazines, and another filled with odds and ends.

In the living room, I admired the artwork on the back wall and the view from the comfortable sofa across the terrace to the valley beyond. A wall-mounted TV and an open copy of a programme guide indicated that this was where Mrs Wallace sat in the evening.

I took a last look around. Apart from the view, there was nothing of interest.

Shutting the door behind me, I looked up the stairway, then to the other doors off this small space, one to the right of the kitchen and one to the left. One, I discovered, opened into a small windowless room with a toilet and tiny wash-hand basin. The other was locked.

Locked. Was there anything more tantalising than a locked door? From being vaguely interested in what was behind it, now I was consumed with curiosity. What was so important, on what was a domestic floor, that it needed to be kept locked away?

The door was old, probably original, and the lock the old-fashioned type. It was possible to peer through the keyhole but the room beyond was in darkness. The key to open it would be too big and awkward to fit on a keyring. I reached a hand to check above the door. All I found was some dust. Life was never that easy.

I was about to give up, take my curiosity and the stolen silver frame and get the hell out of there. But I did hate to give up. The key had to be somewhere handy. I checked above the other doors. Nothing.

My hand was on the newel post and my foot on the lower step before I had an epiphany. The newel post was set about half an inch from the wall. I slid my hand down it and almost laughed as my hand snagged on a nail and my fingers closed over the metal key hanging from it. I was right, it was big, old-fashioned and heavy.

The lock was well maintained, and the key turned without as much as a squeak. The door opened inward. Gentle as I was, it hit something behind with a loud thud. 'Shit!' I stopped; my breath caught in my throat. Then I gave a snort, Carol was two floors up, she was hardly going to hear.

I took a step into the dark room. If I'd been expecting treasures, I was sadly disappointed. Even in the dim light that filtered from under the kitchen door, I could see it was nothing but a storeroom.

It was time to go before Mrs Wallace arrived home and I had to explain my presence in the house. Carol would not be impressed if I was found down there, especially after all the fuss I'd made about her taking ten minutes of my time for free.

Yet, I stayed looking into the shady space. Why would a store-room be kept locked? Did Mrs Wallace suspect her cleaner of making off with supplies? Or Carol, or any of the other staff who came in during the day. Supplies were locked away, yet silver frames were left for any thieving git to take. It didn't make sense and if there was one thing I hated even more than locked doors, it was a mystery.

I felt along the wall till I found a switch. When I pressed it, the glaringly bright light from the single unshaded bulb illuminated the room without providing any clarity as to why this room should be locked. The shelves were full of random stuff... tins of soup, toilet rolls, bars of soap, cleaning products.

Nothing of any value.

The small table behind the door explained the thump. Moving into the room, I straightened the pestle and mortar that had been knocked over. 'Well, well,' I muttered under my breath. The reason for the locked door became apparent as I picked up packet after packet of medication with dawning incredulity.

Carol had said Mrs Wallace insisted on giving her husband his meals. Maybe I was being overly suspicious, but I thought I knew exactly why Mrs Wallace was keeping the door locked, and why her husband's condition had deteriorated faster than the doctors had predicted.

27

After a night shift, I usually fall asleep on the bus journey home. Since most of my recent shifts had been in Bath, the regular drivers knew me. If I were asleep when the bus arrived at my stop, they'd simply give a yell to wake me up. Once, it was a replacement driver and I didn't think to tell him – tiredness can make me stupid – and I ended up in the bus station in Chippenham.

That day, I had too much to think about to feel sleepy. I stared out the window as Bath was left behind and the bus barrelled through treelined streets that always seemed too narrow for its size.

Mrs Wallace intrigued me. I needed to know more about her to understand what I'd seen in that storeroom. It hadn't shocked me. Not much did anymore. I was the murdering daughter of a bigamous father – what could possibly shock me? Anyway, it was impossible to deal, not only with the sick and dying, but with their relatives too, without seeing the worst humanity had to offer. So, I wasn't shocked, but I was intrigued.

Perhaps if I hadn't been quite so bored with my dull mundane life, my going-nowhere career, the unedifying prospect of the same-old same-old for years to come, I'd have let it go. Perhaps too, if I hadn't seen that photograph, if it hadn't brought my father back into my head. He was never far away, but now it was the man he had been before I ever knew him that was invading my thoughts. What had made him choose to do what he'd done? Was it being married to my mother, or had it been my entrance to the world that had forced him to split his life? Did he look at me and worry about our future? Had he seen through to my soul and been afraid?

As the bus chugged along, I stared out the window, forgetting to blink, my eyes watering from weariness.

* * *

There was little natural light in my apartment. The long narrow window above the door faced north and was in the shadow of the two-storey house next door. As a result, even on the brightest sunny day, the interior was in a perpetual twilight. It didn't bother me, and in fact was a blessing when working nights.

I pulled off my clothes, dropped them where I stood and slipped under the duvet. After a night shift, sleep would normally come as suddenly as switching a light out. That morning, I shut my eyes, the thoughts of Mrs Wallace and my father buzzing in my head making me toss and turn. When I finally fell asleep, my dreams were full of staring eyes. I recognised Jemma's and Olivia's. I always did. They followed me everywhere. Awake or asleep. But there was another pair. I wasn't sure, but I'd a sneaking suspicion they were Carol's.

Less than two hours' sleep only filed the edges off the exhaustion that would probably linger until I slept again that night. Rather than getting up, I lay there with my fingers linked behind my head, my thoughts dancing around the intriguing Mrs

Wallace. I wasn't interested in people in general. Most were boringly dull two-dimensional characters trudging through their incredibly banal sad little lives.

I preferred people to be like onions with lots of layers to peel off, never knowing if under the next there was going to be something gross, or if you'd make it to the centre before finding the heart of it was stinkingly rotten.

Sometimes it was easy. People like that ward manager Pippa, peel away one layer and you saw what was underneath – someone who'd be happy to do anything to get what they wanted or keep what they already had. Sometimes it was a little more difficult. I still wasn't sure about Carol.

The unknown Mrs Wallace struck me as being more fun to investigate. I hadn't needed to peel away any layers to see her secret behind the locked door, but I guessed there was more to be discovered, that if I looked, I might find something deviously ugly and rotten at her centre.

I hoped so; I scrambled from the bed and grabbed my bag, then sat back with the silver frame in my hand, staring at the young Mr Wallace, my father's lookalike. I had planned to leave the photo in it as a reminder of the man my father had once been, but I changed my mind. The frame was difficult to open. When I broke a nail, I grabbed a knife to prise it apart. The photograph of Mr Wallace as a younger man had been put on top of an older one of him with a woman, her face slightly averted. She could have been anyone. She could have been my mother. Frowning, I took it out and put it into the book I'd been reading. A photograph of my mother was propped against a book on the shelf. I slipped it into the frame and put my father's lookalike behind. When the frame was reassembled, I made space for it on the bookshelf. It did my mother justice.

My thoughts drifted back to Mrs Wallace. She had been

married before, Carol had said. But not him. I wondered why. Did he too have secrets? I suddenly desperately wanted to know, as if somehow, knowing him would help me understand my father and the road he took.

Carol had been working for the Wallaces for weeks, and unless she went around with her eyes shut, she had to know something. She was such a goody two-shoes though, it wouldn't be easy to squeeze information out of her.

I lay considering my next step until hunger pushed me from the bed. There was no need to get dressed. A scruffy T-shirt that had lost both colour and shape over the years and hung to my knees was perfect lounging wear. I wasn't going out or expecting visitors. That was a joke on me. I never went anywhere except to visit my mother, and nobody visited me. Ever. It was the way I liked it.

The small freezer was full of ready meals I bought in bulk every few weeks from Waitrose. Their meals for one were convenient and tasty although the variety was limited to three: cottage pie, fish pie or beef lasagne. I ate them in rotation, sometimes bringing home a Domino's pizza for a change if I happened to be passing one of their shops. I didn't get deliveries. Officially, I didn't have an address. Nor did I have a letter box.

Theo had broken the news after I had paid over the deposit and first month's rent in advance.

'Give Lily Cottage as your address,' he said, tucking the cash he'd requested into his shirt pocket. There was a plant pot outside the door planted up with a fake box shrub. It had obviously been there for years, the faded leaves strung with lacy cobwebs. He tilted the pot on its side. 'If post comes for you, I'll stick it under here, okay?'

It seemed odd, but I received so little post it didn't seem to matter.

The ping of the microwave jolted me from my thoughts. I used a towel to take the fish pie across to the table. I never saw the point in emptying the food onto a plate. It was simpler, and saved on washing up, to eat straight from the container.

The book I'd been reading was on one side of the table. The bookmark I'd left to mark where I'd left off made it easier for me to flip it open one-handed, and within seconds I was lost in the grim story of the dangerous and psychopathic inmates housed in Broadmoor.

Fiction – even the more graphically violent novels – was too tame for me. It was books about serial killers and real-life murders, the more debased the better, that fascinated and enthralled me. Perhaps it said a lot about me that after an hour reading about the horrific details of some of these inmates' crimes, my thoughts had cleared, and I knew what I needed to do next.

Carol was working straight through to Thursday, so I knew, good girl that she was, she'd go straight home after her shift with the Wallaces that evening. I checked the time on my mobile. It was too early to ring. More relaxed now that I'd decided my next step, I left the empty container and dirty fork on the table, picked up my book and crossed to the bed. Snuggled under the duvet, I was soon back in Broadmoor.

When I finished, I shut the book with a sigh. It was my dream to visit Broadmoor, to see where Peter Sutcliff had spent over thirty-two years, where Ronnie Kray died, and where Peter Bryan, who fried his friend's brain in butter, was still incarcerated. Sadly, it didn't look as if I was going to be able to make my dream come true – sometimes I had doubts about my sanity, but even if I did commit a seriously deranged crime, I wouldn't get into Broadmoor. It only accepted male patients now. Such a shame, but perhaps I was better off staying free.

Climbing from the bed with the book in my hand, I went to the bookshelf and frowned. With my living space so constricted, it was necessary to be strict about what I kept. The book in my hand was a definite keeper and I made space for it on the middle shelf, the one dedicated to institutions like Broadmoor and Wakefield.

The shelf above was given completely to the oldest psychiatric hospital in the world dating back to 1247. Bethlem Hospital, or Bedlam as it was commonly called, giving the English language a word that became synonymous with mayhem and madness. One of the top tourist attractions in London of the 1750s was doing a paid tour of the hospital to see the inmates who were generally chained to walls. It was a tour I'd have loved to have done. I'd bought every book I could find on the hospital.

Other shelves were given over to the notorious and infamous. A recent purchase was a book on Jeffrey Dahmer which indicated it had something new to say about the notorious serial killer. It would be my next read.

I put it on the table to start the following day, the bookmark on top carefully aligned with the edge of the cover. For the remainder of the evening, I'd watch some TV.

But first, I'd make that call to Carol.

The phone rang a few times before I heard her soft, hesitant, 'Hello.'

Her tone was neither friendly nor unfriendly as if she was trying to decide why I was contacting her. We weren't on ringing terms, our meetings arranged by message, and I wondered if I'd made a mistake, if I'd given her a reason to be suspicious. It was done, no point now in shilly-shallying. 'I suppose you're wondering why I'm ringing.' I tried to inject a note of humility into my voice. 'I'm so sorry I was less than helpful this morning. I should have explained that I've been having a problem with sleeping recently and I'm so tired it's affecting my mood.' I pressed the mobile closer to my ear, straining to hear any reaction. When it came, a sigh that I knew meant she'd swallowed my pathetic line, I relaxed. 'I feel so bad about it and would love to have the chance to make it up to you. So how about I take you for lunch on your next day off?' Grovelling was a new act for me. I wondered if I'd pulled it off.

'Lunch? That's very kind of you, but really, it's not necessary.'

There was little gratitude and less warmth in her voice. Either I hadn't been very believable or more intense grovelling was in order. 'I know how much you love your garden,' – this was a complete shot in the dark, she had, in fact, simply mentioned having one – 'so I was thinking of Prior Park garden centre. They do a lovely lunch and the weather being so good, we could sit outside. Go on, let me treat you to make up for my being less than helpful this morning.'

The sigh I heard this time was more reluctant acceptance than understanding. 'I was going shopping for some pelargoniums at the weekend, so I suppose I could have a look there.'

'Great. It's a date. What day suits you best?'

'Friday.'

'Friday!' I gushed, overcompensating for her less-than-rapturous response to getting a free lunch. 'Brilliant, that's perfect for me too. About twelve thirty, that suit?'

'Yes, that'd be fine.'

'Okay, great, I'll see you there on Friday then.' I hung up, tossed the mobile onto the bed and flopped down beside it. Seriously, Carol could be such hard work, and all this to satisfy my curiosity.

She wouldn't know the secret that Mrs Wallace was hiding in that locked room; if she did, Carol wouldn't hesitate, she'd have been on the phone as quick as you could say NMC.

But I was good at ferreting out information people didn't

realise they had, and difficult as Carol could be, as much as she continued to make me uneasy, she was no match for me.

Anyway, I was starting from a positive point; I knew Mrs Wallace was hiding a nasty little secret. I simply needed more information before deciding what I was going to do with that knowledge.

28

Two days later, I was walking along Prior Park Road towards the garden centre that had unimaginatively used the same name. It was a convenient short walk for me from Bath bus station and I arrived with time to spare. A typical modern garden centre, it had lots of indoor and outdoor plants, a well-stocked gift shop, a farm shop, a pet and aquatics section and, of course, a café. Something for everyone.

I half expected to find Carol waiting, but this time I'd beat her to the *being first* spot. Ignoring the plants which held little interest for me, I wandered around the gift shop. So much *stuff*: I wasn't quite sure what some of it was for. The farm shop was of more interest. A loaf of artisan sourdough bread almost tempted me until I saw the price. I poked at it to see if it did anything exceptional, then laughed and moved away when I saw an assistant looking at me with raised eyebrows.

When I checked the time and saw it was twelve thirty-five, I was worried in case Carol had changed her mind. Perhaps I should have sent her a message that morning to remind her, but it was too late. I checked my mobile. There was no message from her; perhaps, unusually for someone who liked to be early, she was simply late. She was coming from Larkhall on the far side of the city, and traffic in Bath could be a nightmare.

I'd done another circuit of the gift shop before I saw her sauntering in, as if being fifteen minutes late was perfectly acceptable. It wasn't, but I was obliged to let it pass without comment, after all I'd lured her to lunch for a reason.

'Hi,' I said, wandering over to meet her. 'There are some gorgeous plants outside, you're going to be spoilt for choice.' I hoped I was right; I'd seen a splash of colour through the door but hadn't thought to investigate.

'That's great.' She waved to the entrance. 'Sorry I'm late, they're doing roadworks on London Road again, and the traffic was backed up.'

'It's why I travel by bus,' I said and pointed towards the stairs to the first-floor café. 'Let's get a table.'

We were in luck and found one outside. The café was self-service, but the staff behind the counter were quick and efficient. We were back in our seats within a few minutes, Carol with a coffee, me with a glass of tap water. Our sandwiches would be brought out when ready. The prices had almost made me weep, it had better be worth it.

'This is nice,' I said. 'I haven't been here for a while.'

Carol sipped her coffee and kept the bowl between her palms as she looked around. 'I don't think I've ever had lunch here before. It's lovely.' She smiled. 'It was kind of you to invite me.'

'It was the least I could do after being so hesitant and grumpy when you asked for my help with Mr Wallace.'

'That's okay, you explained you were tired, and I know what that's like.'

Our sandwiches arrived, hers accompanied by a healthy salad, mine with chips. I tore open two packets of tomato ketchup and squeezed the contents out, picked up one sauce-covered chip with my fingers and popped it whole into my mouth. 'These are good,' I said, picking up a second one.

I needed to get the conversation around to the Wallaces. Subtlety wasn't my forte, but I knew I had to tread carefully if she wasn't going to cite professional confidentiality that would lock me out. I wiped ketchup from my lips with a serviette and tried to sound casual as I asked, 'When are you back to work?'

'Sunday. What about you?'

I shrugged. 'A run of nights from tomorrow. Four on, one off, then a further two before a couple of days off.'

'Sounds exhausting.'

It would be. All, apart from one night, were in the home I disliked the most. I'd sent a further email to the agency requesting private home positions. This time, they didn't reply at all. Not even a standard acknowledgement. 'No, it'll be fine. I'm working in Neptune House, and you know how quiet that can be.' My one night was there, so it wasn't a total lie. I picked up my sandwich and took a small bite. 'You've been with the Wallaces a while now. I'm surprised he hasn't gone into the hospice for end-of-life care.'

'He wants to die at home, and Mrs Wallace promised him that he could.'

'That's so lovely, they're obviously very close.' I took another even smaller bite of my sandwich, afraid to finish too quickly in case she rushed off. 'They're not married that long, isn't that what you told me?' I wasn't sure if her hesitation in answering was due to my question or the piece of cucumber she was nibbling with her unusually small teeth.

I wanted to knock it out of her hand and bring her attention back to me. 'Just a few years, isn't that right?'

'What?' She speared a piece of lettuce with her fork before looking at me. 'Sorry, yes, two years. They'd known each other for a while before that though, she was the receptionist in the doctor's surgery he and his first wife attended.'

This was interesting. I faked a yawn, raising my hand to cover my mouth just that little bit too late. 'Sorry, I still haven't caught up with my sleep. What were you saying...? Ah yes, Mr Wallace and his first wife. When did she pass away?'

'Three years ago. A sudden massive heart attack while they were at a party. She was pronounced dead by the paramedics. She and Mr Wallace had been together for thirty years.'

She made a sad face, so I mirrored it, pushing the corners of my mouth down. 'How sad.' I didn't really think so. Thirty years. A lifetime together. Some people were never happy. My parents had only had seventeen.

'Mr Wallace was devastated. I spoke to the GP when he visited last week. He said that Oonagh, the second Mrs Wallace as she is now, probably saved him. She helped him to arrange the funeral and supported him when he was falling apart.'

If I hadn't been fishing for information, I'd have made a smart comment about him pulling himself together again pretty quickly if they'd got married only a year later. Such restraint is exhausting, and I had to stifle a genuine yawn. 'It must have been such a shock for her when he got sick so soon after marrying.'

Carol took the top piece of bread from the second half of her sandwich, put it to one side, and used her fingers to pick a piece of chicken from the filling. She peered at it carefully before putting it into her mouth. 'No, she knew. He'd been diagnosed with cancer a few months before the wife died and that's why he was in and out of the GP surgery. He was going through his second round of chemotherapy when his wife had the heart attack.'

Oonagh Wallace married a sick man. That was an interesting piece of information. 'I suppose they expected to have a lot longer together,' I said, trying to sound sympathetic.

Carol pushed the mangled remains of her food away and picked up her coffee. 'I'd imagine so. He was doing okay until he got a chest infection a few weeks ago. He never recovered from it and since then, he's had almost twenty-four-hour nursing care.'

'Apart from those few hours when she feeds him his morning and evening meal.'

Carol looked surprised. 'How did you know that?'

I smiled. 'You told me, remember.'

A flicker of annoyance swept over her features in a wave. 'I shouldn't be discussing a patient in my care, it's very unprofessional of me.'

As unprofessional as begging me to help her after I'd worked a twelve-hour shift? 'Don't worry I won't sell it to the tabloids.'

She didn't look remotely amused. Draining her cup, she put it down with a snap. 'That was lovely, thank you.'

There was a finality in her voice that irked me. But I knew when to cut my losses, I wasn't going to get any more out of her. Not that day anyway. 'We should do it again sometime.' I drank the last of my water. 'You want to go and look at the plants?'

Carol checked her watch. 'I think I'll leave it, actually, I need to get going.'

It suited me. I'd found out all I could, I wanted to get home and digest what she'd told me about Oonagh Wallace who was becoming more interesting by the day.

29

I left Carol in the car park and headed down Prior Park Road into
the city. She hadn't offered to drive me anywhere although she
could have dropped me on the London Road where I'd have been
able to get my bus, or near Alice Park where I'd have been easily
able to walk home. It didn't matter. I could catch a bus in the
station which would probably fly past her dented old Toyota on
the bus corridor.

As I approached the station, I had a change of plan. It wasn't a
long walk to Lansdown Road for someone as used to walking as I
was, and thirty minutes later I was standing outside the Wallace
house.

What I had discovered in that locked room near the kitchen
was interesting but putting it together with what Carol had told
me made it fascinating. Reading about true crime and the devi-
ous, infamous perpetrators was one thing, seeing a crime enacted
was something else. I'd seen photographs of Jeffrey Dahmer –
he'd been a good-looking man. From the photographs I'd seen of
Oonagh Wallace, she too was good-looking. But with her I could

manoeuvre a meeting and see her in the flesh. Maybe even become part of the story.

That fascinating thought kept me lingering by the gateway, staring up at the massive house. For the first time, I regretted I didn't have a car. If I did, I could have sat in it and watched the house till she came out. A vague idea crossed my mind. I could ring the doorbell and explain I'd lost something the day I'd been helping Carol, and since I was passing I decided to pop in on spec to see if I could find it. Even to my ears, that sounded far-fetched. Anyway, it came with an insurmountable problem. I'd have to explain why I'd been needed. Mrs Wallace might complain to the agency, and Carol would get into trouble. Might even be suspended. And they'd need a replacement. If I could have guaranteed that I'd be it, I might have been tempted, but I couldn't. Since I wanted to know more about the Wallaces, it was better to keep Carol in situ.

It was irritating to have come all this way for nothing. I walked past the house, turned, crossed the road, and dawdled back. So frustrating to be this close. Crossing the road again, I turned to pass one last time. I could ring the doorbell, say I was collecting for something or other, couldn't I? No, that wouldn't work, charity workers all carried identification. She might ask to see it.

It would be simpler to ring the doorbell, and when she answered, to look surprised and say I was looking for – I sought for a good imaginary name – Sally Prior, no, Sally Park. It'd do.

I walked to the steps leading up to the front door and looked for a doorbell. It took a few seconds to find it, hidden as it was under the ivy that slithered upward from the garden. I pressed once, my ear cocked to listen for its peal. If it did sound within though, it wasn't audible on this side of the heavy front door.

Minutes ticked by before I decided to press again, keeping my finger on it for longer. Perhaps Mrs Wallace wasn't home, but whichever nurse was on duty should answer.

When the door opened suddenly, it startled me, my yelp an automatic response that seemed to amuse the woman who stood framed in the doorway. She waited, one hand resting on the door-frame, her head slightly tilted in an unspoken question. I noticed her nails were short, unvarnished, her hands long and slim. She had an air of elegance about her that I instantly envied. Unlike my thin shapeless physique, her slim body had curves in all the right places. These were obviously, even proudly, emphasised by a turquoise silk blouse unbuttoned a tad too far to show the lacy edge of a similar-coloured bra. The cream ankle-length chinos were a perfect match.

Since I'd been meeting Carol for lunch, I'd made a bit of an effort with my appearance. But there was only so much I could do with my limited wardrobe. I saw Mrs Wallace's eyes drift over my charity-shop navy T-shirt and the Asda cotton trousers I'd bought on sale a few months before. I saw the moment when she decided exactly where I stood on the social stepladder – a subtle change in her expression, from the narrowing of her eyes to the tightening of her lips. Very subtle, but the overall effect was a switch from open and welcoming to shuttered, almost defensive. She shifted position too so that she was behind the edge of the open door, ready to slam it in my face should the situation require such drama.

She needn't have worried. My plan had never been to offer violence. It had been mere curiosity to see what she looked like in the flesh. Photographs could be deceptive, they did, after all, simply catch a moment in time – not the precursor or the conse-quences.

It was time to follow through with my rather lame plan to ask for Sally Prior, or had I decided on Park? I couldn't remember. It didn't matter because standing on the doorstep, being looked at so dismissively, I knew I wanted more than this brief unsatisfactory meeting.

I had always been a quick thinker, nurses needed to be, so when a completely different idea jumped into my head, I went with it. I lifted my hands and laid them against my mouth, shaking my head slowly at the same time and taking a step backwards.

Dropping my hands, I made my lower lip tremble hoping it looked a natural reaction to intense overwhelming sorrow. 'I can't,' I said, taking a further step away. I met her suddenly intent gaze and shook my head again. More frantically this time. 'I thought I could, but I can't do this. I just can't.'

Without another word, I turned and ran down the steps, across the driveway and through the gates. Unsure how far she could see from where she stood, I kept running until I halted, only slightly out of breath, at the end of the road.

My head was spinning as I walked back down Lansdown Road and turned down Upper Hedgemead Road to cut through the park. It had been an interesting day, starting with that meeting with Carol. I still couldn't understand why she unsettled me. I knew little about her apart from where she lived and that she lived with her parents. She'd never offered any more personal details, and I'd never asked. Nor had she asked me. What an odd pair we were.

I pushed Carol from my head to concentrate on the much more interesting plan that had leapt into my head as I'd looked at Oonagh Wallace. I didn't know much about property prices but that house on Lansdown Road must be worth millions. When Mr Wallace took his last trip to wherever he believed in, his widow would be left a very wealthy woman. I guessed it wouldn't be long, she was going to make certain of that.

If my plan worked, she wouldn't be the only one to gain from the poor man's death.

30

Late afternoon, the day was still excessively hot, and I was clammy by the time my bus arrived.

Back at home, I changed into more comfortable shoes and headed for a walk along the river. Walking near water always seemed to help clarify my thinking. My plan, to blackmail Oonagh Wallace with what I knew, was crazy. It meant letting her get away with killing her husband for the money, but I was hardly one to sit in judgement. I'd killed Olivia for the same reason. That the money hadn't been for me wasn't relevant.

If I had more money it would guarantee my mother's care for as long as she lived. I could even think about giving up nursing. The thought made me smile for a second, a fleeting pleasure before reality swiped it from my face. What would I do instead? Spend more days in the nursing home with my mother? I'd been a nurse all my working life. Although I'd not made much of my career, it was what I did, what I was.

I could get a bigger apartment. The thought didn't appeal, I didn't want more space, more stuff. Where I lived, the cosy comfort of it, suited me.

The only downside to it was my landlord, Theo. I'd seen him watching me. At first, I'd given him a friendly wave, said good morning or whatever was appropriate. When I realised my greeting was met with a stare and nothing else, I stopped speaking, and eventually dropped my pathetic wave too. However, I found it impossible not to acknowledge him in some way and resorted to an uncomfortable jerk of my head in his direction. He never responded but I felt his eyes following me as I walked away. I could feel them, boring into my back. Sometimes, if I passed his house, I could see a curtain twitch and knew he was there, looking down at me.

There had been no issues with my accommodation that needed his attention and as a result, I hadn't needed to speak to him. It struck me that I'd not seen him for a few days, nor had he been at his window, staring at me.

Should I be worried? He lived alone; he was elderly and grossly overweight. Maybe he'd died alone, as my father had done, and was lying in his house, eyes wide and vacant staring at the ceiling. His body would slowly decompose as maggots made a meal of him.

I imagined his body putrefying. The noisome stink of it.

I couldn't get the idea out of my head. I could go back, ring his doorbell. And if he answered? *Hi, I'm just checking that you're alive.*

I barked a laugh that frightened birds from the nearby hedge, they flew up, squawked, then settled down again.

No, I wouldn't ring his doorbell. But I could check his letter box. If he was lying dead somewhere in the house, the tat that was constantly being delivered, the flyers for this that and the other, would have built up.

The idea hastened my return, and I crossed the fields to the footpath and turned into our shared driveway. From the outside, nothing looked amiss. But death didn't advertise itself with flags and banners. I approached the front door. Bay windows on either side were dressed in net curtains heavy enough to prevent the curious from peering inside. I know, I'd tried that first day when I'd come to view the apartment.

A letter box was set into the centre of the wooden door at waist height. Although I knew I couldn't see through the windows on either side, I wasn't sure someone inside couldn't see out. Theo could be watching me, waiting for me to ring the doorbell.

I should have turned away but the idea that he really could be inside, dead and decomposing, was fixed in my head and I knew it would be impossible to relax unless I knew for sure.

Ignoring the possibility that he was peering out at me; I pushed open the flap of the letter box and slid my other hand inside. I'd only been inside the house once when I'd first called to see the apartment. I didn't get further than the hallway and there had been little to see. A nondescript painting on one wall, a small hall table with a drawer my fingers itched to open. The only other thing I remembered from that brief visit was the post basket on the back of the front door. There was no draught-excluder brush to block my way, allowing me to slide my hand all the way into the bottom of the basket. It felt empty. Even if he didn't receive much post, there'd be flyers advertising all kinds of crap. There'd be something.

Part of me was disappointed. I'd have liked nothing better than to have dialled 999 and to have emergency services arriving. It would have been exciting to have watched the police using a battering ram to access the house and thrilling to see a dead body.

In my role as a nurse, I'd seen dead bodies numerous times over the years, and I'd had to dial 999 more than once. But this would have been different. This would have been a drama and I'd have had a star part and, unlike my starring role in the deaths of Jemma and Olivia, this one I could talk about.

My fingers were still feeling around in the empty basket when I heard the distinct sound of a door banging from somewhere within. Startled, I dropped the letter box flap. It was well sprung and came down hard on my wrist. I swallowed the yelp of pain and yanked the flap open again. Too quickly, too carelessly, a silver bracelet I'd donned that morning, in a vain attempt to look a little dressed up for my meeting with Carol, caught on the hinge of the flap. I struggled to release it aware of the faint sound of footsteps on wooden floors. Upstairs, I guessed. I was safe for a minute, but if he came down, he wouldn't miss my hand poking through his door.

I was left with no option. I'd have to take the bracelet off. A good plan, but nothing was going my way. With the evening sun on my back making me sweat, my usually dexterous fingers were hot and clumsy as I tried to move the lever to open the lobster-claw clasp. I wiped sweat from my eyes, dried my hand on the leg of my trousers and tried again. Finally, the damn thing opened. I took my hand out, then tried to pull my bracelet free but it was stuck fast. When I heard footsteps on the stairway, I dropped the letter box flap gently and scarpered.

I was giggling in relief as I pushed open my front door. The loss of the bracelet was an irritant though. It had belonged to my mother, was one of the few expensive things I had, and I really didn't want to lose it.

Later, when I'd had something to eat and my equilibrium was restored, I'd go back and try again to release it. Theo wouldn't notice it until opening the basket for his post in the morning. Without the sun beating down on my back or feeling under pressure, I was sure to be able to get the bracelet free.

Only one window from the house was visible from my apartment. A landing light on the first floor – it came on as soon as it was dark and stayed lit till ten. I had to go to the front of the house to see if any other lights were on. I waited till midnight before I put my front door on the latch and headed around to recover my bracelet.

A security light came on, but I knew where the sensor was. As soon as I got close to Theo's front door, I was safe. A few seconds later the light went off. When I pushed open the letter box flap, apart from a faint glow drifting down the stairs from the landing, the hallway was in darkness.

I was so busy looking for any sign of movement within that it was several seconds before I realised what was missing... the bracelet. I reached inside, hoping it had perhaps fallen into the basket but if it had, it had fallen through a gap to the floor. I leaned my forehead against the door and swore softly. No: it had been caught in one of the hinges of the flap. It couldn't have fallen either in or out without someone releasing it.

My landlord must have found it.

His post basket had been empty, so he'd know it didn't belong to whoever delivered the post that morning. But there was no reason to think he'd guess it was mine. Unless, of course, he'd seen the security light come on and looked out his window in time to see me scurrying around to his door.

I gave a hollow laugh. At least I knew he was alive.

31

I stared impotently at Theo's door for several minutes before taking a step away. The security light flashed on, blinding me and I stumbled and almost fell. I waved my arms to balance myself before hurriedly moving away as curtains at the upstairs window twitched.

I don't think he saw me. I hoped not, because contrary to the impression I liked to give people, I wasn't particularly brave and, unless I was in the driving seat, confrontation of any sort made me shiver and took me back to a time I wanted to forget. To those months of bullying and name calling. It was better to keep people at a distance until I could deal with them on my terms, as I had then. *Deal with them* – I almost smiled at the euphemism.

If Theo had seen me, he'd probably call around in the morning and demand an explanation. A good time to make myself scarce. If he didn't get an answer, he'd assume I was working. If I could stay out of his way for a few days, he'd give up. He might connect my visit to the bracelet he'd found in his letter box, but he couldn't prove anything. Anyway, I'd done nothing wrong.

On the contrary, and it was so unlike me, I was trying to do the right thing and look out for a neighbour. That'll teach me.

Determined to be up and gone early, I set my alarm for seven, and did the minimum ablutions before slipping under the duvet. I put that damn bracelet from my head and fell asleep thinking of the house on Lansdown Road.

* * *

I didn't bother with breakfast the following morning. There were plenty of cafés in Bath where I could indulge myself. Apart from avoiding Theo for a few days, my plans were loose.

I'd timed it well and my bus arrived a minute after I got to the stop. It was rush hour, so traffic into Bath was more than usually slow. It didn't bother me, I sat, stared out the window and let my thoughts drift. With no plans, I stayed on till the bus arrived at the station.

To get the kind of breakfast I liked, at a price I could afford, meant wandering outside the touristy area, but although I was hungry, I wasn't in a hurry. Finally, almost an hour later, my rambling took me through Victoria Park and out onto the Upper Bristol Road. There I found just the place. Minutes later, for only a couple of quid, I was tucking into scrambled egg on toast and drinking decent coffee.

I had finished the food, and was sipping the end of my coffee, before I admitted that I'd no idea what the next step would be in the nebulous plan that had slid into my brain the day before. It needed a bit of substance if it was ever going to have a chance of working. If Carol were more forthcoming with information, I'd have been tempted to give her a shout, but I'd give her a few days in case my more frequent overtures made her suspicious. I wondered, without much interest, what she did on her days off, then put her out of my head to concentrate on the Wallaces.

It wasn't till I had finished the coffee and the caffeine had made its way to my brain cells that an idea came to me. I hadn't learnt much from Carol but everything she had told me had been filed away... just in case. And now one of those little pieces of information took on a shiny glow. Oonagh Wallace played golf every morning. I remembered Carol stressing *every* and raising her eyes to the ceiling as if golf was some kind of abnormal obsession.

I checked my watch. I'd begun my day early; it was still only nine thirty. If I hurried, I could make it to the Wallace house before Oonagh got back from her golf. And on the way, I'd come up with a plan to gain access and have a better snoop. If I didn't, I'd simply wing it. I was a nurse, after all, an expert in swerving, making do, acting dynamically and getting things done.

It took me thirty minutes to walk to the house during which time I'd come up with what I thought was a clever idea to gain access. When I arrived, I climbed the steps to the front door, pressed the bell, and waited expectantly. When nothing happened, I did a double press, two short jabs, to let whoever was inside know I meant business.

It was another minute before the door was opened by a small stocky woman wearing an old-fashioned nurse's dress at least one size too small. I didn't expect to recognise her, the agency had hundreds of nurses on their books and apart from induction and yearly mandatory training, we didn't get to meet others. She regarded me silently, without curiosity.

The ball, it appeared, was firmly in my court. Just where I liked it to be. 'Hi, I'm terribly sorry to bother you. I know you must be so busy' – probably gorging on biscuits and coffee and watching TV – 'my name is Lissa. I'm an agency nurse. My friend

Carol Lyons looks after Mr Wallace most of the week. You've probably seen her name in the reports.' I smiled and waited for some sign of acknowledgement, some agreement that she did indeed recognise the name. There was no change in her bovine expression. If she recognised the name, she was giving nothing away. It cost nothing, apart from my patience, to persevere.

'Carol was in a bit of a bind the last day she was here. The care assistant who was supposed to help her in the morning was in an accident, and they couldn't get a replacement.' I was taking a chance in assuming this nurse wouldn't know about the day I had helped, and my story would only work if it had occurred within the last couple of days. I tried another smile. 'You know the way it goes sometimes. Anyway, I was coming off a night shift elsewhere and when I heard I offered to help.'

Almost the whole truth. I waited to see a softening in her expression. If it was there, it was well hidden. I liked the ball in my court, but I was tired bouncing it up and down at my feet and was conscious of the minutes passing. 'I don't want to delay you, but I wondered if you'd found a gold stud earring.' I put my hand up and pulled at my earlobe.

'I haven't, no.'

It speaks. 'I didn't realise it was missing until that night, too late to ring Carol and ask her to have a look. And of course, she's been off since.' I rubbed my earlobe again. 'It has huge sentimental value so I thought it would be better if I came around; I'll be devastated if I can't find it.'

I guess I wasn't much of a storyteller because she showed little sympathy. Instead, she looked behind, cocked her head, then turned back to me with the same dull, uninterested stare. 'Listen, I'm sorry, I need to go,' she said and proceeded to shut the door.

Time to make a move. Before she had time to react, I put my hand on the door, enough weight behind it to stop her shutting it.

'I'm sure I lost it while we were moving Mr Wallace. He lurched, and his hand brushed against my head. It must have happened then.' If I could have cried on demand, I'd have done so. Unfortunately, it wasn't one of my skills. However, by luck, I'd hit on something she could relate to.

'He did the same to me this morning. I need to learn to duck faster.'

Given an inch, I hurried to take a mile. 'An occupational hazard, isn't it?' I dropped my hand from the door. 'I know you're busy looking after Mr Wallace. I don't want to delay you by sending you on a search for my precious earring, but if I could come up, I know where I was standing and might be able to find it.'

Whether it was her sudden understanding that we were all in this together, or maybe my stress on the word *precious*, to my surprise, she stood back pulling the door open. 'Mrs Wallace isn't here, but I'm sure she'd understand, after all you were kind to have helped out.'

Her initial reticence to speak to me quickly vanished and by the time we'd climbed the stairway – she leading the way one plodding step at a time – I knew all about Jolene. She didn't, as it turned out, regularly work with Mr Wallace. 'It's usually Carol or Michelle covering the day shift, but Michelle needed a few days off for a wedding and Carol couldn't cover them all so they rang me. I don't do private homes usually.' She stood at the bedroom door, her hand on the doorknob. 'I prefer to have more support, if you know what I mean.'

I bit back the caustic comment that leapt to the tip of my tongue. I'd worked with nurses like Jolene who did the minimum to get by, and happily delegated everything they could to junior staff, or worse, left it for whatever nurse was doing the next shift. I almost felt sorry for poor Mr Wallace to be left in her care.

But when we went in and I saw him, I realised my sympathy was wasted. It had only been a few days since I'd seen him, but he'd deteriorated dramatically. I didn't feel any sense of pride in knowing I'd been right, that he wasn't going to last as long as his GP had indicated. I'd given him days, maybe a week. Now, with a grey cast to his skin, a bluish tinge to his lips and a mottling of the fingers that lay curled on the white sheet, I was giving him hours.

'He's too frail to sit out any more,' Jolene said crossing to an armchair that had been pulled close to the window. A small table positioned within hands' reach held a flask, a mug, and an open packet of chocolate digestives. She picked up the book she'd left splayed on the seat and took its place. 'You don't need me to help you look for your earring, do you?' She didn't wait for an answer. The book must have been good, she buried herself in it and ignored me. And Mr Wallace.

I stepped closer to the bed. He was sitting upright in a nest of pillows. His breathing was shallow and, as I moved closer, I could smell the stink of death that came with every feeble exhale.

To my surprise, he opened his eyes, looked at me and said a very quiet, 'Hello.'

'Hi,' I said. 'I didn't mean to disturb you; I was looking for an earring I'd lost.'

'Okay.'

His lips were dry and scaly. 'Would you like a drink?'

'Please.'

I picked up a glass of water and held a straw to his mouth. He sucked on it twice, then pushed it out with the tip of his tongue. 'Thank you.'

'You're welcome.' I put the glass down and picked up a tub of Vaseline. 'Your lips look very dry, this will help.' I used my finger to slick some over his lips. 'Better?'

'Much, thank you.' He gave me a faint smile. 'I don't know you, do I?'

'No, I'm Lissa. I was here once with Carol, helping.'

'Carol.' His smile grew. 'She talks a lot.'

It made me laugh. 'She does.' I looked to where Jolene was still buried in her book. 'Is there anything else I can do for you?'

'Stay with me a minute?'

There was a chair nearby, I hooked my foot around it, pulled it closer and sat. 'Of course I will,' I said, taking one of his cold hands in mine. I didn't know him, it was only my second time to meet him, and the resemblance that he'd had in his younger years to my father hadn't carried through to this older man, but he was a man dying alone. As my father had. That alone kept me sitting there for a long time.

Only when his breathing deepened and slowed did I take my hand away and get to my feet. Sunshine was slanting through the window. Jolene held her book up to the light and turned a page. I wanted to go over, rip the book from her hands and hit her across the face with it. Make her suffer for her lack of care.

I didn't, of course, I couldn't afford to lose my job.

I wondered if Oonagh knew how close to the end her husband was. She'd be relieved. After all, this was what she was working towards.

I hadn't cared, but that was before I'd spoken to the man. Now, I wanted more than money, I wanted her to be punished for what she was doing.

32

Jolene remained buried in her book, oblivious to the needs of the man in her care. I'd have to see what I could do about her.

Conscious of the time ticking away, and of the need to be gone before Oonagh Wallace returned, I made a half-hearted attempt to look for the earring I said I'd lost. I moved the hoist and peered into corners. My forehead was concertinaed to show concern on the off-chance Jolene might drag her eyes from her book and look my way.

She finally looked up as I lifted a chair and dropped it noisily. Her confused expression took seconds to clear, then she laughed. 'Shit, this book is so good I'd forgotten you were here. Did you find what you were looking for?'

I raised and lowered my shoulders, letting out a loud huff as I did so in a dramatic indication of failure. 'No such luck,' I added, in case my amateur theatricals were lost on her. She didn't strike me as too bright. I lifted my hands and tilted my head towards the bathroom. 'I'll go wash my hands then get out of your hair.'

I closed the door over, turned the tap on full, quickly washed my hands and used some tissues I pulled from a box to dry them rather than using a slightly dubious-looking hand towel. I left the water running and took a step towards the bathroom cabinet, pleased to see the key dangling from the lock. I'd had a glimpse inside when I'd been there with Carol, but I wanted to make sure I was right about what I'd found downstairs in that locked room. It took seconds to confirm my suspicions. Mr Wallace's current medication was stored here. The medication I'd seen downstairs in that locked room was a combination of medication he was no longer prescribed, and older tablets his late wife had been on. All should have been returned to the pharmacy for disposal, but it seemed Mrs Wallace had found a better use for them.

Back in the bedroom, I noticed the dying man hadn't moved. Neither had Jolene. 'Right,' I said drawing her attention. 'It was a wasted journey, I'm afraid. If you happen to find it sometime when you're tidying or something,' – as if the lazy lump would ever stir herself to do anything – 'you could put it in a safe place, leave a note for Carol and she'll let me know.' I flapped a hand in her direction. 'Don't bother getting up, I know the way.' I looked back towards the bed. 'You wouldn't want to leave Mr Wallace unattended.' My sarcasm was wasted on her.

I moved closer to the bed. 'Goodbye.' I laid my hand gently against his cheek. 'It's okay to let go now, you've done your bit.' Sometimes people clung to the life they believed they had. I could have told him the truth, that his beloved wife had been killing him for some time. I didn't though: I might discover she had reason, that this man she had married in good faith had proved to be a monster. Perhaps the superficial similarity to my father cut deeper, and Mr Wallace had as big a secret to hide as my father had done.

Perhaps this was why I had become so obsessed with him and his wife.

Mr Wallace didn't open his eyes or acknowledge my words in

any way. Even in the few minutes I'd been there, he'd grown closer to his exit from a life that could be cruelly unfair. I thought back to the cycles of neglect and indulgence that had honed my childhood – maybe life was simply cruel. With a final glance towards Jolene, I left the room.

Outside, I checked the time. Twenty minutes to eleven. In the hallway, I opened and shut the door loudly, much as I had done on my previous visit, although I doubted whether Jolene cared if I left or not, then I turned, slipped through the door and down the stairs.

The key to the locked room was in the same place. A minute later, I was inside. I used my phone to take a few shots of the pestle and mortar and the open packets of pills belonging to both Mr Wallace and his first wife. Photographic proof would be essential for what I'd planned.

Then I was done, the door locked, key returned, and I was running up the stairs. I was at the top when I heard the distinct sound of the front door opening. Panic had me wondering whether to run back down and try to find an alternative exit, or failing that, somewhere to hide. Panic... it was a sure road to failure. A few deep breaths calmed me. Oonagh Wallace was sure to head upstairs to check on her husband. To see how close she was to her destiny.

I opened the door a crack and peered out, shutting it again when I saw her standing at the foot of the stairway checking through her post. No matter how tightly I pressed my ear to the door I couldn't hear if she moved up the stairway. I waited a full minute before looking out again. This time, the hallway was empty. My exit was feet away. I slipped through the door, closed it gently after me and tiptoed across the hall and got the hell out of there.

And then I was outside, giggling as relief surged through me.

I had the photographs I needed. Blackmail was a new direction for me. A killer and a blackmailer – my criminal curriculum vitae was expanding.

33

If I got off the bus at the stop I normally used in Bathford, I had to walk past Lily Cottage before I could get to my apartment, so I stayed sitting till the next stop. It was only a ten-minute walk back, and I was able to sneak inside without being seen from the house.

I kept the TV off. If Theo came to my door, he'd be met with silence. If he knocked, I'd simply ignore it. I don't know why I was being so stupid about the situation. I could go around, explain what had happened, we'd have a laugh about it, and I'd get my bracelet back.

Except, the way he stared at me made the breath catch in my throat.

Why did I stay? I'd asked myself that several times since I'd moved in. The answer was simple. I loved my cosy little apartment. Loved that it was separate, isolated, that I had my own front door and didn't have to make polite conversation with other apartment dwellers I passed on the stairways or met in the lift. Dealing with people all day, it was a relief not to have to bother being polite when I got home.

Weighing up the advantages, the chill he gave me was almost

easily dismissed. Almost. That I couldn't rid myself of it completely should have prevented me from going anywhere near his house. It should have prevented me from worrying whether he was alive or dead, and certainly should have stopped me sticking my damn hand in his blasted letter box.

I shook my head at the stupidity of it all and regretted the loss of my mother's silver bracelet. It had been the only pretty thing I'd had. Or had been anyway. I looked at the silver frame I'd taken during that first visit to the Wallace home, then reached for the book where I'd put the photograph I'd taken from it. Out of focus as the black and white shot was, the young Mr Wallace was still clearly identifiable. The woman by his side might have been his first wife, it could have been anyone.

I put it safely back between the pages of the book.

Usually, I'd have music blaring. Country and western songs telling a sad story, or Carrie Underwood singing about making men pay for their crimes. If the beat of my music crossed the narrow gap between my garage apartment and the house, Theo never complained.

So usually, I was free to blast out my music and keep the silence at bay. Because even at night, unless I was trying to sleep, silence unnerved me. In it, no matter how many years had passed, unwelcome thoughts of the lives I'd ended took the opportunity to slip in with sharp and vicious barbs, determined to cause me pain. But if I played music, Theo would know I was home. He'd knock on my door, maybe keep knocking until I answered. The biggest downfall to my apartment, and one I was certain was illegal, was there was no second exit. If he stayed at my door, I was trapped.

I'd been there before, by Jemma's bullying, by Olivia's detrimental hold on our finances, and it had led me to kill. I wasn't going to kill Theo merely because he stared at me. Anyway, killing him would lead to complications. Who knew what would happen to his house afterwards, and to mine.

I put Theo from my head with difficulty and thought instead about my visit to the Wallace's that morning. I wondered if Mr Wallace was still drawing breath or if he had finally let go his feeble grip on life.

From the dying man, my thought went to the nurse, Jolene. It was such a shame I couldn't do something about her, but all I could do was to hope for his sake, that she wouldn't be returning. Perhaps in time, I'd have forgotten about her, if she hadn't appeared in the Bartholomew Care Home.

In charge of my mother's welfare.

34

I tried to visit Mother every two to three days. If I was off, I'd spend most of the day in the home, helping her to shower and dress, to have her meals, and I'd sit with her beside a window in the lounge or take her for a walk in the grounds in her wheelchair. Only the changing seasons outside marked any difference to the routine – a summer hat or a warm coat. If I was working a run of nights, I'd sleep for a few hours after the final night, then visit in the afternoon.

After my fourth shift in a row, I arrived to find Mother in her bedroom watching TV. I say *watching* but there was nothing so dynamic about what she was doing. She was sitting facing the TV and it was switched to a property programme. Escape to somewhere or other. It could have been anything, there was no indication she cared.

'Hi, Mum,' I said, bending to plant a kiss on her cheek. I frowned. Someone had been heavy-handed with her make-up. 'Wait till I fix you up a little, then I'll take you for a walk in the sunshine.' I pulled a handful of paper tissues from a box and brushed them over the circles of rouge on her cheeks, blending them upward and out. She was still such a pretty woman. Her hair was washed and blow-dried every Monday into the same style she'd worn since I was a child.

I used the same tissues to pat the colour on her lips, then stood back. Better. I ran my fingers through her hair to fluff it up and smiled. Much better. All through my ministrations, she stared straight ahead, through me, as if I wasn't there.

Years before, I'd have kept up a running monologue, asking her questions, answering them appropriately, sometimes putting on a different voice. It amused me if nothing else. Over the years the amusement had waned and now, mostly, we sat in silence. There was a time too, when I'd told her about my life, hoping for a glimmer of interest: when I went to university, when I qualified as a nurse and was offered that position in the Bath United. Sometimes I still told her things – my move to the apartment in Bathford and the irony of being back in the village where I'd grown up.

I found a wide-brimmed straw hat on a top shelf of the small built-in wardrobe. The crown was squashed almost flat, and it took some careful manipulation to push the material out without breaking it. 'Here you go,' I said once it was made presentable. I pressed it down over her hair and tilted it slightly. 'Perfect.'

A wheelchair leaned against the wall. I unfolded it and fixed the seat cushion in place. 'Right, Mum,' I said, putting a hand on her elbow and tugging gently. She rose without argument. It was all she would do. Now and then, usually when a new nurse started full of energy and optimism, they'd try to get her to walk, to put one foot in front of the other. I'd seen the more enthusiastic ones down on their hands and knees, actively moving one foot at a time, sliding each forward an inch while other staff supported Mother with a hand under each elbow. I let them at it, didn't bother to say we'd tried for a long time, spent a ridiculous amount of money on physiotherapists and a variety of walking aids, all to no avail. It wasn't that Mother couldn't walk, after all, it was that she didn't want to.

I manoeuvred the wheelchair behind her and put on the brakes. 'Okay, Mum.' I placed a hand on her shoulder and pressed gently. 'Down you sit.' Usually she would respond immediately, dropping to whatever was placed behind her with a childish certainty that there would indeed be something there. But now and then, for no reason that was obvious to anyone, she'd refuse to respond to the signals. 'Mum, sit down and we'll go outside for some fresh air. You'd like that, wouldn't you?'

Sometimes, I suppose, I fell into the same trap I had criticised Carol for – doing things for *my* sake rather than Mother's. It was such a lovely day; *I'd* prefer to spend some of it in the home's pretty grounds rather than being stuck inside. My dear mother never showed the slightest interest in going into the grounds, nor gave any sign of being happy or sad while we were outside. I stopped pressing down on her shoulder. 'Would you prefer to stay here?'

That I even bothered to ask the question both amused and saddened me. How many years would have to pass before the faint glow of hope finally flickered and died? How many more times would I ask, and stupidly wait for her to answer? When she sat, with a suddenness that startled me, it would have been nice to have seen it as a positive action, her version of *yes, let's go*. Nice, but foolish. She'd simply grown weary of being on her feet. Nothing more.

With a sigh, I settled her feet onto the footplates, readjusted the hat that had become a little askew, then headed from the room and down the long corridor towards the front door. It ran past the nurses' station. By this stage, I knew the regular staff by name and expected to have to stop and have a word with whichever nurse was on duty that day. Polite meaningless words laced, on their side, with sympathy.

As we approached, I saw that I was in luck. The nurse was in conversation with the relative of another resident and I could slip past with just a wave. I would have done, would have smiled inanely, and pointed towards the exit. I might even have mouthed *I'm taking her out for a walk*. It was recognition that prevented any acknowledgement at all. The home rarely used agency staff, but it seemed they had needed to that day, and it was someone I recognised despite the smarter uniform. The lovely Jolene.

Jolene. Looking after my mother.

I wanted to storm over, grab hold of her and shake her till her bones rattled and her teeth fell out. I wanted to shriek until the manager arrived. Then I'd point a finger, tell of her neglect of Mr Wallace, and have her thrown out. But I could do nothing. I hadn't reported her then, I couldn't do now.

I kept walking, pressed the code on the security pad to open the front door and pushed my mother's chair through.

* * *

The grounds of the home were criss-crossed with wheelchair-friendly pathways dipping in and out of the shade offered by some lovely old trees. Usually, I'd give a running commentary, where we were going and what we were seeing, as if Mother couldn't see for herself. But meeting Jolene had thrown me. If only I could go to the manager and tell him my concerns, but what could I say? That I'd seen her neglect a patient in her care? His first question would be where? And his second, had I reported it? It would be awkward to explain why I'd been in the Lansdown house; it might open a huge can of lying worms. And his second question? I had sincerely felt sorry for poor Mr Wallace being left in Jolene's care, but not enough to report her for it. Not until I saw her that morning, and realised my mother could be in danger from her neglect.

Mother was getting older, her immobility had repercussions that medication could slow but not prevent. If she became unwell, I'd stay with her of course. But I couldn't look after her twenty-four hours a day. When I shut my eyes, I needed to know she was being cared for, that she was safe, and I'd seen what constituted care in Jolene's eyes.

That the home rarely used agency staff wouldn't prevent the need being there at any time. And there was no guarantee it wouldn't be her.

I needed to ensure that could never happen.

35

It was a particularly nice afternoon with a blue cloudless sky, and it was warm enough without being sticky-hot. I pushed the chair around until we reached a bench overlooking the rose bed. It would be a nice spot to sit for a while, the heady scent from the roses a pleasant alternative to the chemically clean air of the home. A good place to linger and allow the irritation that had been simmering since I saw Jolene to fade. Only then could I come up with a plan.

The sun was breaking through the branches of the tree that had been giving us shade. I moved Mother's chair a little, readjusted her hat, and shifted her arm away from a sneaky beam. 'What do you think, Mum? What'll I do with Jolene?'

If she had any opinion on the woman, she was keeping it to herself. I used to wonder, when she'd first disappeared into herself, if she'd wake up one day and tell me all the things she'd been storing in her head. All the opinions and the comments she'd wanted to make over the years.

All the words of love she'd saved up for me.

I pictured us, wrapped in each other's arms, and weeping from a surfeit of emotion. All the love she'd saved up, it would envelop us, and I'd once more be loved as I had in those long-ago days of indulgence.

Such foolish thoughts. I stood abruptly. It was time to get going, supper, as they designated the evening meal, came on the dot of five thirty. When I visited, I helped her with her food and preferred to do so in the privacy of her room. It was more relaxing than sitting in the dining room among the other women, some of whom were not slow to criticise everything and everyone they saw. Especially someone new, which I, despite my frequent visits, still appeared to be. I had heard comments on my clothes, my hair, the way I sat, even the way I held the spoon I used to give Mother her food. I survived a few visits before requesting she had her meals in her room when I visited.

On our return, I saw the medication trolley in the corridor and heard Jolene's voice drifting from one of the resident's bedrooms. I smirked. Mrs Downs was notoriously difficult especially when it came to her medication. She took several tablets, and liked to be told what each was for. Every time. And then she'd make a huge palaver of taking them, coughing and spluttering over each one. She'd been a resident for several years and had become more entrenched in her ways with every year. Jolene would be with her for a while.

Officially, nurses were supposed to bring the medication trolley with them. Not leave it sitting unattended. Officially, but mostly we did exactly what Jolene was doing, lock the trolley, leave it in the corridor and go into the resident's room. *Lock the trolley.* She wouldn't have left it open, would she? She couldn't be that careless. I stopped the wheelchair beside it. I could see Jolene's back. Her posture was slightly stooped as she bent over the tiny frame in her blanket-strewn armchair and she was speaking loudly, as if Mrs Downs was deaf rather than pedantic and stubborn.

I rested my hand flat on the lid of the trolley, then slid my fingers to the edge and curled them under. With my eyes fixed on Jolene, I pulled upward, unable to believe my luck when the lid lifted. A plan came to me then, fully formed, and foolproof.

I'd seen the open trolley often enough over the years and knew exactly how it was laid out. Most of the residents' medication came in cards and these were hung on specially designed hangers in the medication room. There was a different hanger for each medication round, the nurse would take the correct one and put it into the trolley at the start. Some medication wasn't suitable to be packed in this way and came in individual packets. It was these I wanted to reach. I didn't need to open the lid all the way. Holding it open with one hand, my other slipped in, felt around and picked up a packet. It was easy to press one pill into my hand, return the packet and search for another. When I had three different tablets, I was happy and dropped the lid shut.

Back in Mother's room, I helped her into her armchair, positioned the table in front of her and waited. Most of the other residents on this floor went to the dining room for lunch, so Jolene would be along soon. Worried she might recognise me and ruin my plan, I did my best to change my appearance. My hair, short though it was, was tied back with a band. I pulled it out and fluffed my hair. As disguises went, it wasn't great, but my mobile phone would help. Its cover opened like a book and with it open and held in front of my ear, and my fingers spread, a large part of my face was hidden.

When I heard the trolley stop outside, I began an imaginary conversation. 'No, that's absolutely fine, I can go there directly from here.' I nodded my head as if agreeing with whatever was being said. When I saw Jolene's figure appear, I dropped my voice slightly. 'No, that's not a problem, honestly—' I tapped a finger of my free hand on the table. 'You can leave the medication here, nurse, thanks, I'm used to giving them to Mum.' I spoke more rapidly into the phone. 'Believe me, I can make it. No problem.' I kept up my side of a ridiculously inane conversation – seriously I have no imagination – until I heard the trolley rattling away down the corridor.

I peered into the medicine cup she'd left on the table. Six tablets. The same ones every day. Three of which were supplied in packets, not on cards. I fished them out, replaced them with the three I had purloined earlier and sat back with a smile.

This was going to be perfect.

I still had about six minutes before supper arrived. Plenty of time to put the cat among the pigeons.

I was in luck and the manager, Stefan Albescu, was in his office. Through the open doorway, I could see his fingers flying over the keyboard, his forehead creased in a frown of concentration as he stared at the computer screen. If he was having a rough day, I was about to make it worse.

I rapped my knuckles against the door and when he looked up I smiled apologetically. 'Sorry to disturb you, Stefan, but I have a problem.'

'A problem?' His tone of voice inferred this was impossible, but then he smiled, shrugged and waved me to a seat. 'It seems to have been a day for them.'

He'd been manager of the home for almost eight years. Efficient, supremely professional, kind to the residents, fair to the staff, he was the best manager the home had had in the years Mother had been there. We had a cordial relationship. It was easy:

he ran a good home so I rarely had need to complain. That worked in my favour.

I put the medicine pot on his desk. 'As you know I frequently visit at mealtimes and give Mum her meal and her medication. Being a nurse, it's instinct to check them and,' – I tilted my head at the container – 'unless there's been some major change in her medication since I saw her last two days ago, these aren't correct.'

'If there'd been any change, we'd have let you know,' he said, reaching a hand out to pick up the container. He peered at them. 'I'm not terribly au fait with your mother's medication regime.' His eyes met mine and I could see the cogs turning. 'Give me a minute to see what's what.'

He was on his feet and out the door before I had a chance to reply.

When there was no sign of his return several minutes later, I pushed the chair back and crossed to the door, ducking back behind it when I heard raised voices approach.

'I don't know what's going on!' Jolene's voice, high and whiney. 'I don't make drug errors. I'm very careful. If there was an error, it was down to the disorganisation of the drug trolley. A total mess.'

Stefan walked to the entrance door, pressed the code to release it and pushed it open. 'You know the old saying, a poor workman blames his tools. You made a serious error. I'll be having words with your agency and will be reporting the error to the NMC.'

He was too professional to slam the door in her wake; I wasn't and punched the air in satisfaction before returning quickly to my seat. The Nursing and Midwifery Council took any breach of their code seriously and medication errors were dealt with severely. Jolene would be struck off the nursing register. Patients and residents, anyone unfortunate enough to have been in her care, would be a little safer.

Stefan was very apologetic. 'It shouldn't have happened and

thank goodness you were here today and noticed.' He pressed his lips together. Jolene's supposed crime reflected poorly on him and on the home. 'You have our apologies and assurance this won't happen again.'

It was an assurance he shouldn't make. Unfortunately, mistakes did happen, medication errors were made. Usually, they had no repercussions. A lack of care, however, was a different matter. It would be a while before I could forget poor Mr Wallace.

'I've always been happy with the care here. I'm sure it won't change.' I'd make damn sure it wouldn't. 'It was a once-off accident, Stefan, please, think no more of it. I'm impressed you acted so swiftly.' More than impressed, I was delighted.

I was back with my mother just as one of the dining room staff was walking towards her room with her supper tray.

'A bit late today,' she said, putting the tray down on the table in front of my mother.

'No problem. It looks good, thank you.' I waited till she was gone before pulling my chair closer. 'Chicken curry, Mum. Your favourite.' It had been. In a different time, a different life. One of the meals she'd often cooked. From scratch. Crushing spices, marinading pieces of chicken. I'd sit and watch, my nose twitching as the aromas hit me. And then, in the glow of the overhead light, we'd sit, Mother, Father and I, and we'd laugh, talk and eat the meal. *Such happiness.*

Was it real? I don't know if it was, or if over the years I'd painted my past in pretty colours, reinventing it to make everything easier. I was no longer able to separate the life I'd had, from the life I longed to have lived.

Sometimes, like now, I'd drift off and forget my role. Mother wouldn't reach out and nudge me, wouldn't complain to be kept waiting for the next mouthful, wouldn't say the food was cold when I did eventually remember what I was supposed to be doing.

After lunch, I'd read snippets from the newspaper I paid to have delivered every day. I had asked that the staff take time to read even a little of it to her when I wasn't there, but sometimes I'd find the previous days' newspapers in such a pristine shape that I knew they hadn't been opened.

Annoyance at their neglect would be balanced by a reluctant understanding. They felt, no doubt, that their time was better spent than reading the news to a woman who showed no evidence of caring what was happening in the world. I could have saved myself a great deal of money, and read the same newspaper over and over and my mother wouldn't have known the difference.

'Let's see what's happening today, Mum.' I unfolded the paper on the table and started to read it, page by page.

'That's it, Mum,' I said, helping her to drink the last drop of tea. 'I'm going to head home now, okay?'

Sometimes, when I leaned close and pressed my lips against her cheek, I'd be certain she was going to say something, going to reach up with her hand and pat my cheek, turn her head to meet my lips with hers, look me in the eyes and silently beg my forgiveness.

Sometimes, I was really good at fooling myself.

36

I always switched my phone off while I was visiting Mother, wanting to give her my undivided attention. As I left that evening, and walked down the avenue to the road, I reached for it and switched it on. There were the usual messages from the agency confirming shifts I'd already agreed to, and a missed call. I wasn't too surprised to see it was from Mother's solicitor, Jason Brooks. Although there was no longer any need for his services, he kept in touch and offered me advice – whether I wanted to take it, or not.

But he was a nice man, and probably the nearest to family I had, so I returned the call as I walked slowly along. 'Hi, it's Lissa,' I said when it was answered.

'Lissa, thanks for getting back to me. Are you at work?'

'No, I was visiting Mum.'

'Ah, right. I called in myself last week. I thought she looked well.'

'She doesn't change very much really.' I stopped at the end of the avenue and leaned against the trunk of a sycamore tree. It wasn't unusual for Brooks to ring me, but there was something in his voice that said this was more than a mere courtesy call. 'How're things?'

'Good, good. Listen, I was wondering if you were free for lunch sometime?'

Lunch? Now, this was unusual. We'd had several meetings over the years, all were held in his office. I might have had a biscuit with a cup of instant coffee but that was about as far as it went. I had no worries his intentions weren't honourable. He was happily married to a stunningly beautiful woman, and I, well, I was just me. 'Lunch sounds great. I'm free tomorrow if that's any good.'

'Tomorrow... hang on... yes, that would suit perfectly. How about The Ivy in Bath, around one thirty?'

'Sounds lovely. I'll see you then.'

'Excellent.'

When he hung up, I stayed leaning against the tree, tapping my phone against my chin. I had no idea why the solicitor would want to see me. I also had no idea where The Ivy in Bath was, but that, at least, the internet could throw some light on.

* * *

The Ivy, on Milsom Street in Bath, was the kind of restaurant people like me didn't go to. By that I meant people with an extremely limited wardrobe. I pored over the photographs on their website: intricate plasterwork, chandeliers, comfortable-looking leather seats, white linen-covered tables laid with silver and fancy glasses. Not a place to wear my best chinos and T.

I didn't even have my pretty silver bracelet to add a bit of a shine to an outfit. I wondered what Theo had done with it. If he had guessed it was mine and had seen me lurking, he hadn't approached me about it. Desperate as I was, I wasn't stupid

enough to go knocking on his door to confess my crime. Stupidity
– it was a crime in my book.

I lay awake worrying about what to wear. As if I were heading
off on a hot date with a gorgeous man. At least I assumed this is
what that would feel like. I'd never been on a date, hot or other-
wise. Although I had grown comfortable with my body as it was, it
didn't stop me remembering the cruel taunts of my childhood. My
nose was still big, my mouth too wide. And if men looked at me, I
knew what they were thinking and never gave them the chance to
get the words out. It had nothing to do with trust. Not all men
were like my father. *Bigamists. Liars. Cheaters. Destroyers of dreams.*

In the morning, I stood and investigated my small wardrobe.
Perhaps I was expecting the fairy godmother to have made an
appearance overnight. If she had, she must have given up in
despair. My rags were still rags. But I wasn't meeting Jason till one
thirty. I had time.

At nine, I was outside a charity shop on Walcot Street. It was
one of my favourites. Although I rarely bought anything, I was on
friendly terms with the manager, a woman of indeterminate age
with a head of hair that was very obviously a wig, especially on
days when she had, by accident or design, put it on back to front.
She usually swathed her body in what looked to be garments she
was unable to sell. They didn't fit her short rotund body, but she
wore so many, the smaller, shorter pieces overlayed with wider
baggier ones, that she was respectably if bizarrely covered.
Despite her eccentric style, she had a good eye, and I'd seen her
pick out an item for a customer that suited perfectly.

She was pinning a mixture of coats to an outside rail with an
extended window pole when I arrived. I waited till she'd finished
before offering a greeting. 'Hiya, Maggie.'

'Lissa, what's bringing you out so early?'

'Desperation.' Throwing myself on her mercy seemed like a

good plan. 'I'm being taken for lunch to The Ivy today and have nothing to wear that doesn't make me look like Orphan Annie.'

She reached up and adjusted her wig. It was still backwards; her adjustment didn't make any difference and my fingers itched to grab it and twirl it around. I resisted. This was my favourite shop and I didn't want to lose it. Plus, I genuinely liked her, despite or maybe because she didn't give a fuck what anyone thought of her. 'Can you help me?'

'I suppose you have less than a fiver to spend on it,' she said.

She knew me so well. 'I could stretch to ten at a push.'

'Ten.' She sighed, shook her head, and turned to disappear into the bowels of her shop.

It was narrow, but it stretched back a long way, with each section jammed to overfill with clothes of every type. Customers were allowed to explore but it was a little like looking through the woods for a tree. Maggie had every item inventoried in her head under that crazy daft wig. If there was something suitable there for me, she'd find it.

She was back a short while later, her hands filled with a tumble of material. She dropped it on the countertop and pulled it apart. Three dresses came from the tangle. Dresses! The last time I'd worn one was as a student nurse before trousers and tunics became the standard uniform. Unlike that white uniform, these were floral and twee, and not something I'd have chosen.

'Try them on,' Maggie said as if she'd read my mind. 'You might be surprised.'

There was a tiny changing room. Small as I was, my elbows banged off the sides as I pulled off my T-shirt and slipped the least gaudy of the three she'd chosen over my head. I had to drag the curtain back and step outside before I could see myself in the full-length mirror. My smile was automatic. Maggie was right. I was surprised. Pale blue with tiny darker blue flowers, it was gathered at the waist and gave my stick-insect figure some shape. 'This is perfect.'

'It suits you,' she said. 'It's fourteen quid but I can let you have it for ten.'

'Deal.' I took it off, dressed and joined her at the counter. 'Here you go.' I handed over a ten-pound note.

'You have a good time,' she said, and waved me off to go and deal with another early-bird customer.

It was only one twenty when I arrived outside The Ivy. Too early, as usual. Jason would be on time; he was that kind of man. I had a choice – stand in the doorway looking desperate or cross the street to Waterstones and look at books. The second seemed the better option and was a pleasant way to spend the time. It also allowed me to keep an eye on the front of The Ivy. When I saw Jason arrive, I gave him a minute to sit, put the book I was flicking through back on the shelf and left.

The reception for The Ivy proved to be a desk set in the entrance hall. The woman who stood there, smiling that forced smile that came with the job, greeted me pleasantly. It wasn't her fault that I immediately felt dowdy. In her short black clinging dress, her face beautifully made up and her hair in those curls that screamed she'd taken loads of time over it, she looked stunning.

The inside of the restaurant was even more impressive than I'd expected. As I followed the woman through the restaurant to a seat in a quiet corner towards the back, I had time to take in the lovely space and the fashionably dressed clientele. With each step I felt more out of place.

Jason's welcoming smile was a relief. He rose and came to

greet me, kissing each cheek with practised ease. 'It's so good to see you, Lissa. It's been a while.'

'Must be three months,' I said, sliding along the leather seat. 'You came in to visit Mum when I was there.'

'Let's decide what we're having, then we can chat,' he said, handing me a menu.

He had the best poker face; I had no indication what this ominous-sounding *chat* could be about. Some aspect of Mother's care I supposed, but what, I wasn't sure. I was almost tempted to ask if we could get whatever it was over with so I could enjoy my lunch, but I didn't. Jason had been kind to me over the years, I'd do things his way.

I'd already looked at the menu online, so didn't have to embarrass myself by asking what a couple of the dishes were. When the waitress came, I was able to order with a certain carelessness, as if I ordered such delicacies as white onion soup with truffles every day.

It was delicious, as was the duck that followed, and the sticky toffee pudding I finished the meal with, resisting the temptation to scrape my spoon across the plate to capture every morsel.

It wasn't until we were drinking coffee that Jason brought the conversation from mundane chitchat to the real reason he'd invited me to lunch. 'I've been worried about you,' he said.

About me! It was unexpected and brought sudden unwanted tears to my eyes. 'That's so kind, but you've no need to be, I'm fine.'

On the curved leather seat, he wasn't seated far from me. He reached across and picked up my hand.

He shook his head. 'So tiny,' he said. He kept it wrapped in his bigger, warm hand and looked at me. 'When I saw you in the home a few months ago I was shocked by how thin you were. You've been preying on my mind ever since. I'd hoped perhaps you were going through a tough patch or something, that you'd look better today.' He squeezed my hand. 'I think you're even thinner. You're not looking after yourself, Lissa. I spoke to the manager in the home, he says you visit every time you're not working and spend hours there.'

'She's my mother, of course I visit her. She needs me.' I saw him take a breath. *Please don't say it, please, please don't say she doesn't need me, that she'd be as well cared for if I never visited, please don't say it, because if you do, I'll hate you.*

He pressed my hand gently. 'She's very lucky to have you.'

Relief made me smile. 'Thank you.'

But Jason wasn't finished. 'But you need to make time for yourself, Lissa. Maybe take a few days, go away for a break.'

'Good idea, yes, I'll do that.' I kept the smile in place with difficulty. Go away? Even if I could be persuaded to leave mother, even the cheapest hotel would break my budget. Plus, I was trying to put money aside to buy a car.

'I've done some research into alternative accommodation for your mother.' He must have seen the instant horror on my face because he immediately held up a hand. 'Hear me out, please. You're paying that top-up fee and for all the extras. You can't have much left over, and I think that's why you're neglecting yourself. There are homes, just as good, where the full fee would be covered by the state. You'd have money for yourself, Lissa. To have a life.'

He was being kind, but he didn't understand. 'She deserves the best, Jason. Don't forget, I've been to some of those homes that cover the full cost. I know the compromises they make. So no, but thank you for caring, she'll stay where she is.'

Jason knew when he was beaten. 'I tried.'

His air of sad resignation made me laugh. 'You did, and it is much appreciated.' It was; it was good to have someone who cared for me. 'If you want to make sure I'm well fed, you could invite me to lunch more often.'

This made him laugh and we ended our lunch chuckling together.

I could have told him that I had an idea to increase my income, but I didn't think he'd approve of my plan.

37

On the way home, I sent Carol a message asking if she was free for coffee. I hadn't heard from her since we'd met in the garden centre. Not even a thank you for the lunch I'd splashed out on. That had been a waste of money. Unlike my dress. I smoothed a hand over the material. If we met for coffee, I'd wear it and surprise her. It was more suited to the type of places we normally frequented than The Ivy.

I needed to have up-to-date information on the Wallaces before I proceeded with my plan. He may have already died. It wouldn't make a difference to what I intended doing but it would change my approach.

To my surprise, I had a reply a few minutes later.

Yes, would like that. When?

I was starting a run of two nights. It would have been sensible to wait till they were done. More sense to have abandoned the plan altogether. It was crazy, flaky, but now that I had the photographic proof, it might just work. Sadly, it needed Mr Wallace's demise to put into action. After all, I couldn't blackmail the grieving widow until she was one.

I tapped out a message:

How about tomorrow? 2ish? Cafe Renaldo?

Perfect.

* * *

The night shift was exhaustingly busy. Instead of the three care assistants there should have been, there were two, which meant we were chasing our tails the whole shift. I came home totally exhausted and fell into a comatose state for three hours. My first thought on waking was to ring the agency and say I couldn't work that night, that I was sick, exhausted. That I couldn't go on, that the solicitor was right, I needed to get myself a life, needed to stop working every damn hour of the day. I'd move Mother to a cheaper nursing home where the state covered the cost. I'd stop paying for daily newspapers, hairdressing, manicures. I'd abandon her – just as my father had done. Just as she had abandoned me.

Then I threw the covers back and got up. Café Renaldo was near the bus station in Bath and the time was creeping quickly towards two.

There was no temptation to cancel. Carol might take umbrage at such a late change of plan and be unwilling to meet again, and I needed what she knew. I looked at the dress I'd left hanging on the back of the wardrobe door and shook my head. I'd been fooling myself. Nothing I could wear would make me look any more presentable. I pulled on a pair of chinos and a clean T, slung my tatty bag over my shoulder and left.

I kept walking when I saw the front door of Lily Cottage open. I hadn't seen Theo for a while, only that glimpse of a figure at his upstairs window the night I'd lost my bracelet. I didn't want to see or talk to him that day. Far too weary for polite conversation, certainly too tired to keep a rein on my tongue. I might have asked him for the return of my bracelet and goodness knew what can of worms that would have opened.

He might have called my name; I wasn't sure nor was I turning to find out. Then I was out on the footpath and crossing the road to the bus stop.

I arrived several minutes too early for my two o'clock meeting with Carol. The café was busy, but it was the kind of place where people didn't tend to linger for long. As I stood looking for a spot, I spied a couple beginning the ritual of gathering their belongings in preparation to leave and hurried to take possession.

I wasn't planning on spending any money this time. When Carol arrived five minutes after the hour, I waved to attract her attention, and when she crossed to the table, I greeted her with a smile. 'I was lucky and managed to get a table for us.'

'Well done,' she said, dropping her bag on the spare chair.

'I didn't want to risk losing it by queuing for coffee.' As hints went, it wasn't subtle.

'I'll go and get it. What'll you have?'

The night shift had been too busy to allow time for more than a mug of coffee and slice of toast while I was writing up the notes that morning, and lunch in The Ivy seemed like a distant memory. It was tempting to ask for the all-day breakfast, but I didn't want to push my luck. 'A cappuccino and a scone would be nice.'

She nodded and left to join the queue.

My strategy had worked. I sat back and relaxed. It was all

going to work out. If I got the information I needed from Carol, then I'd put my plan into action. If it worked, I'd be better off; if it didn't, I wouldn't have lost anything.

The queue was slow moving. I looked to where Carol was standing quietly, not shuffling impatiently as I'd have done. She turned, caught my eye, and held my gaze without changing expression. As before, I had the oddest sensation that I knew her from somewhere. It was something about her eyes: there was a knowing look in them that made me shiver. She only looked away when the person in front of her moved forward.

I was imagining it. Tiredness could do odd things to the thought process. I kept my head down until I heard her return.

'Here you go,' she said. She rested the laden tray on the edge of the table and balanced it there while she offloaded the array of food and drinks.

She'd gone for the all-day breakfast and my mouth watered as the aroma of sausages and bacon wafted in my direction. My scone was a poor choice in comparison. 'Lovely,' I said as I cut it in half, buttered both sides and emptied the contents of a plastic container of jam onto each. It wasn't sausage and bacon, but it was pretty good. Or maybe it was just that I was so hungry. So tired. And suddenly just incredibly weary of everything.

'You're very quiet, you okay?'

Carol's plate was almost empty. Had I dozed off? I reached for my coffee and slurped a mouthful. It was still warm, but only just. 'I've had a few busy shifts.' I didn't say I'd been working that night, unwilling to get into a discussion about how ridiculous I was to be going out instead of resting. I ate half the scone, drank some more of the coffee, mentally begging the caffeine to rush to my brain. There wouldn't be a better opportunity. 'How's it going with Mr Wallace?'

She immediately assumed the *face*, so I knew without being told that he'd died. Mrs Wallace had the outcome she'd wanted.

'He passed away,' she said.

Euphemisms like p*assed away* – a far gentler expression than the cut to the chase *he died* – were commonly used by everyone working in the caring sector. I remembered an embarrassing moment many years before when I was working in the hospital. One of the first times I'd needed to inform a woman that her relative had died, I'd used *he's left us*. Unfortunately, she assumed he'd been transferred to a different ward and asked where he'd gone. The man had been a particularly obnoxious person and, given the choice, I'd have said *directly to hell*. Fortunately for my career, the words didn't get said and I realised my error in time to use the more direct, 'No, I'm afraid I mean he's died.'

As Mr Wallace had done. How long he'd have lived without his wife's deadly input was impossible to tell. Maybe years. Years when she'd have had to tend to his needs. How much better off she was now. 'Were you with him at the end?' Another euphemism. I could have used *when he croaked* but it wouldn't have done me any favours. Carol was very professional and straightlaced.

'Yes. I was glad to be there both for him and Mrs Wallace. I'd got to know her well over the weeks.'

I had to choose my words carefully. 'It must be a relief for her that he's at peace.'

'Oh yes.'

'I mean,' – I spoke as if the thoughts were just coming to me, not as if I'd been thinking about it for days – 'he's been sick since before they married, so it's been hard for her.' I picked up the second half of the scone and took a bite. It was really very good and taking the edge off my hunger. 'I'm guessing he went downhill more quickly than they expected, am I right?'

'You know as well as I do, that there's no guarantees about the course of a disease as insidious as cancer. He was unlucky, that's all.'

'Yes, I suppose.' I drew out the last word, loading each letter with doubt. I hoped it would encourage Carol to ask what I meant. When she didn't, I was forced to be more explicit. 'Of course, you'd have noticed if she was helping him along.' When this was met with silence, I decided to go for it. 'You said she fed him his meals. It'd be easy enough to slip some crushed tablets into his food.'

She drew back, eyes wide, whether in surprise, horror or shock I wasn't sure. 'What!'

Definitely horror. I held my hands up in surrender. 'Sorry, it was just a thought. I've been reading far too many psychological thrillers recently; they have me looking at everything through a shattered lens.'

'Seriously, you need to be careful what you say, Lissa. That's the kind of nonsense that gets people talking.'

'Yes, and frightening doctors enough into asking for a post-mortem.' I was half thinking out loud. But I wasn't wrong, if there was any hint of doubt about Mr Wallace's demise, they'd have had no choice. The serial killer doctor, Harold Shipman, had cast a long shadow.

'That isn't going to happen,' Carol said, her voice firm. 'Mr Wallace's GP saw him the day before he passed, and it was he who came to make the official declaration of death. He signed the certificate without issue. It was entirely expected, and your silly talk is just that... silly.'

I tried to look suitably apologetic. 'Sorry.' I looked towards the service counter. There wasn't a queue. 'Fancy another coffee?'

Her hesitation was obvious. Perhaps she'd thought she'd spent long enough in my company. I felt stupidly and unexpectedly hurt. 'Maybe even a scone? They're good.' Was I begging? What a pathetically sad creature I was.

'No, no scone, but another coffee would be nice.'

'Great.' I got to my feet. 'Back in a tick.'

There was still no queue, and my order was taken immediately. When I turned, I caught Carol staring at me, a strange expression twisting her face. She looked away immediately and when I reached the table, she'd rearranged her features and even managed a smile as I placed the brimming cappuccino in front of her.

'I hope I didn't offend you,' I said, stirring sugar into my coffee. 'Of course you'd have noticed if anything had been off with Mrs Wallace.'

'She's a very nice lady. It hasn't been easy on her. I think she expected they'd have far more years together.'

Carol seemed to see only the good in the woman. I remembered how she'd looked at me only moments before and wondered what she saw in me.

38

Carol knocked her coffee back in a couple of almost frenetic mouthfuls. It had cost nearly four quid; she should have savoured it. Despite my best efforts, I managed to pry nothing more out of her regarding Mrs Wallace. When Carol spoke of her, it was in glowing terms that didn't hint she knew anything about the woman's ulterior motives.

It didn't make me doubt my interpretation of Mrs Wallace's actions at all. Perhaps it was my history that allowed me to see a side of people that wasn't obvious to someone who never painted outside the lines like Carol.

'I have to go,' she said, dropping her empty cup on the saucer. 'I've a lot to get done, I'm starting a run of five days tomorrow with a new client.'

A new client? How many times had I asked for a private client? Carol had to have pull in the agency. She wasn't a better nurse than me. I swallowed my annoyance to ask, 'A new client? Where is it this time?'

Carol picked up her bag and pushed back her chair as if to say she wasn't lingering any longer. 'In Kingsdown, Wormcliff Lane. Handy enough.'

Wormcliff Lane. Less than two miles from me. It would have been perfect; I could have walked, saved the bus fare. 'How do you do it? I'm still being placed in nursing homes and hospitals.' I smiled as if I didn't care, as if I was quite happy with my lot.

She was hunting inside her ridiculously large bag. A leather one. Not a charity shop purchase. Only when she'd pulled out a large bunch of keys, did she decide to answer. 'I've been lucky, I suppose. The manager of the first home I worked in emailed the agency to say that families had said how helpful and empathetic I was. The request for a nurse to look after Mr Wallace came at the same time so I suppose they thought I'd be perfect. And I know Mrs Wallace emailed the agency to say how happy she'd been with the care I'd given her husband. I'm assuming that's why I got this one in Kingsdown.'

'That's great, well done.' I should have guessed. Carol was the kind of woman who'd go out of her way to say all the right things to the right people. I'd worked with her sort: the ones who'd be busy cosying up to the managers and administrators, leaving suckers like me, who couldn't be bothered with that kind of nonsense, to do all the work.

'When are you working again?'

I could tell she'd asked because she felt it necessary to reciprocate the interest not that she really cared. Or maybe she wanted to gloat when I told her I was, yet again, working in the crummiest nursing home in the region. 'Oh, I need a rest. I'm taking a few days off.' I stretched and yawned loudly to back up my lie.

'Right, good,' she commented, not bothering to hide the fact that she didn't give a toss. I frowned. I knew why I met her, but why did she bother to meet me when it was obvious she didn't particularly care for my company? Maybe she was as curious about me as I was about her.

Outside the café, I knew she wasn't going to offer me a lift – she never did – so rather than crossing to the bus stop to stand there looking pathetic, I lied and told her I was going to do some shopping. We walked together until she needed to turn off for the Charlotte Street car park, then I walked a little further to the next bus stop.

Lost in thought, I boarded the bus when it came, sat in the seat I always chose if it was free, and rested my head against the window as the bus trundled on its way. I got off at my usual stop in Bathford and wandered along to my apartment. Perhaps if I'd been more conscious of my surroundings and not completely absorbed in my thoughts, I wouldn't have walked smack-bang into Theo.

He was a big man, tall and broad, and walking into him was the equivalent of walking into a wall. It rocked me on my feet and sent me stumbling backwards. I would have fallen had he not, with a quick reaction that surprised me, grabbed hold of my upper arms with his big hands and held me as I regained my footing.

'You need to be careful,' he said, looking down into my eyes. 'A little bit of a thing like you could easily be badly injured.'

It was clear from the odd look in his eyes that he wasn't talking about my stupid stumble. The night of the letter box fiasco he obviously *had* seen me. It was too late to explain, to say I'd been trying to be a good neighbour, that I'd been concerned not to have seen him. That I was bloody well trying to be nice. Too late.

I pulled away, mumbled, 'Thank you', and darted past him. I fished in my bag for my keys as I walked and stabbed them into the lock without delay. I could feel his eyes on me. Typically, anxiety made me clumsy, the keys dropping to the ground. I risked a glance towards the gate as I bent to scoop them up. He was still there. Still staring.

Once inside, I pushed the snib down on the lock. Who was I fooling? If he wanted to get in, his bulk would have made short work of the flimsy door. Perhaps I needed this sudden dart of fear to solidify my plan to blackmail Mrs Wallace. Money would allow me to move. Isolation had its benefits, but, as I was beginning to learn, it also had its drawbacks. There had to be something between the high-rise tower of apartments I'd lived in before, and this.

I remembered the view from the Wallaces' home. The spacious rooms. I flopped onto the sofa and looked around my cosy home. Could I get used to living somewhere bigger? Perhaps I loved small because it was all I could afford.

I rested my head back. Something needed to change and soon. My plan could work. It needed concentration though and that was impossible as tired as I was. There was only one thing to do. Since I'd started with the agency, I'd been careful never to take a day's sick leave. I'd never refused a shift either, no matter how difficult it would be. Each time, thinking reliability would work in my favour and they'd give me easier, cushier placements.

Since it hadn't, and they gave these jobs to the likes of goody-two-shoes nurses like Carol, they could bugger off. Harnessing my irritation, I grabbed my bag, pulled out my phone and rang the agency before I could worry about the repercussions.

'I'm really sorry, I can't work tonight,' I said, assuming a croaky faint voice. 'I seem to have come down with something.' *Something*. It was suitably vague, meaning I could ring back in a day or two and say I was miraculously cured. 'I'm going to have to cancel my shifts for a while.' After that night, I had two off. By then, I hoped to know what I was doing.

'So sorry to hear that.' The agency administrator didn't sound in the slightest bit sympathetic. Unsurprising really, the poor thing would spend the next hour or so desperately ringing everyone trying to cover the shift. 'I'll take you off the roster until we hear from you.'

'Thank you, that would be best. Hopefully, I'll be better soon.' Soon? That depended on what happened with Mrs Wallace. I tossed the phone on the seat beside me and sighed. It was tempting to dive straight in. Go around to Lansdown Road now and get the ball rolling. But although I wasn't unwell, I was too weary to think straight. It would be better to start with a clear head the following day.

I had an early dinner and watched a bit of TV. Perhaps it was the tiredness, or the thoughts that were swirling around my head, or maybe it was simply that the crime series I was watching wasn't very good, whatever the reason, it wasn't making any sense to me, and I switched it off.

Instant silence. No rumbles from apartments on either side, or heavy-footed movement from anyone living above. This was my perfect home. But I had to admit, Theo worried me. There was something odd about him. I gave a snort of laughter. Maybe I was getting paranoid, hadn't I thought the same thing about Carol?

No, that wasn't quite right, I hadn't thought she was odd, it was just something in her eyes. A familiarity that puzzled me.

My sigh was loud in the silence. It would be hard enough to get to sleep without thinking of either Theo or Carol. Like most night shift workers, my circadian rhythm had gone a little berserk. It didn't help that the warm June had been followed by a hot, sticky July. There was little airflow in the apartment even with both long narrow windows open, and often I'd wake with a slick of sweat on my face and between my breasts.

Switching out the light, I opened the door. It was still daylight, so I didn't need to worry about triggering the security light as I crossed to lean against the wall of Theo's house. In the shade, it was pleasantly cool. But if any air came through the open door, it stayed hidden when I shut it behind me.

I hoped tiredness would defeat the heat and I'd manage a few hours' sleep. Dropping my clothes on the back of a chair, I slid under the sheet and shut my eyes. When I woke, it was dark and I stretched out a hand and felt blindly for my phone, groaning in disbelief when I saw the time. Midnight. Three hours sleep would be of little help. I needed to get some more.

Maybe I would have done, if the security light hadn't come on outside, lighting up the room and making my heart hammer.

39

When the security light went out, I was able to breathe again. It was probably a fox looking for food; they drifted in from the surrounding fields looking for a quick meal at the expense of human wastrels. I'd seen them in the early morning, bold as brass, walking down the middle of the road.

My eyelids drooped, maybe counting foxes was as good as sheep and I'd fall back to sleep. When the security light lit up the room again, my eyes instantly flicked open, and any thought of sleep disappeared in a puff of fear.

I lay rigid, my eyes fixed on the open windows as if someone, or something, was going to slither in. It was a crazy thought; the windows were over six feet from the floor, plus they were too narrow to allow access for a human. In the middle of the night though, it was easy for my mind to conjure up shapeshifters and other escapees from a Steven King novel.

'It's a fox.' I whispered the words as if there was something lurking outside the door. Something listening. It would have made sense to get up, throw some clothes on and open the door to frighten away whatever was out there. But unlike the air I was trying to lure in earlier, I didn't want what was out there to come inside.

When the light went out, I held my breath. Seconds, minutes passed. Then it came on again. Teasing me. On and off for the rest of the night, on and off until daylight drowned its light. Only then did I drift into a sleep populated with monsters that had me twist and turn and wake with a cry that seemed to hang in the air.

The dim light of day had squeezed through the narrow windows giving just enough light to chase most of the shadows away. I was angry with myself for my foolish imaginings, angry with the damn foxes, or rats or whatever rodent had set the security light off again and again.

Because that's what it had to be.

There was no reason for Theo to be hanging around outside. Listening at my door. He was sure to have a key. If he meant me harm, he could have come inside.

Whenever he wanted.

For the first time, I realised that nobody, not one single person, knew where I lived. I had willingly fallen in with Theo's request to give Lily Cottage as my address, but I'd never needed to.

If I vanished – if Theo made me vanish – who would know?

40

If anything could shake the sleep from my brain, it was the thought that nobody knew where I lived. I hadn't mentioned my new address to the agency, or to Jason Brooks when I'd met him for lunch, not even to Mother's nursing home. I had had no need to. Everything was done by email, text message, or phone call. Nobody was going to send me a birthday or Christmas card. No one was going to send me Valentine's Day flowers.

Only in hindsight did I realise how crazy it all was – including my ability to shut my eyes to anything apart from what I wanted. What a stupid, stupid, *stupid* woman I was!

Anger drove me from the bed to stamp barefooted up and down the small space I had been pleased to call home. The walls seemed to be closing in on me. In desperation I slammed my fists against them. All I succeeded in doing was jarring my elbow. It didn't make the space any larger. It didn't stop the self-flagellation. Anger faded to self-pity. If I wasn't such an idiot, men like Theo wouldn't take advantage, if I was nicer, the agency would have given me the cushy jobs, if I had been a sweeter, prettier child, my father wouldn't have wanted to spend so much time away from our little family.

Self-pity was always hard to shake off, and only by forcing my mind to concentrate on my plan, did I succeed. I was going to call around to Lansdown Road and speak to Mrs Wallace. I hoped I'd find her playing the part of the grieving widow, floating around in funeral weeds, eyes downcast as she mentally counted how much she was going to inherit.

Perhaps she continued to play golf, explaining to anyone who might ask that she'd promised her dear departed that she would. Brief as our meeting had been, she struck me as a woman who could play a part. She and my father would have made a good team.

There was little point in arriving too early, but I didn't want to hang around the home I was beginning to hate. Instead, I dressed and went to visit my mother.

* * *

Although the home didn't allow visitors until the day staff were on shift, they made a concession for me. It suited them of course. If I arrived early, as on that day, I'd help Mother have a shower and get dressed.

While there was never any indication she heard or understood what I said, I chatted as I helped her with her ablutions, telling her about Mrs Wallace and what she'd done to her husband. I rubbed a soaped flannel in lazy circles over Mother's back and tried to avoid the spray from the shower head.

'I guess she thought she'd waited long enough so decided to give nature a helping hand. She probably started months ago,' I said, soaping Mother's arms. 'Maybe switching some of his prescribed medication with those that had belonged to the first wife. Probably helpfully popped them out for him in the morning, leaving them by his early mug of tea or something.'

Yes, I could imagine the glamorous Oonagh clearly. And if her poor misguided husband happened to comment on the different shape or colour of the pills, she'd shrug and say it must be a different make. He'd never have suspected. How would he? Despite constant proof of their existence, nobody ever expected a monster to appear in their life.

Once Mother was dressed, I sat her in her armchair and went to the kitchen for her breakfast. Her tray was laid out already. I added another cup and saucer for me, made a pot of coffee and three slices of toast and took it all back to her room.

Mother was happy to watch TV while having her breakfast. I use happy in the loosest sense of the word. She didn't show emotion of any kind. The frown marks that divided my forehead weren't on hers. No emotion – no frowning – no lines. A quiver of resentment made my expression tighter, the lines deeper, and I'd guess if someone asked, they'd say I was the older, not Mother.

'I'm going to make some changes, Mum.'

Did I imagine a sharpening of her expression?

'No, don't worry,' – I reached for her hand and held it in mine – 'I'm not planning on moving you from here. It's my own situation that's going to change. You'll be glad to hear, nobody needs to die this time.

'At least,' I frowned, 'I don't think so.'

41

I stayed with Mother until after lunch. 'I'll be back tomorrow,' I said as I kissed her smooth cheek. 'I'm not working for a few days. Perhaps, if things work out, we could go into Bath for a day. I could get a taxi to take us there. We could have lunch somewhere or go to the Royal Crescent, sit in their garden, and have a glass of wine. What d'you think? Wouldn't it be lovely?'

I'd gone into the hotel once and had been mesmerised by how beautiful it was. Luckily, although I did get a few curious looks from staff, they didn't charge for walking through the hotel to the hidden garden behind. It had been a blue-sky summer's day and most of the tables scattered throughout the garden were occupied by beautifully dressed people sipping drinks. I hid my scruffiness behind a huge tote bag as I walked around inhaling the ambience. It was the kind of place my parents would have gone to. Probably the same kind of place my father would have taken his other wife too. It looked like the sort of place she'd have felt right at home in.

If my plan worked out and I had more money, I could bring Mother there. We'd be just as good as the rest.

Hoping I was leaving her with happy thoughts, I left the home and headed for Lansdown Road.

* * *

It was almost two when I arrived in front of the imposing house I assumed now belonged to Widow Wallace. I wasn't nervous. If my plan worked, it would be life-changing. If it didn't, my life would go on as it had done for years. *And years.* As it would go on for years to come.

I checked in my bag for the photograph I'd brought, flicking my fingernail against the edge. I hoped my dress would make a good impression. My plan was a two-parter and this first part was simply to gather information. The more I had, the more likely I was to succeed with the second part, the blackmail. All I wanted was a few thousand, ten perhaps, enough to buy a small car. It would make my life so much easier. Perhaps I would find somewhere more suitable and cheaper to live further from the city. A small cottage in a big garden. No neighbours in sight. Wales, maybe, deep in the countryside. I could drive to visit my mother, even take her out for the day.

Putting my dreams aside, I climbed the steps to the Wallace's front door. At the top, I smoothed a hand over my hair, settled the strap of my bag on my shoulder, took a deep breath and pressed the doorbell. *Let the games begin.*

When I heard the door opening a minute later, I rearranged my features into what I hoped looked partially apologetic, partly determined. I hoped she'd remember my last visit. It would make this one easier and more effective. When she looked at me blankly, I could have been flattered with the thought that I looked so much more sophisticated in my pretty dress, but I had enough self-awareness not to fool myself. She didn't recognise me, because women like her never noticed women like me.

'You probably don't remember me,' I said with a tentative smile. 'I called around last week but chickened out when you answered, and I ran away.' Her eyes drifted over me. Perhaps she was admiring my dress. 'I came back.' It was stating the bleedin' obvious, but I was hoping I'd managed to inject enough pathos in the three words to stimulate some smidgen of curiosity.

She stood with a hand on the door. I had been right about the widow's weeds; she was indeed dressed in black but there was nothing funereal about the chiffon blouse, the slim-fitting skirt, or the strappy stiletto-heeled sandals. 'I remember you,' she said.

My sigh was deliberately over-dramatic. 'I'm so sorry for running away last time.' I shook my head and gave a tentative smile. 'It's not an easy thing I'm doing.' I had her now, I could see the light of curiosity in her eyes. 'I'm here to see George Wallace.'

The hand that was lightly gripping the door tensed, the knuckles whitening. She pulled her lower lip in with small white teeth. She was good: it was a completely believable act.

'Is he here?' I drew myself up. 'This time I'm not running away.'

Her mouth opened and shut, then to my disbelief, and admiration, she started to cry.

'I'm sorry,' she said. She raised the handkerchief she held in her free hand and dabbed each eye delicately. 'You'd better step inside. I'm afraid I have bad news for you.' She didn't shut the door behind me, as if expecting my stay to be brief. 'I'm not sure why you're looking for my husband but I'm afraid it's too late. He was very sick for a long time and passed away at the weekend.' Her voice was soft, thick with tears. If I hadn't known better, I'd have believed she was sincerely grieving.

It was my time to shine now. I'd seen enough people faint in my day to be able to do a creditable effort. It was a step backward, hand raised to my mouth to cover my open-mouthed gasp, another step backwards, stumbling this time, then a half-turn to rest my hand on the wall. 'No.' Just the one word, but on a wail. I hoped I hadn't gilded the damn lily.

'Oh dear,' she said, taking a step towards me.

I kept my face hidden in the curve of my arm. Unlike her, I had never mastered the ability to cry on demand. Rubbing my eyes with my fingers would have to do. I hoped they looked sufficiently irritated and red when I straightened and turned to look at her. 'I can't believe he's dead.'

She dabbed her eyes again. It's a cliché that some women can cry and still look beautiful. I've never seen a woman yet who didn't look haggard and ugly after a crying session. Whereas she didn't look precisely ugly, she looked more haggard than I'd expected. Probably had been up late like Scrooge counting her pennies.

'He was sick for a long time. The end when it came though was sudden.' Her lower lip trembled. 'It's been hard.'

'If only I had come in the last day.' I swallowed loudly. It was the closest I could get to gulping. 'I can't believe I won't get to see him.' I looked towards the open door. 'I suppose I'd better go.' It was a risk; she might have let me leave, but most people would have a natural curiosity about a woman who'd arrived – for the second time – and asked to speak to your late husband.

'No, please don't,' she said, crossing to shut the door. 'Come, I'll make us some tea and you can tell me why you wanted to see George.'

Don't you just love when things fall into place so perfectly? I followed her through the door and down the stairs. The kitchen door was wide open so the small vestibule at the bottom of the stairs was brightly lit. I noticed she didn't glance towards the locked door on the left. I wondered if she'd managed to get rid of the evidence. Easily done, any pharmacy would accept unwanted medication for disposal with no questions asked.

'Have a seat.' She waved to the table overlooking the garden and the view beyond. 'Would you like tea or coffee?' When I hesitated, she added, 'Or there's wine, if you'd like a glass?'

I'd have loved a glass, but I wasn't a big drinker, and my tolerance was poor as a result. The last thing I needed was to make a mess of things when everything was going so well. 'Tea would be good, thank you.'

She moved around the spacious kitchen, filling the kettle, opening, and shutting cupboards. I kept my bag on my lap, waiting for the right moment to whip out the photo and present her with my carefully practised words.

'Here you go,' she said, putting teapot and mugs on the table. She sat before realising she'd forgotten the milk and jumped up with a muttered, 'Sorry, hang on.' She stayed on her feet as she poured the tea. Picking up the jug, she added milk when I nodded. Only then did she sit.

'My name is Oonagh; George was my husband.'

'Lissa... Lissa McColl.' It seemed as good a time as any. 'George is... was... my father.'

42

I'm not sure what she was expecting, but this wasn't it. Her eyes opened wide in shock and she drew in a noisy ragged breath.

I reached into my bag and took out the snap of George Wallace and the unknown woman I'd found in the photograph frame. 'This was taken almost thirty years ago.' I placed it on the table and slid it towards her before tapping it with a finger. 'That's George, isn't it?'

She couldn't lie; he hadn't changed that much over the years. Giving it a brief look, she got to her feet and crossed the room to pick up a spectacles case. She opened it, took a wire-rimmed pair out and slipped them on, then lifted the photograph and looked at it silently for several seconds. 'And the woman?'

'Cathy McColl. My mother.' It was better, in my web of lies, to use the truth when I could. 'She had a breakdown many years ago and has been in care ever since. I was going through some of her stuff recently and found this.'

Oonagh put the photograph down and took off her glasses. She held them by one arm and swung them to and fro.

'When I found it, I took it in to my mother and asked her

about it.' I sighed. 'Since her breakdown, she doesn't talk much, but when I put this into her hand and asked if this was my father, she said, "yes, it was."' It would have been ideal had I been able to squeeze out one miserable tear. I rubbed my eyes, hoping it would suffice. 'She told me his name was George Wallace. But that's all she would tell me.'

I reached forward and tapped the photograph with a finger. 'It didn't take me long to find out about the logo on the wall behind them. It's the University of Bath's. It took me a bit of digging to discover one of the lecturers was called George Wallace, less time to find out where he lived.'

'She looks very young.'

I had to be careful. If my story was that I was the result of their passion, George would have been about forty and swept away by his love for my twenty-year-old mother. 'I think she was about twenty.'

Oonagh's eyes opened even wider, but she shook her head and said nothing.

'She left university without graduating. I always wondered why; I suppose I've had my answer now.'

The glasses still swung back and forth, Oonagh's expression now indecipherable. I hoped she was wondering what ramifications this would have on her inheritance.

'When I was old enough to ask questions, my mother told me my father had been the love of her life.' I smiled sadly. 'I'm so sorry I was too late to meet him.'

The glasses Oonagh held were being swung with such ferocity, I could feel the waft of the breeze they made, and half expected to see the lens flying across the room. 'I'm really sorry,' she said, 'but I'm afraid you're wrong.'

I was going to launch into a long spiel about having a DNA test done, and planned to yank out one of my hairs in a dramatic fashion as if in proof of my certainty. Matching DNA from hair samples was only ever sixty per cent successful, but it didn't matter, it would never get that far. I just wanted to keep her talking. My words were poised for take-off, 'I—'

She held up a hand to stop me, got to her feet and crossed to the American-style fridge that dominated a corner of the kitchen. When she returned, she was holding a bottle of wine and two glasses. She didn't ask if I wanted any. Instead, she unscrewed the lid from the already half-empty bottle and poured with little care. Wine slopped over the edge of the glass and puddled on the table around the base. When the bottle was empty, she placed it in the middle of the table. Between us. Like a weapon.

She lifted her glass and downed half in one long gulp.

I didn't want a drink but, I wasn't sure why, my mouth was suddenly dry. The wine was cold, sharp. Different to the cheap sweet stuff I bought on occasion. A sip would moisten my mouth. It didn't, so I did as she had done and gulped half. It might not help; I didn't think it could do much damage. There was something in her expression that was bothering me. It looked very like sympathy... pity even.

'I'm afraid, your search hasn't ended. George and your mother may have had a relationship, but he can't have been your father.' She took a smaller sip of her wine, looking at me as if waiting for a reaction.

I didn't give one. She was so emphatic; I knew I'd been an idiot. I should really have considered why George Wallace had never had children. It didn't matter, but I didn't like being caught out.

'George had chickenpox as a child,' Oonagh said. 'It left him sterile.'

43

Oonagh picked up her glass again. She swilled the contents around, then emptied it in one long gulp before lowering it. 'I'm sorry, you must be very disappointed.'

I lifted my glass and held it in front of my face. As a shield it was little use, but it was all I had, and gave me time to rearrange my features into some semblance of disappointment. She wasn't to know I didn't give a toss, but I could hear it in her voice – she felt sorry for me, for the poor fool who was searching for her father. She'd be freer with her words now and I'd gain more information, more knowledge. It was my first blackmail; I was determined to make it a success.

Oonagh continued to hold her empty glass, twirling the stem around in her fingers. 'Your mother is in care, you said?'

'Yes.'

'That must be hard. I was lucky, I was able to keep George at home until the end. It was what he wanted.' She sighed heavily. 'It wasn't easy to see him so sick though.'

'That must have been difficult.' I pushed the corners of my mouth down in a clownish sad face. 'Had he been unwell for a long time?' I was interested to see her full act. She might do as I did and stick as closely to the truth as possible.

'He had cancer. It had been diagnosed before I met him, but he'd had treatment and the prognosis was good. We hoped we'd have years together.'

Lie number one. Shame I couldn't take out a notebook and keep a tally. I had to remember I wasn't supposed to know the truth. 'How long had you known him?' I thought for a moment she wasn't going to answer, and I was trying to figure out what my next question should be when I heard her sigh.

'Only a few years. When I met him, his first wife was still alive. She died suddenly and he was grief-stricken. He was going through chemotherapy at the time and was struggling to keep it all together so I offered to lend a hand.' She sat back in her chair, her eyes drifting to look out the window to the garden and the view that swept away down the hillside. 'I'm not sure why I'm telling you this...'

Her voice faded away. Afraid she would stop just as it was getting interesting, I assumed my best sympathetic voice and said, 'Sometimes it's good to talk.' Most times, it's better to keep your trap shut, but that didn't suit my purpose at all.

'Yes,' she agreed. 'And sometimes it's easier to speak to a stranger.'

Exactly what I'd hoped. I waited but when she seemed to have become stuck, I nudged gently. 'You helped him to deal with the loss of his wife. That was kind of you.'

'Kind?' She continued to stare out the window. 'Yes, I suppose that's how it started. I was simply being kind to him.'

Being kind to him! Lie number two. She'd eyed up the lonely, vulnerable, sick, *rich* widower and cast her web. The poor man, he hadn't had a chance.

She'd been staring out at the view but turned to look at me. 'George was the sweetest, most lovely man.' Her smile was so filled with sadness that it took me aback and made me blink. My brain struggled to process something so unexpected that I instantly felt out of my depth. Treading water, I desperately tried to reach for something solid to cling to. 'You were married very quickly.'

Instead of answering, she got to her feet, returned to the fridge, and took out another bottle of wine. 'A temporary crutch,' she said waving it at me.

I hadn't finished my wine, but she topped it up anyway before filling her glass. 'George did love his wine,' she said. 'Here's to you, wherever you are.' She lifted the glass to the ceiling, then took a deep gulp, emptying half. 'There were lots of people who looked askance at us when we married, only three months after his first wife died. To be honest, I was shocked he'd asked me so quickly, and at first, I said no.' She looked at me. 'Do you know what he said?'

I shook my head.

'He said he'd been blessed to have met another woman to love, that he had no idea how much time he had left and wanted to spend however long that was with me.' Her smile was rueful. 'I'd been married before, many years ago. It hadn't lasted and hadn't given me any reason to try again, but George...' She took a sip of her wine, balancing the glass against her lower lip for a long time. 'He was the most amazing man. When I was with him, I believed in everything.'

In everything his money could buy, more likely. I struggled to keep my thoughts focused. I knew the truth; she'd married him for the money. I wasn't going to be fooled by this very good act. 'You agreed to marry him.'

'Yes. Crazy as it was, I did.'

She smiled and shook her head as if she still couldn't understand why. It was such a good act... almost believable.

'Of course,' she went on, 'we expected to have years together. Then he got that damn chest infection. He was a week in hospital with it, and so frail when they discharged him that we decided to have a home nurse for a while.' She ran a finger around the rim of the glass. 'It was hard to allow someone else in, but he was a proud man, he hated me seeing him at his worst. We thought he'd pull through, you know, that once he got his strength back, he'd be fine.'

I watched the waterworks start up again. God, she was good.

Oonagh pulled a tissue from her pocket and wiped it over her eyes. 'I suppose the chest infection allowed the cancer to take hold because he never did get stronger. But, even when his condition worsened, we still thought we'd have time together. We kept the nurses, day and night, but I made sure there were hours for the two of us to be together. I'd sit with him, hold his hand, read to him, or we'd watch a movie. He insisted I went back to my golf and when I came home, I'd entertain him with stories of the other golfers and how well or badly I'd played. Our life had changed, but I still loved being with him.'

Lies, all of it. 'He went downhill quickly then, did he?'

She didn't appear to notice the bluntness of my question. 'Yes.'

Of course he did. I wondered if she'd researched which medication to give him to shorten his life, or if she'd just crushed whatever she had willy-nilly, hoping that somehow, they'd do the job. I'd seen what she had to work with. Two different types of cardiac medication: either would have done the job in large enough proportions, both together would have hurried the process. It wasn't rocket science. Working in the doctor's surgery as she had done, she'd have had access to enough information to help her along.

'When he died, even though I knew it was coming, I was stunned... lost... as if all the lights in the world had been switched off at the same time, and all that was left, all I could see, was darkness, shadows, shades.' Her sigh was long and seemed to float through the air.

She was lying, she had to be, I couldn't have been so wrong. I was reminded of my mother's reaction to my father's death. She'd had all the light switched off in her life, and she'd stayed there locked in the darkness.

'Even now, when I come through the door of this huge empty house, my first thought is to go to him. Maybe heat up his next meal, spend time helping him to eat.' She gave a soft laugh, her eyes filling again with the memory. 'In the final few days, he didn't want to eat at all, you know, but he did, he'd take a few spoonfuls of it simply to please me. It was the way he was.'

Food she'd made for him. Food she'd poisoned. At least the poor man went to his death oblivious to her treachery.

'It's funny,' Oonagh said.

Nothing seemed remotely funny to me, but I had a feeling the grieving widow wasn't talking to me. I'm not sure she even realised I was still there. 'What is?' I asked when her monologue seemed to have ground to a halt.

She turned to look at me in surprise. 'Sorry?'

I knew I'd been right; she'd forgotten I was there. 'You were saying something was funny.'

'Funny,' she frowned. 'Ah, yes, sorry. It was thinking about helping George with his meals. It was a running joke between us because I'm a terrible cook, we used to either eat out or get a takeaway.'

Once again, she drifted away into her memories. *Careful or you'll get trapped in them, as my mother was.* 'And when he was no longer able to eat them...' I nudged.

'Poor George.' She smiled. 'He loved his food, but that chest infection really drained him, and he didn't have the energy to chew so food had to be sloppy stuff he could easily swallow. I promised him when he got better, we'd go out for a steak, but he never did get better.'

Of course he didn't, because she was poisoning him. 'You cooked food and liquidised it, did you?' I waited for her to say, 'yes', pushing down the twinge of sympathy that was growing for this woman, angry for being so easily swayed by her unexpectedly good performance as the grieving widow.

'I tried.' She laughed, a short sound tinged with self-directed criticism and derision cut off by a gulp of despair. 'Imagine how badly I felt when I couldn't even do that for him.' She wiped tears away with a flick of her fingers. 'I was lucky. One of the nurses who came to look after him volunteered to make meals up for him. She'd make a few, put some in the freezer for the days she wasn't here and a few in the fridge. They were perfect: smooth and tasty. He ate most in the early days, and even towards the end, when he was struggling, he admitted they were good and managed a few spoonfuls.'

'One of the nurses made the meals up for you?' Another lie, but not Oonagh's this time. I remember, as clearly as if I was hearing it now, Carol telling me that Mrs Wallace had prepared his meals.

'Yes, we were so lucky. Carol, that was her name, she was a godsend. So kind and compassionate. Nothing was too much trouble for her. She said she had time to spare during the day so was happy to organise the meals for me.'

It didn't matter. Carol may have prepared the food, but it was Oonagh who gave it, she who added the pills. But now that she'd started talking, she wasn't in any hurry to stop and soon, I knew the truth. And my plan – that pathetic plan to learn more about

Oonagh to strengthen my hopes of success with the blackmail –
went up in a puff of smoke.

'Carol used to grind his medication to a powder too, so it was
easier for him to swallow,' Oonagh explained, unaware that every
word was shattering my stupid plan. 'She'd leave it in a little dish
wrapped in cling film and all I had to do was to add it to his food.'

Carol ground his medication?

'We were blessed with her. The day after George died, she
called around to see if there was anything she could do for me.
There wasn't, but she insisted on helping in some way, so volunteered to get rid of all the old medication that had been stored
down here. It was so kind of her, really.'

The medication that had been stored. The open packets. The
pestle and mortar. Carol? 'Very wise of her.' I'd been wrong about
so much, could the thought that was beginning to sprout in the
corner of my mind possibly be right?

I picked up the bag I'd dropped on the floor beside my chair. I
needed to get away to absorb all I'd learnt. 'I'd better be going.'

She got to her feet when I did. 'I hope you find your father,
and that he turns out to be as kind as my George was.'

'Thank you. I'll keep looking.' I looked around the huge room.
'It's a big house to be living in alone.'

'It never seemed that big when George was here. He was such
a larger-than-life character; he filled every space he was in.'

Curious now, I asked, 'Will you stay here alone?'

'Oh, dear me, no. Not even if I had the choice, which I don't.'
My look of surprise made her smile. 'It's a big house to maintain.
George released equity in it several years ago. Now that he's dead,
it will be sold.'

That twinge of sympathy came again, this time I allowed it.
'What will you do?'

'I kept my apartment. I was planning to rent it out but never got around to it. Now, I'll wait till George is buried, then return to it and the life I had...'

Once again, her voice faded, as she drifted into her memories. It was a moment before she spoke, a moment when I mentally kicked myself for misjudging her. For seeing what I'd wanted. People like my father who lied and cheated, not those who sincerely loved.

'It will be the same,' she said, her voice a little stronger. 'But it will be different. George has left such a big hole, but my life is richer for having loved him, for having known someone so amazing even for such a short while. There'll be some money, so I won't need to go back to work.' She wagged her head and smiled. 'For a little while anyway.'

'Right.' I couldn't think of one other word to say. I'd misjudged this woman and had been completely fooled by Carol. I'd had everything wrong.

Goody two-shoes, Carol, how I had underestimated her.

44

I'd been so wrong that I was shocked. Wrong about Oonagh Wallace. Wrong about Carol. It was small consolation to guess I was right about one thing though... George Wallace's end had been hastened along. How could I possibly have guessed it had been by the saintly, empathetic, supremely compassionate nurse, Carol.

I left the grieving widow behind and walked back into the city for my bus home. Everything Oonagh Wallace had told me was examined in minute detail. George had never recovered from his chest infection because someone, aka Carol, was making sure he didn't. His decline was attributed to his underlying cancer. Who'd have suspected?

Obviously neither Oonagh nor the GP had; but they hadn't been inside that locked room. They hadn't seen the open packets of the first Mrs Wallace's medication, or the pestle and mortar used to crush the tablets.

Carol. The crafty bitch. She'd made up meals for George, added a selection of crushed medication to each, and waited for the inevitable consequences.

It wasn't the doing that puzzled me now, it was the why.

I had killed. But I'd had a good reason, both times. I'd got rid of a bully; I'd ensured my mother's care would continue. What possible reason could Carol have? It wasn't as if she'd gain financially even if Oonagh had been left that enormous house. Carol might have been given a gift voucher, a box of chocolates or even a bunch of flowers. People never gave nurses what they needed – money – as if we were above it all, as if being handed over an envelope stuffed with cash would be beneath us.

But if it wasn't money, what was her motivation?

She'd sung Oonagh's praises almost every time I'd met her. Was that it? Did Carol think Oonagh would be better off without him. Perhaps, she had assumed, as I had done, that the widow was going to be left wealthy. Maybe, Carol had designs on the widow herself. I didn't think the widow would swing that way, but then what did I know?

Did it matter?

It bothered me, and I wasn't sure why.

Maybe it was seeing Oonagh's genuine grief. I guessed she'd have clung to every last hour of George's life, and as long as he wasn't in pain, wouldn't have chosen to end it by a minute. It was the kind of love my mother had had for my father. The kind of love neither of my parents had ever had for me.

It was the kind of love that should be nurtured to the very last breath. Carol had chosen to shorten the little time Oonagh had had with George. I wanted to know why.

Jolene, the nurse I had set up to punish for her lack of care, perhaps she wasn't the kind of nurse I should be afraid of. Nor should I be afraid of nurses like me, who killed for a reason. Far more terrifying, were those who killed for no reason at all. Because they could choose anyone... even my mother.

The thought horrified me and brought me to a dead stop in

the middle of the footpath causing a trio of women who were walking behind to divide and walk around me. They turned to stare, and one made a half-hearted movement as if to ask if I was all right. Whatever she saw in my face made her change her mind, link her arm through each of her friends', and hurry down the hill into the city.

I stayed there for several minutes, thinking of my mother. Her vulnerability. How my life would be changed if she died. The loss. It was unbearable, brought tears to my eyes and made me cry out loud startling a cyclist who was passing, his bike wobbling dangerously before he regained control and cycled on. He didn't look back. Why would he? Who cared about a stupid woman standing in the middle of the footpath making an idiot of herself?

I trudged on, my dragging feet rising dust from the summer dry footpath. On automatic, I reached my bus stop and waited, not bothering to check the timetable. I leaned against the wall, barely blinking. It was twenty minutes before the right bus stopped and I climbed on and sat with my nose pressed to the dirty glass of the window as the bus carried on regardless.

It wasn't a driver who knew me, so didn't know to stop and let me off. Lost in my thoughts, it wasn't until someone sat heavily on the seat beside me that I looked through the window and realised I had passed my stop.

It took twenty minutes to walk back up the hill. Exhaustion weighed me down. I just wanted to get home, crawl into bed, and put the world and all its worries out of my head. *My home.* Any thought of moving to something better was gone. I was stuck here. Next to my creepy neighbour.

Or did Theo consider *me* creepy? I was, after all, the one who'd stuck my hand into his letter box, losing my lovely bracelet as a result. What had he done apart from looking at me oddly? And lurking outside my front door at night, making the security light flash on and off with deliberate intent. I mustn't forget that.

Hoping not to see him, I kept my eyes down as I went through the gateway and picked up my pace till I reached my front door. My keys already in my hand, I opened the door, slipped through and shut it behind me. With a worrying drift into paranoia, I pulled one of the chairs over and wedged it under the door handle. Even that didn't seem to allay my stupid fears and I almost laughed to see myself step backwards away from the door without taking my eyes from it, as if the big man was going to put his shoulder to it and break my pathetic defences down.

If I could sleep, things would seem better. Convinced I was right, but still too wary to completely relax, I kicked off my shoes, lay fully clothed on the bed and shut my eyes. Sometimes, despite everything, our bodies know when they've had enough. Mine did, and I fell into a deep sleep within seconds. I would have stayed there, held peacefully in oblivion, if it hadn't been for the heat. Although the sun didn't manage to negotiate the narrow space between the garage and the house, it did shine on the black rubber roofing and turned the always warm space into a furnace. I could have left the windows ajar. They were long but not very high and only opened out about two inches. With them open, the room was warm; with both shut, the heat was oppressive.

There was no logic in leaving them closed. Nothing harmful could slip through the narrow gap when they were open. The dank space outside discouraged most flying insects and the woodlice that crawled through were irritating, not dangerous. It didn't matter, the windows stayed shut. I stayed hot. And awake.

Awake and restless, my thoughts churning around and around, and always, *always*, when they stopped, it was Carol's goody-two-shoes face that was there staring at me with eyes that hid so much.

When night came, darkness settled around me with no cessation of the crushing heat. I pulled off my clothes and lay naked on the bed. I was tempted to open the windows then, had almost decided it was worth it, had got as far as sitting upright, when the security light outside switched on turning the windows into long strips of light. I flopped backwards with my eyes glued to them until they went out. In the darkness, I held my breath, letting it out in a frustrated whoosh when the lights came on again seconds later. On and off they went for a long time. I barely blinked, afraid to miss something, anything, that might happen in the microseconds when they were shut.

When the darkness lasted several minutes, my eyes strained to see if there was any change in the shadows. If there was movement. If somehow, someone or something had managed to sneak inside. I knew I was being ridiculous, but the knowledge didn't make me any less fearful.

My body was rigid, my eyes the only part of me moving, darting back and forth. Then they stopped and widened. It had happened before, many times over the years, and I shouldn't have been surprised. Stress brought them out, and I was so damn stressed I could hear my heartbeat thump thumping in the silence, the beat speeding up as the eyes that had appeared in the darkness shimmered overhead and stared down at me. Only eyes, but I recognised them: Jemma's sad blue ones, Olivia's more world-weary paler ones.

They alone knew what I had done. They alone had the power to punish me.

I had managed to get rid of Jolene without resorting to physical violence. Carol wasn't going to be so easy. And whatever I did, it needed to be a permanent solution. There was only one way to guarantee that. I watched the eyes looking down on me.

Soon there would be a third pair to join them.

45

The security light stayed out and I managed to get a few hours' sleep. Not that it did me much good as I tossed and turned the whole time in a loop of dreams where my mother was being killed by Carol.

There were tears on my cheeks when I finally woke, and I knew I had to get in to see my mother to reassure myself she was all right. It was only six. There wasn't a bus till seven. Too long to wait in fear, so I rang and spoke to the night nurse. Kerry had been there for years, reliable and caring. I'd spoken to her before, several times: it wasn't the first time I'd been worried about my mother in the wee hours. Just the first time I'd worried she was in danger from the very people supposed to be keeping her safe.

'Mum is okay?' I asked after brief greetings.

'Yes, she's fine. I checked in on her a few minutes ago, sometimes she wakes early but she was still out for the count.'

I felt a surge of paranoia. Out for the count, or dead? I wanted to beg her to go back, check, wake her if necessary. If Mother died, I'd be lost, and my life would be empty.

Wouldn't it?

Or would I be free of the millstone around my neck that was weighing more heavily by the year? The thought bounced into my head, startling me – shocking me – I'd never thought this before. Had I? If my mother died, would I be lost, or free?

Kerry was speaking, the words floating by without being heard. Something about being on a run of nights and being tired. I didn't know, or care, and interrupted her without compunction. 'What nurse is on today?'

There was a slight hesitation, as if in protest at my cutting in, before she answered, 'Jenny O'Brien.'

Jenny. One of the good ones. I could relax knowing Mother would be in good hands. I would still go in to double check, but I wouldn't have to rush in on the first bus. 'Great, tell her I'll be in to visit later.' I hung up without waiting for a reply and lay on my bed for several minutes. Had it been the first time I'd thought my life would be better without my mother? I wasn't sure. It wasn't a thought I would allow to linger.

I was going to be a serial killer; I didn't want to be a monster.

* * *

Although the night nurse had put my mind to rest, the shocking thought that my life would be better without my mother made me decide to get the first bus to see her after all. After a quick shower to wash away the stink of body odour, I pulled on fresh clothes and had a glass of water in lieu of breakfast.

The chair was still rammed under the handle. Before taking it away, I pressed my ear to the door for several minutes until I was certain as I could be that nobody lurked outside. When I returned the chair to its usual place, I listened again. Even then, as sure as I was that there was nobody waiting for me, I only opened the door a crack and peered around the edge. My nose crinkled at its first breath of fresh air for several hours. It was so sweet, that when I had courage enough, I opened the door wide and fanned it gently backwards and forwards to encourage the stale stinking air inside to depart. As I did, my eyes were fixed on the corner of the house, afraid I'd see Theo rounding it any moment. The passageway was so narrow, his bulk would fill it and block my exit. On the other end, the gate that led into the garden was always kept locked. I knew because I'd tried it several times.

When it came to a toss-up between ventilation and avoiding Theo, the latter won. I shut and locked the door behind me and speed walked down the driveway out onto the footpath. Only when I was at a distance, did I turn and look back. Nothing to be seen, no monsters chasing me. I didn't slow down though and walked quickly to the bus stop. Too early, I was forced to stand and wait for several minutes before it crested the hillside, stopping when I waved frantically as if afraid it was going to ignore me and drive past.

It was still early when I got to the home. The night staff, probably desperately trying to finish the work before their shift ended, didn't rush to answer my ring on the doorbell. It didn't matter, it was a beautiful summer's morning, already warm but too early to be sticky hot. I sat on the low wall beside the door and rested against the building. If I'd shut my eyes, I probably could have slept to the lulling chorus of the birds in nearby trees. I imagined the night staff opening the door to find me slumped on the wall. Their reaction would depend on who it was. Kerry, who would recognise me, would probably have shaken me awake. Other members of staff, less sensible, and to whom I'd be a stranger, would probably take fright and ring for an ambulance.

I wasn't one for fuss, so kept my eyes open with difficulty. The short amount of sleep, wracked as it was with crazy dreams, had brought me little rest. It seemed a better idea to stay on my feet. The bus driver had been playing one of my favourite Pink songs. I hummed it now and swayed gently to the beat as I approached the door and pressed my nose to the window to see if I could catch a glimpse of anyone coming.

Unfortunately, as was always the way, a care assistant had that very moment arrived at the door. She was as startled to see my face pressing against the glass as I was to see her and both of us leapt backwards. My retreat took me to the edge of a step. I stumbled before tumbling over the low wall I'd been sitting on and coming to a halt, inelegantly, in the shrubbery.

The care assistant, whose name I didn't know, opened the door, and rushed to my assistance. 'Oh God, are you okay? I'm so sorry for startling you.'

The shrub I'd landed in was getting its revenge, clinging to my clothes, scratching and catching me. The care assistant, though willing, wasn't very able and hindered rather than helped. By the time I managed to extricate myself, both my arms were adorned with painful scratches and the T-shirt, one of the few I'd bought new, had acquired a rip that stretched from armpit to neckline.

'Oh God,' the care assistant said again, as if an appeal to the deity might be of assistance. Unless he was going to arrive with a needle and thread, and was an expert in invisible mending, I couldn't see the point in calling for him.

'I'll stick some dressing tape over it, it'll be fine,' I said, holding the edges together with one hand. 'I'm Lissa McColl.' When this didn't elicit a response, I elaborated. 'Cathy McColl's daughter.'

'Oh Cathy! Yes, I heard you often come in early. I've just started. Still learning the ropes.' She looked back to the door. 'I'd better get on. A busy time.' She giggled as if realising she'd said something stupid. 'You'll know of course, being a nurse.'

There didn't seem a need to comment and I followed her into the building.

'You sure you're okay?'

'Fine, don't worry about me. You head off, I can find my own way to Mother's room.'

With a grateful grin, she scooted off down the corridor and vanished into a room.

I was feeling a long way from okay. My mother was asleep. Usually, I'd wake her with a gentle kiss on her cheek, or a slightly less gentle shake. Not that morning. I shut the door behind me, sat in the comfortable armchair and rested my head back. The scratches on my arms stung. My hip hurt from the contact with the wall as I'd fallen over it. My head hurt too, from the thoughts that were ricocheting inside my skull. I shut my eyes, then opened them and looked across the small room to where my mother slept peacefully. Not a care or worry to interrupt her sleep. Nothing to make her twist and turn restlessly. Did she have nightmares, perhaps hearing the words announcing my father's death again and again?

Her expression was relaxed. Few wrinkles marred her pale complexion. Her hair, cut and coloured by experts, was brushed back from her forehead. I ran a hand over my mostly grey, carelessly chopped hair, and used a finger to trace the deepening lines that divided my forehead and separated my eyebrows.

I pushed to my feet and crossed to the small en suite bathroom. The cabinet was packed with the same moisturiser my mother had always used. I'd insisted the status quo was maintained even as the prices of what she used doubled, then trebled as the years passed. I opened a jar of her day cream, dipped a finger in and spread it across my cheek. It felt nice. Cool.

There was an array of cosmetics to choose from. I went through them all, picked out an eyebrow pencil and coloured over my sparse pale brows. Impressed with the result, I added mascara and dark red lipstick before taking a step backward to assess the change. My inexperience showed. I'd been heavy-handed and looked like a clown. Worse, with my ripped T-shirt, I looked like a down-on-her-luck hooker. I rubbed a hand over my face, smudging the mascara and lipstick. The result was a fright, made worse when I rubbed harder, hurting, mashing my face with the flat of my hand until all my features were distorted by swirls of black and red.

The en suite was so small that when everything overwhelmed me and I swayed, the toilet seat was directly behind to catch me. As a nurse, I knew what to do, and I lowered my head between my knees and waited for the world to stop spinning. I had no fear the staff would come in. Once I was there, they left Mother's care to me, so I was able to remain sitting hunched over in the silence of the en suite until I felt able to stand.

It was a shock to look in the mirror and see what I'd done, and it took several applications of cleanser to remove all traces of my stupidity. If only everything was that easy. If we could take a handful of cleanser and wipe away the things we regretted doing. The things that had happened in our past. The thoughts that painted streaks of darkness in our heads, a darkness that leached out to touch everything we did.

I was being foolish: it was tiredness talking. I'd done what was necessary, no more. Only cowards refuse to act for fear of the consequences.

With my face restored to its usual colourless, plain, ugly self, I went back into the bedroom. Mother was still asleep. I opened her wardrobe, and quietly moved hangers in the packed interior until I found something suitable. A cotton shirt I'd bought for her the year before. She'd only worn it once and wouldn't miss it. I dragged off my torn grubby T-shirt, tossed it into the wastepaper basket and pulled the clean shirt on.

Then I sat back on the armchair and shut my eyes. Seconds later, they opened again, and I stared across to my sleeping parent.

If she was dead – how different my life would be.

46

I continued to regard my mother with more than usual curiosity. Only when she stirred, stretched and yawned before opening her eyes, did I turn away. When I looked back, she was watching me. Wishful thinking frequently had me assign emotion to the times, like now, when she looked at me with unusual intent. As if she'd read my mind, she suddenly looked heartbroken, the same way she did that fateful day my father died.

Had I said the words aloud? Did she believe I wished her dead? Because of course I didn't. I might give some thought to how easier my life might be if I didn't have the financial burden of her care to weigh me down. It didn't mean I wished her gone. She was my mother. All I had left.

'Hi, Mum,' I said, getting to my feet and hurrying to her side. I perched on the edge of the bed and leaned down to press a kiss to her forehead. 'I've been waiting for you to wake. How about we get you out of that bed, have a nice shower, then we can have breakfast together. What d'you think?' I didn't expect an answer. Maybe it was my imagination, but her expression faded from stricken to the usual neutral lost one she'd worn since that day so many years before.

Keeping a monologue going, I jollied her into the shower ducking the splashes of water as I soaped her. Sometimes, without saying a word, she'd simply refuse to co-operate. Digging her heels in with the streak of stubbornness that seemed to have come at the same time she'd lost everything else. That morning, perhaps she understood I was feeling a little under par, because she did as I wanted when asked, lifting her arm, her leg, stepping in and out of the shower. Like a child. And I spoke to her like one too, chivvying her along, telling her how good she was being, how pretty she looked when she was dressed, how beautiful when I put her make-up on with far more care than I had given to applying it to my face. But then my mother was a very pretty lady, her nose a refined size, lips a perfect Cupid's bow, eyes a startlingly dark blue.

My father had been a handsome man too. I'd no idea where my remarkable-for-all-the-wrong-reasons features had come from. Mother had said they'd come from him, but she'd been wrong. Or she'd lied to make me happy. Perhaps they'd come from the same twisted genes that had made me a killer.

'There you go, Mum,' I said, sweeping a brush through her hair. 'Shall we have breakfast in the dining room this morning for a change?' I pulled up her wheelchair as I spoke. Although I was used to small spaces, the room was feeling claustrophobic and with the heating on despite it being mid-summer, it was stiflingly warm.

The dining room wasn't far. The double swing doors into it weren't locked, but the interior was dark, blinds shutting out the early-morning sun. 'Hang on, Mum.' I wheeled her chair inside and slid my hand along the wall to find the switch and flood the room with light. It took a bit of fiddling to get the blinds pulled up and allow daylight to brighten the room. 'That's better,' I said, switching out the glaring overhead beams.

I knew my way around and within a few minutes had a pot of tea and a plate of toast on the table. There didn't appear to be any cereal, I didn't think she'd mind. 'Here you are,' I said, holding a triangle of buttered and marmaladed toast to Mother's mouth. Like an automaton, it opened, I popped the morsel inside. It shut, and teeth chewed, lower jaw moving around and around. A cow chewing the cud.

There were two slices for me, both long gone before she'd finished hers. It didn't matter, I had no plans and it suited me to stay away from the garage. When had I begun to think of my accommodation as a garage rather than my home? Possibly around the same time as I'd realised my landlord was more than creepy, that he might, in fact, be dangerous.

With another piece of toast being chewed slowly, I sat back and looked around the elegant stylish dining room. Several round tables were surrounded by comfortable chairs, loose removable covers ensuring they always looked clean. Floor-to-ceiling windows looked out onto a small courtyard furnished with large pots. In the summer, they brimmed with flowers, in the winter, elaborate metallic sculptures took their place. Fitted with tiny lights, they turned the space into a winter wonderland.

This was what the extra money was needed for, all the little things that made it first class, not economy.

Here, Mother was well looked after and safe.

Safe. I needed to make sure she stayed that way. And that meant dealing with Carol. She might never work in the Bartholomew Care Home, or be in charge of my mother's care. But she might.

I'd do anything to keep my mother safe.

Even kill.

I'd killed before, there was nothing to it.

47

As Mother slowly chewed her way through the two slices of toast and drank her third cup of tea, I took out my phone and tapped out a message to Carol.

I'm off today, fancy meeting for coffee later?

Not lunch, I'd stay with Mother, help her with hers and get mine for free. Officially, I was supposed to pay for the privilege, but the only time I'd been asked for payment I looked at the manager with a raised eyebrow until he gave an embarrassed laugh. 'I suppose you do help out quite a bit.'

The subject was never raised again. It was fortunate the management didn't realise how much advantage I took: the slices of bread I tucked into my bag, the rolls of toilet paper and bars of soap I acquired. Pennies compared to the thousands of pounds I paid to them.

Mother had finished her breakfast before I had a reply from Carol.

Sounds good. Where and what time?

Manvers at three?

Okay. See you then.

I'd no idea what I was going to do. Nor did any enlightenment come to me during the remainder of the morning as I sat in the lounge with Mother while the activity co-ordinator did stupid things with bits of foliage and flowers. She insisted on putting pieces into Mother's hands despite knowing she never interacted. Perhaps, she, like me, lived in perpetual hope.

Before lunch, I pushed the wheelchair around the grounds and pulled up to our usual seat under the trees. Leaving Mother to look at the roses, I shut my eyes and tried to think of some way to remove the risk that was Carol from the world.

I could stick with what had worked for Jemma and Olivia. A sharp weapon inserted into the right place. That there was such a choice of weapons freely available made it an easy choice, but age had brought reservations, and a slight dislike of the messiness attached to stabbing someone to death.

There was also the traditionally assumed choice for females – poison. Perhaps. Whatever I finally decided, there was little I could do before our meeting later that day. The idea was to find out a bit more about Carol. Maybe find a weakness to exploit.

I looked across to where my mother was staring blankly ahead. If she noticed the beauty of the roses that were swaying gently in the warm breeze, there was no obvious sign. Nor did her dainty little nose twitch when the breeze swept their sweet scent over us.

My weakness. Not my mother as such, but that lingering

desperate need for her to wake up, turn to me, and tell me how much she loved me.

* * *

When I pushed open the door of the café at six minutes to three, I still had no idea what I was going to do apart from gathering information. That a similar plan had backfired dramatically when I visited Oonagh Wallace didn't stop me hoping for success this time. Being early allowed me to be in control, to watch Carol as she came through the door, and to try to read her unreadable expression.

The café was spacious but popular and I stretched my neck to peer into the far corners in search of an empty table. There wasn't one. Perhaps I looked desperate, because a couple in the corner waved and made *we're about to leave* gestures, tapping their chests and pointing to the door with stupid grins on their faces as if thrilled to be able to be so kind.

'Thanks so much,' I said, waiting as they gathered up bags, books and mobile phones before leaving with a smile.

It was a good table. I could sit with my back against the wall and look out the window to the street. I'd be able to see Carol before she saw me and was aware of my scrutiny. Perhaps even her facial expression might tell me something important. I was always good at grasping at straws.

A woman with a tray balanced in one hand craned her neck in search of a seat. Her eyes landed on my table with its clutter of empty cups and crumbs of past snacks. Perhaps she thought I was done and would be leaving shortly, because she approached with a determined smile on her face. Before she reached me, I'd pulled the two spare chairs nearer, depositing my bag on one, resting my hand proprietarily on the other, prepared to defend my right for possession if I needed to. Maybe it was my stance, or the expression on my face, but when she was almost within touching distance, she stopped, lowered her eyes, dropped her smile, and turned to cross to the other side of the café where she found one empty seat at a table with three other women.

I don't know what she said to them. Something derogatory no doubt because, almost as one, they turned to look in my direction, eyes wide, mouths pursed. Then they put their heads together, that coven of witches, and cackled for the rest of the time I sat in the café guarding my table.

Without reason, as it happened. Ignoring the coven, I turned my attention back to the entrance, waiting for Carol to arrive. She was late. Maybe she thought her time was more valuable than mine. That she was more important. As the minutes ticked by, irritation started to hum along my veins.

I checked my mobile. No message to say she'd been delayed. My thumb hovered over the keyboard mentally writing a message that didn't sound pathetic or, God forbid, needy. Better to be blasé and wait unconcernedly, as if I was happy with my own company and she was an unnecessary addition.

By the time ten minutes became twenty, then thirty, the hum of irritation had become a festering boiling anger that faded fast as the realisation hit me. It wasn't that she was late, more that she wasn't coming at all.

Stupidly, because we weren't really friends, I was overwhelmed by the stinging sense of abandonment. It didn't help that the coven chose that moment to launch into an ear-splitting cackle that reverberated around the café, drawing all eyes, making the staff behind the counter look over in concern. It was the perfect opportunity for me to make my escape without drawing attention to my pathetic plight. Gathering my belongings, I fled the café.

48

There didn't seem to be any option for me but to make my way home. There may have been a very good reason for Carol's failure to turn up. Perhaps she'd had an accident. Maybe she was dead. That of course, would be the best outcome, because I still hadn't come up with a way to rid myself of her.

I was at the entrance to my now despised accommodation before I remembered to keep an eye out for Theo. Then it was too late, he was there, the bulk of him, slap bang in the middle of the driveway.

It was so tempting to make a dash for it, to slip between him and the wall, or run through and flatten the colourful border that edged his garden on the other side. Either would have been a risk. A big man, he had long arms, big hands, he could have easily grabbed me as I passed. Plus, it was cartoon-ridiculous, wasn't it? The big man and the ugly little gremlin.

'Hello.' I forced myself to act as normal as I could manage, but whether it was because there was nothing normal about our relationship or because finally I could admit, if only to myself, that I was sincerely stupidly, pathetically scared of this big lump of a man, the one word came out like a rusty squeak. I swallowed, and managed a better, 'Lovely day, isn't it?' Talking about the weather was what people did, wasn't it? And monsters like him, murderers like me, we could behave like everyone else when needed. 'Well, great talking to you,' I said, despite his not having opened his mouth. He didn't then either, but he did, thank goodness, move to one side to let me pass.

I resisted the desire to run to my door. I did, however, rummage inside my bag, so I had the key in my hand ready to slip into the lock, get inside and lock the door after me. I would have done too if he hadn't sneaked up behind me as if he'd floated. How could such a great big lump move so swiftly, so damn quietly? He was there, his breath hot and heavy on my cheek and billowing down the neck of my T-shirt. The stink of garlic and onions made me instantly nauseous as I turned to stare straight into his big jowly face, his tiny piggy eyes glaring down at me.

'You dropped this,' he said in a curiously high-pitched voice.

My eyes were glued to his face. I was afraid to look down to see what he was holding, convinced I'd see my silver bracelet lying like a traitor across his palm. I was searching for the right words to explain why he'd found it in his letter box – a difficult search because what possible reason could I have for sticking my stupid hand into it. *I was worried about you*, sounded lame and unbeliev-able. It also wasn't true. I hadn't so much been worried about him, as worried about the effect his death might have on me. Nobody who had murdered once, never mind twice, wanted police snooping around.

'Here,' he said.

He was so close, the smell of him overpowering, overwhelm-ing, making my legs weak and my head spin. Darkness spread like tentacles from the little specks that spun around my vision. Spreading, spreading, until that's all there was.

* * *

I've no idea how he got me from the door into my apartment and onto my bed. Had he picked me up in his sumo wrestler arms, held my body close to his chest while he carried me over the threshold like some sleeping virgin bride? I don't know, and when I opened my eyes to see him loom over me, the *how* I got there was the least of my worries.

'You fainted,' he said.

'Yes.' I waited for him to move back so I could sit up. Instead, he stayed hovering above me, his fleshy wet lips opening and closing like a gormless goldfish. I half expected him to drool, to see a long stringy rope of it ooze from his mouth and sway in the draught from the open door before attaching itself to my bare flesh. The thought made me shiver and it was that that made him move.

'You're shivering. You must have caught a chill or something.' He reached for the blanket that lay folded on the end of the bed, shook it out and, with surprising gentleness, draped it over me. 'Should I ring for a doctor, d'you think?'

Ring for a doctor? It was such an unexpected, anachronistic thing to say that I almost laughed. Perhaps his only experience with illness was garnered from watching old-fashioned TV series where local doctors made house calls. It wasn't the time to be admitting that I wasn't even registered with a GP practice. 'No, I'll be fine,' I said, relieved he'd taken a step backwards.

'You're too thin. I bet you don't eat properly.' He looked around the room as if looking for evidence to support his theory.

'I'm just tired.' That was true. Weary of everything. This man. Carol. Playing parent to my mother.

'Right.' He turned back to me. 'You should try to get some

sleep. I've put your phone on the table. You were lucky it didn't break when you dropped it.'

My phone? 'I dropped it?'

He shrugged beefy shoulders. 'I think you were pulling your keys out; it must have got caught and you didn't notice.'

My phone. Not the damn bracelet.

'Anyway, if you're sure you're okay, I'd better get going.'

I rested a hand over my forehead. 'I'm fine. Thank you. You were kind to help me inside.'

'It was like picking up a kitten,' he said and with a nod he was gone.

He shut the door after him, and I was left in the semi-darkness wondering if I could ever get anything right.

I lay for several minutes without moving, trying not to think. Which of course is impossible. I even tried to think of a brick wall, that trick George Sanders used in the *Village of the Damned* to stop those scary alien children reading his mind. It didn't work any better for me than it had for him. Or maybe my thoughts were simply too monstrous to be contained.

Theo had removed my shoes after he lay me on the bed. A thoughtful thing to do. Had he planned to remove more? Had my waking stopped him? The thought of his plump damp hands touching me made me shiver and pull the blanket up under my chin.

He'd been kind though. Taking off my shoes. Covering me in a blanket. Offering to call a doctor. The last made me smile and relax. He couldn't be all bad, could he? And on that unanswerable question, I fell asleep.

A loud knocking on the door woke me, disorientated, thoughts flailing around in my head trying to find purchase. It took seconds for everything to clear, more time to remember what had occurred – that I'd fainted, and Theo had picked me up and carried me to bed. After which, bizarrely, I'd fallen asleep. Not for long: exhaustion still fuzzed my brain. Long enough though for the light to have dropped from semi to complete darkness. Complete darkness? If someone was knocking at the door, the security light should be making the room glow. Perhaps, they'd been knocking for a long time, long enough for the security light to have switched off.

Or perhaps, Theo had switched it off and was outside now, waiting for me to answer. Did he want to take up where he had left off earlier?

Or perhaps he simply wanted to check that I was feeling okay. I suppose it was in a landlord's interest to ensure his lodger didn't die on his premises. That would be awkward and troublesome. Especially, if he wasn't supposed to be renting it out in the first place.

When the knock came again, a rhythmic rat-a-tat-tat, I threw back the blanket and swung my feet to the floor. I waited a moment, afraid to stand too quickly, imagining collapsing to the floor again and Theo having to break down the door to rush to my rescue. His soft marshmallow body would hit it with an ineffective squelch, and he'd be forced to run at it again and again. With a snort, I wondered whether it would be the door or his flabby skin that would burst first.

'I'm coming,' I shouted, and pushed to my feet. My hair was plastered to my head, and I guessed I looked a mess. It didn't matter. I'd reassure him, tell him I was okay and send him on his way.

I turned the catch and pulled open the door. The words of reassurance that were waiting to be said, the ones I hoped would send Theo away happy, were swallowed with a gulp as I stared at my visitor.

49

'Are you going to invite me in?' Carol said, looking behind her as if worried about standing there in the darkness.

All she had to do, the stupid woman, was to take a step backwards to trigger the security sensor and flood the area with blinding light. I'd have liked to have told her to get lost. I didn't though. I still had no plan for getting rid of her, but I was curious about two things. Why she hadn't turned up that afternoon, and how she knew where I lived.

I know I hadn't told her. In fact, I hadn't told anyone. So how did she know?

'Sure,' I said, stepping back and giving a wave. 'Welcome to my humble abode.'

She bent and picked up a cardboard box. 'I come bearing gifts.' She placed the offering on the table, then straightened and looked around, a curious expression on her face. 'Interesting accommodation.'

Interesting? It was a converted garage! 'Yes, I love it, so comfortable and well-appointed.' I sounded like an oily estate agent trying to convince a reluctant potential client. 'Plus, more importantly for me, it's not too expensive and it's all mine.'

She slung her bag over the back of a chair and sat. 'Really sorry about this afternoon. Something unexpected happened that I had to deal with.'

And you couldn't let me know? You left me sitting in that café looking pathetic. Something unexpected – no details – she was lying. 'No worries. I had a really good book with me so was happy to sit with my lunch and get it finished.'

'Good.' She patted the side of the box. 'To make up for it, I stopped on the way and got us coffees and pastries.' She opened the lid as she spoke. 'A cappuccino for you, right?' She held it out to me, a slight smile curving her thin lips, as if daring me to refuse her peace offering.

I might have done. Might have got on my high horse and said no, but confused thoughts were still tangled in my head and caffeine might be the remedy. 'Thank you,' I said, and took the seat opposite.

She pushed the box towards me. 'Have one. I wasn't sure what you'd like so I got pain au chocolat and jam doughnuts.'

'No, thanks.' I was unwilling to eat something that would ooze either jam or chocolate when I bit into it, because I knew either would drip down my chin and make me look as stupid and confused as I felt. I took a mouthful of the coffee. It was good and I took another longer drink praying the caffeine would rush to my brain and help me make sense of what was going on. Because something was. I just wasn't sure what.

Carol shrugged and reached into the box for a jam doughnut.

It was a perfect round sugary ball, and I felt my mouth water in anticipation. 'They look good. Maybe I will have one after all.' I waited until she'd taken a bite from hers to judge the level of jamminess at its core. When nothing dripped from hers, I took a tentative bite from mine, more a nibble really, and wanted to cry as jam gushed into my hand and dripped in a red sugary mess to the table. If it had been possible, I'd have thought Carol had set me up, but it wasn't possible, was it? She'd hardly made the damn things herself.

'I hate it when that happens,' she said, taking another bite from hers.

I put the doughnut down, positioning it on top of the splodge of its innards that marked the table, then got to my feet and went to the kitchen sink and rinsed the mess from my fingers. Carol had finished her doughnut when I returned. Instead of doing as I had done, she brushed her sugary fingers on the leg of her jeans sending sparkling crumbs flying to the floor. It was such a careless, thoughtless act that it took my breath away.

I needed more caffeine to get my brain working. Lifting the paper cup, I drained it in a few gulps.

'Good coffee, isn't it?' Carol said, sipping hers with ladylike decorum.

It was so tempting to pick up the remnant of that stupid doughnut and fire it at her. But with my current run of luck, I'd probably miss. 'What are you doing here?'

She did a good cartoon impression of being outraged, rearing back in the chair, mouth and eyes wide. 'Honestly, that's not very nice! I told you. Trying to make amends for earlier.'

I hadn't believed her the first time she said it, but now the lie was more obvious. It was her expression; it didn't look remotely apologetic. The caffeine hadn't yet cleared my thoughts, but I'd had enough of this woman. 'How did you know where I lived? I know I've never told you.'

'No,' she agreed. 'You didn't tell the agency about your change of address either.' She shook her head and tutted loudly. 'You really should have done, you know. Very naughty of you, plus bloody annoying to put me to the trouble of having to follow you.'

Nothing was making sense. 'Why—'

Carol banged the table with the flat of her hand. It sent the disposable cups toppling, the remains of the coffee from hers trickling out and sending a stream racing across the table. It hung on the edge for a few seconds before starting to drip drip to the floor. 'Why?' She swept her hand over the table sending cups and the box of pastries to the floor. 'I recognised you. From the very beginning. And I could see in your eyes that you recognised me too.'

Carol was right. I thought I'd recognised her from the start. I just hadn't realised she'd felt the same. My head was feeling muggy. Muggy, but I could still think. I had recognised her, she'd recognised me. From where? My thoughts whirled backwards through the years. It had been something in her eyes that had seemed so familiar. I drew a quick breath as my thoughts ground to a halt in a playground many years before. *Jemma.* I remembered her eyes; they'd haunted me ever since. Why hadn't I realised? She'd had an older sister. 'You're Jemma's sister?'

50

Carol laughed, a loud chilling sound that filled the small space and bounced off the walls. There was a hint of madness in the sound, more than a touch in the eyes that glared at me across the table.

'I'm right, aren't I?' It made sense. I'd killed Jemma, and all these years later her sister had come to get her revenge.

The manic laughter had brought tears to Carol's eyes. She lifted a finger, wiped one away and flicked it towards me. I saw it coming, a bizarrely long stretch of water, too grossly enormous to be a teardrop. I ducked to avoid it. It must have looked hilarious because her laugh rang out again. 'Your face,' she said pointing.

My face? I reached a hand up. To make sure it was still there. She wasn't making any sense. 'I am right, aren't I?' I asked again.

She seemed to be finding it all so damn funny, shaking her head and snorting. 'No, you're not right, you idiot? Who the hell is Jemma?'

Jemma, the girl I killed years ago. *Had I said that aloud?* There was no change to Carol's expression so possibly not. If I had, she'd be looking horrified, shocked not amused. 'Someone I knew a long time ago.'

'You think you recognise me because I look like some girl from your past?'

Did I? It had been something in Carol's eyes that seemed familiar to me. If not Jemma, perhaps some relation of Olivia? I had known nothing about the woman my father had bigamously married apart from the one salient fact that he had loved her more than my mother – more than me.

'That's not what you recognise in me, Lissa,' Carol said, her voice low and almost kind. 'You recognised in me, exactly what I recognised in you. Not a person, you stupid woman. It's far more elemental than that – you recognised the killer in me, as I recognised it in you. We both like to kill.'

Her eyes... is that what I had seen? A reflection of my own base nature? Perhaps. She wasn't correct though. I didn't *like* to kill. I just needed to on occasion. But she, I could see it now that her mask was off. Hidden behind her carefully contrived façade of caring nurse, was a woman who killed because she liked to.

'I kept an eye on you. Bored myself rigid meeting you for lunch and coffee trying to suss out your MO. I pumped the agency admin for gossip, but it seemed you were as careful as I was, there were no hints of any wrongdoing. No suspicious deaths on your watch.'

I was ridiculously horrified. 'I have never, ever killed a patient in my care!'

'Really,' she said, looking genuinely surprised. 'How strange. I do, and with such loving care that the families think I'm wonderful. So do the staff I work with. And the agency. That's why I get the plush jobs, you see. It's a great career move.' The corners of Carol's mouth turned down. A sad clown face made for effect. 'I was very careful to keep my tracks covered.'

I remembered Oonagh Wallace singing her praises. 'You did a good job.'

'Yes.' Carol nodded in acknowledgement. 'I had thought we were kindred spirits. That we could maybe, you know, share our experiences.' She bared her teeth in a snarl. 'But then you went to visit Mrs Wallace and I knew I was wrong about you.' The burst of anger faded quickly. 'Oh yes, I know all about your visit. I've kept in touch with her, and it so happened I called to see her that very afternoon.'

'She...' I couldn't think what I wanted to say.

'Yes, she told me about the odd woman who called with a bizarre story about being George's daughter. When she described you – she was rather cruel about your nose – I knew it was you.'

'You got rid—' I waved a hand.

'Of the evidence? Yes, it was all so easy. I was being so helpful to the grieving widow.'

I remembered how sad Mrs Wallace had been. How I'd completely misjudged her. It seemed suddenly important to get Carol out of my home. 'Right,' I said and stood. No, I *tried* to stand. Something was wrong. I looked at my hand. It was in front of me, my fingers extending the width of the table, too long and heavy for me to move. And my legs, they'd rooted into the concrete floor of the garage. I imagined them pushing through it, deep into the ground underneath, roots creeping to the earth's core. 'There's something—'

'Wrong?' Carol grinned, her mouth stretching to fill her face. Long pointed teeth parted to show a gaping dark hole, a huge one big enough to swallow me whole. 'What makes you think there's something wrong? Are you feeling out of sorts perhaps?'

I looked to where my empty coffee cup lay on the floor. I'd drained every drop of it. Yet again, I'd got it wrong. Carol hadn't fixed the damn jam doughnuts, but she had put something into the coffee. 'Poison?' I tried to get more words out, but that was it.

'Gosh no!' Carol raised a hand to her mouth in mock horror. 'Although poison is regarded as a woman's weapon, it's not something I'd want to tinker with. Well, not precisely.' She stretched and linked her hands behind her head. 'Once I decided we weren't kindred spirits, I knew I had to get rid of you. I've acquired a variety of medication over the years. It proves very useful. I was helping in the operating theatres of Bath United last year. They leave all kinds of stuff lying around so I grabbed a couple of ampules they use for anaesthesia. Muscle relaxant, to be specific. You won't be able to move for a few hours till it wears off.'

She wasn't lying. Try as I might, I couldn't move, not even eyelids that had shut on the last blink and refused to open again. Unable to move, to speak, and now to see, terror overwhelmed me.

'Mind you,' she carried on calmly as if she was discussing the weather forecast. 'You won't be able to move then either.' She giggled, curls of laughter that wriggled into my ears, and burrowed into my brain. 'I suppose you can guess why.'

It wasn't hard. Whatever she had planned for me, being alive at the end wasn't the outcome. Oddly, I didn't care for myself, but who'd look after Mother and make sure she'd have the things she loved. A tear squeezed from between my eyelids. I could feel it sliding slowly, then gathering momentum. It ran into the corner of my mouth, I couldn't move, but I could taste the salt.

Now that I was incapacitated, it looked as if Carol was in no hurry to finish up. I could hear her shuffling in her seat, as if settling in for the long haul. Perhaps that was her plan, to sit and watch me die. She didn't want it too easy. If she had, she could have given me more of that drug to stop me breathing. No, she was drawing it out for her amusement. If I could speak, I'd beg her to let me go. I'd tell her my mother needed me, that she couldn't live without me.

Would she see it as the lie that it was? My mother didn't need me, she never had, never would. It was me who needed her, me with my stupid pathetic desire for her to love me. The home would look after her without my input. She might not get the brand of make-up she liked or the right shade of lipstick. It didn't matter, she wouldn't care or even notice. I was doing it for me. All these years. To show everyone what a bloody wonderful daughter I was, how much I loved her, how good I was. How deserving of love.

Both my eyes and nose were running, my face wet with a mixture of tears and snot. I was glad I couldn't see Carol's expression, the disgust that would be written across it.

I could hear more shuffling, then the squeak of the chair as she got to her feet. I strained to listen, trying to pinpoint where she was, what she was doing. What she was going to do to me.

'I'm just tidying up,' she said, as if she could read my mind. 'I need to get rid of the evidence that you had company. We don't want to give the police ideas, do we?'

It sounded like she was planning to make my demise look like suicide. I was grateful, it meant my death wouldn't be protracted and possibly painful.

'You have some interesting books,' she said.

I heard a rustle as she slid one from the bookshelf, the clicking sound of pages being flicked. Some serial killers were particularly sadistic. I hoped she didn't get any ideas.

The creak of the chair told me she'd sat again. 'Once I knew where you lived, I spent some time watching you. You live a quiet life, don't you? I didn't see one visitor. Makes my job a lot easier.'

More shuffling. I wondered if it was time.

'That security light was a bit of a pain.'

The security light? Poor Theo, I'd blamed him.

'But I was able to have a good look around. That's why I know you have a gas cooker. Cylinders, that must be so inconvenient.'

The cylinders were located to the far side of the garage, out of view. I so rarely cooked that I'd never had to change the one that was connected when I moved in. 'I'll keep an eye and change if it's necessary,' Theo had said. Being kind. He'd only ever been kind and how did I repay him? With suspicion. And now he'd have to deal with a dead body in his illegal apartment. If there was a way to relieve him of this hardship, I'd have taken it, but my hands were tied, or might as well have been.

I strained to open my eyes but all I managed to do was give myself a headache. Or maybe that was the drug. It was probably to blame too for my hallucinations.

The squeak and scrape of the chair as Carol stood alerted me to her movement, but nothing prepared me for her next action. If I'd been able, I'd have screamed in shock as my chair was tilted back to a forty-five-degree angle and dragged across the floor. It was dropped back on its four feet with a bang. I'd probably have fallen from it if a hand hadn't clamped itself like a vice onto my shoulder.

It wasn't hard to guess where she'd taken me. To my small kitchen and the gas cooker. I'd be found with my head stuck in the oven.

It seemed my destiny was to be as ungainly in death as I had been all my life.

_____

51

There was nothing I could do but to listen to the sounds of my impending death being organised behind me. My funeral dirge. The clink of the oven door opening, the clunk as it was carelessly dropped down, the metallic rattle from the racks inside. It seemed a fitting end for a life that suddenly seemed pointless.

My life. All those years waiting for my mother to wake up and tell me she loved me. What a pathetic snivelling fool I had been. I should have left her, as she had left me, as my father had. If I could have laughed, I would've done. What a time to have an epiphany, to realise the waste I'd made of my life.

'Any last requests?' Carol snorted. 'Oops, silly me, you can't answer, can you? How frustrating for you.'

Among so many regrets – never having travelled outside the UK, never having fallen in love, woken up beside a man, *slept* with a man, so very many regrets – the one that really rankled was letting Carol get away with what she was about to do. I couldn't even do what Jemma had done all those years before. I couldn't look Carol in the eye and imprint myself on her so that I would haunt her for the rest of her miserable life, the way Jemma haunted me. I didn't even have that satisfaction.

Or maybe serial killers weren't haunted in the same way. It was small comfort that I would die never having had that accolade.

'Right.'

Carol sounded satisfied. Good to know something was going right for someone.

'Okay, Lissa, this is it. End of the road for you. When I hear, as I'm sure I will, that you were found dead, I'll be sure to show a proper level of sorrow. Hell, I might even go to your funeral. It would be nice for you to have at least one mourner, wouldn't it?'

I wanted to tell her she was wrong, that Jason Brooks would go. The solicitor had always been kind to me. Would he shed a tear when he heard? My mother – would she be told? Would it make the slightest smidgeon of difference to her life if she was told that her darling loving daughter had taken her own life because she obviously couldn't take it any more. Would she weep for me when she heard?

I desperately wanted someone to cry for me.

Carol was shuffling behind me, close enough that I could smell her breath, rancid and stinking as if it oozed from her rotten core.

'Just need to get you onto the floor,' she said. It was disconcerting to feel my body being moved and jolted as she tilted the chair backwards. She was being surprisingly careful, lowering me slowly until my head was resting on the floor and my knees were pointing to the ceiling. I guessed it was all in her plan to make it look like suicide. No bruises to alert the police that someone else might be involved.

Her hands were on me, pulling me off the chair to the floor, grunting and muttering as she worked. My cheek was pressed to the cool linoleum. I was bizarrely grateful to feel anything, to have a connection with something solid.

Carol took the chair away. I listened to her footsteps crossing the floor, the clunk as she replaced the chair where it should be. All would look completely normal – apart from my body and my head stuck in the oven.

'Right,' Carol said again. As if there was anything right about what she was doing. Anything at all right in my world. I wasn't in any position to debate the point. Her hands manoeuvred me, sliding me on the floor, pulling my arms. Then, grunting, she hauled my upper body upward and laid it down. Onto the oven door I guessed, feeling the edge of the door pressing into my ribs, and a greasy smell that indicated my lack of housekeeping skills.

My chin was repositioned, my hands lifted and placed palm down on the door either side of my head. When one immediately flopped to the floor, she took a swipe at my head, connecting with a loud crack. As if it was my fault my poor arm wouldn't stay where it was placed.

This time, when she pulled it up, she caught hold of my hair and yanked it up, slipped my hand underneath then dropped my head on top. 'That's better,' she said, satisfied. 'That's the scene set, Lissa. What a shame you can't see what a good job I've done.'

I heard her move around me, her foot brushing against my hip as she leaned forward to examine the workings of the cooker. Luck was with her. It was an old one. Perfectly serviceable but without many of the safety features modern gas cookers had. If the flame went out, for instance, the gas didn't automatically cut off. The gods were on Carol's side.

Working the oven was a two-handed procedure, one to turn on the gas, one to press the ignition for the flame. Carol would only need the first. It took only seconds for her to figure it out, then I heard the soft hiss as gas started to flow. I could smell it and knew this was to be my end.

So many regrets... so many...

52

The afterlife was edged in light with a multitude of colours like dust motes in the sun. That was my first thought. My second was that it was comfortable and warm, and I felt safe. I drifted, wondering if this was it, that my destiny was to live this way for endless days. It didn't seem so bad, so perhaps it wasn't hell. Despite the two people I had killed, perhaps I was being given a chance and this was Limbo, and I was awaiting redemption before my ascension to heaven.

That thought was lazily bouncing around when I realised something that made me happy – wherever I was in the under-world, it seemed I could move. I lifted my hand, then opened my eyes to look at it. I expected to see it floating in a sea of light. Not silhouetted against the face of a man I'd never expected to see again.

'You're awake!'

Theo. Sitting beside my bed, holding my other hand in his big soft, sweaty paw.

I was awake. Not dead. My eyes flicked around, taking every-thing in. The underworld was a curtained cubicle. Probably in the Bath United. The information came to me in chunks, dazzling me. I remembered the smell of gas so clearly. I hadn't imagined it. Hadn't imagined Carol's craziness. 'What happened?' Theo squeezed my hand. It was strangely comforting.

'I was worried about you after you fainted and went to check how you were. That woman,' – he screwed up his face – 'she was coming out. That made me suspicious to start with. You never have visitors.'

So he had been keeping an eye on me, I wasn't totally wrong about everything. Just about Carol.

'Then,' Theo said, 'I caught the smell of gas, so I pushed her, and she fell back into the apartment. I saw you then, your head in the cooker.' He gave me a shaky smile. 'You gave me a fright; I can tell you. For a second, I thought I was too late, but when I picked you up, I could feel you breathe so I took you outside and lay you on the ground. Then I locked the door with that evil woman inside.'

Inside with the gas. 'Is she dead?' What a perfect outcome that would be.

Theo's eyes widened. 'No, of course not. I turned off the gas before I picked you up. The police took her away.' He shook his head. 'She was screaming, trying to bite them, telling them that she'd killed stronger men than them, and she'd do it again. Mad as a hatter, I'm guessing.'

No, I didn't think so, or at least no madder than anyone else. She'd have known she was caught and had put on an act for her captors. A clever manipulative woman, she'd work the system to her advantage. It would be psychiatric care, not prison for her. But whatever happened, whenever she was released, she'd never nurse again. My mother was safe. Carol wouldn't be causing me any more trouble.

Theo was waiting for my comment. 'Oh dear.' It was all I could manage.

Theo laughed. 'She tried to kill you, and that's all you have to say.'

'It's a lot to take in.' I was trying to remember if I had given Carol anything she could use against me. She said she'd recognised the killer in me. That wasn't going to prove anything. I had a vague memory that I'd mentioned Jemma's name, but no more than that. I was safe.

'The police want to talk to you, of course. They said they'd come to see you tomorrow when you'd be feeling better.'

I felt fine. Whatever drugs Carol had given me had obviously worn off. 'How long have I been here?'

He checked his watch before answering as if to make sure he was giving me correct information. 'Six a.m.'

Six! I'd been out for hours.

'A doctor examined you when you came in. He took some blood too.' Theo looked behind him. Perhaps he thought the doctor would magically appear at the mention of his name. 'He said he'd be back when he had results.'

That could be hours yet. I didn't fancy staying there for any longer than necessary. 'There's no point in me hanging around waiting. I feel fine.' Without warning, I pulled my hand back and pushed into a sitting position. No dizziness. Nor was there when I slid my feet to the floor and stood. It was a chill from the floor that alerted me to what was missing – my shoes. 'I can get a taxi home.'

'No,' Theo said firmly. 'I have the car with me, I can drive you home.' His expression turned apologetic. 'Well, not home actually. It's a crime scene, you understand. They might be finished, but I think we'd better wait till the police say you can return.'

Could I afford to stay in a hotel? This was Bath, nothing was cheap.

'You can stay with me,' Theo said quietly. 'I have plenty of room.'

While I was considering his invitation, the curtains parted and a young man wearing scrubs and a frown came through. He stared at me in surprise.

'This is the doctor,' Theo said.

'Good,' I said, resisting an almost overwhelming need to say *Doctor Who*. Maybe the drugs weren't completely out of my system. 'I want to leave. I feel fine and there's no point in me taking up space unnecessarily.'

The doctor shrugged. 'No problem.' He lifted the clipboard he was holding. 'I've had the results back. You were given quite a concoction of drugs, but none should have any long-term complications.' He smiled. 'Looks like the muscular paralysis has worn off already. As long as you're not planning to drive, I'm happy to let you go. You're a nurse, you know to look out for anything out of the ordinary. Either come back here, or go to your GP, if you've any issues.' And with a nod, he was gone.

'Let's get out of here,' I said to Theo. 'And yes, thanks, I'd be grateful for a place to stay for tonight.'

* * *

I'd never been further than the hallway of Lily Cottage before. If I'd thought about it, I'd have pictured a typical old man's abode, worn and uncared for, smelling of unwashed clothes and poor personal hygiene.

The reality was completely and surprisingly different. He took me into a comfortable and elegant sitting room and made me sit, bustling around me, placing plumped cushions behind my head. 'I'll get you a drink. Tea or coffee?'

I was thirsty. 'Tea would be nice, thank you.'

'Okay, I'll be back in a jiffy.'

And he was, with a tray laden with a pretty cup and saucer, a matching milk jug and sugar bowl, and a fat teapot in a different floral pattern. 'Here you go,' he said, filling one cup and adding milk when I nodded. 'Now you drink this while I go next door and cook you up a breakfast.'

Maybe it was the after-effects of everything that was causing me to feel incredibly lethargic. I sipped the tea, refilling the cup when it was empty, and sipping that. I was on my third cup, my thirst finally quenched, when he returned.

'Breakfast is ready. I thought we could have it next door. It's a lovely morning and there's a nice view over the garden.'

The room that stretched across the back of the house was a stunning space decorated in cream and duck-egg blue. The kitchen was modern and sleek. A table sat in front of double doors that looked over a huge lushly planted garden. It was incredibly beautiful.

'Now, you sit here,' Theo said, holding out a chair for me. 'You'll get the best view of the garden.' He hurried over to the cooker and brought back a hot plate. 'Bacon, eggs and sausages. Sorry, no beans.'

'Wow, this is great.' And it was. I hadn't realised till that moment how hungry I was. Theo sat with his breakfast, and we ate in companionable silence until we were both finished.

'Coffee?' He held up the pot and poured when I nodded.

'This is very kind of you,' I said. It was. I'd given him no reason to be so good to me.

His expression was serious, almost sombre when he looked at me. 'It's the least I can do. I should have replaced that cooker a long time ago. Modern ones cut the gas flow when the flame goes out.' He hesitated, then said, 'You don't have to tell me,' he said, 'but why was she trying to kill you?'

Why? My head was still too woozy to be completely sure, but I think it was revenge. She'd seen me as some kind of co-conspirator, and I'd let her down by asking questions about George Wallace. Perhaps she saw me as some kind of loose cannon. I liked that thought. I needed to get my story straight though if the police were going to come asking questions the following day. I needed to be careful not to implicate myself. I couldn't say I'd known about Carol's attempt on Mr Wallace prior to his death. If she was going to stick with her insanity route, she was unlikely to contradict anything I said, so that left me free to tell a tale that buried her, and kept me safe. It was good practice to try it out on Theo.

'She's a nurse, and I think she might have helped a man in her care to die.' I shrugged. 'It was something she said that alerted me. She was taking medication belonging to him to the pharmacy to be disposed of. I was surprised, because it's protocol to keep all medication for two weeks after someone dies, in case there's any question about the death. When I mentioned that, she laughed and said that was exactly why she was getting rid. She tried to brush it off as a joke, but there was something about the way she said it. I wasn't happy.'

I shook my head and put on my sad face. 'I stupidly allowed her to see I was shocked, and I think she must have guessed I was going to report what she'd said.'

'And were you?'

I looked at Theo's round placid face. He was a genuinely kind man. He'd never understand that I had been planning to take matters into my own hands, that I'd planned to ensure Carol could never hurt another person. 'Yes, I was going to tell the agency that I was worried. They'd have had no choice but to follow it up.'

'They'll do a post-mortem and discover the truth, won't they?'

'Yes,' I said. 'It will be devastating for his poor wife. She'd trusted Carol. She shouldn't have.'

Theo stirred sugar into his coffee, the spoon clinking against the sides of the cup. 'You'll have to take time off, won't you?'

I looked out across the beautiful garden. It would be nice to stay there and relax. 'No, I can't afford to, I'm afraid.' I'd already taken too much time off.

I don't know why, but I found myself telling Theo about my mother. He was a restful man, didn't interrupt with silly questions, merely nodding now and then to indicate he was listening. 'I love her and want her to have the best.'

'You're a good daughter.'

The very words I wanted to hear from my mother. They brought quick tears to my eyes and a tremble to my lips. The after-effects of the drugs were making me soft and stupid. I needed to be careful.

53

Without a word, Theo got to his feet and left the room. I sat and drank my coffee, looking out at the garden. I remembered those thoughts I'd had when I was about to die. They lingered: all those things I'd never done, the idea that I'd wasted my life. But I had a duty to my mother; her care wasn't going to change.

When Theo returned a short time later, he was holding a photograph frame. It looked lost in his big hands. He stared at it for a moment before handing it across the table.

Surprised, I took it and looked at the image. A young girl. Her head thrown back in laughter, her lips parted, hair tumbling around her face. If Jemma had grown up, this is how she'd have looked. I stared at Theo in horror. 'Who is this?' The words came out louder and harsher than I'd expected, and I could see him look at me in surprise.

'It's my daughter. Lizzie.'

Lizzie, not Jemma. Of course, it wasn't Jemma, what was I thinking? 'I'm sorry,' I said, my voice quieter.

'No need to apologise. You've been through so much I really

don't know how you can sound so normal. I admire you, Lissa. I'd like to think that Lizzie would have been as brave.'

Would have been? I looked at the photograph again. 'She's dead?'

'Yes. She was about your age. Always full of life. Always laughing, the way she is in that photo.' His face froze in a mask of misery. 'She was on a beach holiday with three friends. They went swimming. Only two of them came out. The authorities said Lizzie must've been caught in some undercurrent and wasn't a strong enough swimmer to get free. She was swept out to sea. Her body was found a week later.'

What could I say but the standard, pathetically useless, 'I'm so sorry'?

He nodded in acceptance. 'It's been hard. I miss her every day.' He jerked a thumb over his shoulder. 'It was Lizzie's idea to convert the garage. She wanted to be independent and thought it would give her an income while she studied.' He laughed, shaking his head at the memory. 'She put adverts up everywhere before heading off on that holiday.'

I remembered the tatty advert I'd seen. Now I understood.

'I thought I'd taken them all down.' He smiled at me. 'It seems I missed one. When you rang, I was going to explain but,' – he shrugged – 'you sounded so sad. Then you told me your name.' Colour flushed his cheeks. 'The similarity staggered me, and when you arrived, and I saw how like Lizzie you were...' His sigh was a sad lonely sound that seemed to deflate him. 'I wanted you to take the apartment, to have someone real to chase away the ghost.' He rubbed a hand over his face, suddenly looking older, frailer. 'You wouldn't understand. My wife died when Lizzie was eight; since then, there had been just the two of us. I miss her so terribly.'

I wanted to tell him I understood completely, wanted to share my story, but I was afraid doing so would diminish his. A sad case of *my loss is worse than yours*. Was the death of a child a greater tragedy than that of a parent? I dropped my gaze to the photograph again, to the sunny smiling girl with her future ahead of her, a great life, a loving father. Compare her loss to that of my father – that cheating, scheming, bigamous liar. There was no contest.

What about Jemma? How had her loss impacted on her family?

And Olivia?

All the pain I had caused.

Theo reached for the coffee pot. 'Some more?' He waited till I'd shaken my head before topping up his cup with the remnant of the pot. The small cup was lost in his hands as he cradled it. He took a sip and continued to hold it as he spoke. 'I bet you thought I was a creepy old man always looking at you, but you reminded me so much of Lizzie.'

I looked at the photograph again. He had to be joking. 'I don't see the similarity.'

'It's there. You both have gorgeous wide mouths built for laughter.'

Gorgeous wide mouths? Laughter? When had I laughed last? When my mother was alive; when my father was? I touched the tip of a finger to the face in the photograph. 'She doesn't have my big nose.'

'It's perfectly in proportion,' he said. 'You're a lovely looking girl.'

He was seeing me through eyes coloured by love for his dead daughter. Did it matter?

* * *

The days passed quickly. The police arrived to take my statement, assuring me that Carol wouldn't see the light of day for a long time.

'As well as the attempt on your life,' the detective said, 'she's confessed to administering medication in order to bring about an early death to several people in her care.'

'She's a serial killer,' I said.

The detective shut his notebook and put it away. 'Yes, she is.'

'I wouldn't like to be a serial killer.'

He was possibly used to hearing strange utterances but was obviously taken aback and looked to his fellow detective for help. This man, who'd not said a word since they'd arrived ten minutes before, merely raised an eyebrow and said nothing. Abandoned, the detective chose to ignore my remark and got to his feet. 'For the moment, it's been decided that Ms Lyons isn't capable of standing trial. Should that change, we will of course let you know.'

I signed my statement, and that was that.

* * *

'They said I can go home,' I said to Theo after they'd gone.

'You could,' he said, 'or you could stay here.' He waved a hand around the living room where we sat. 'I rattle around this big house, it's nice to have someone else here. You could have your own key and come and go as you please.'

Replace his daughter.

'I have another proposition for you,' he said.

Or maybe to replace his wife.

Luckily, he wasn't looking at me to see my disgust and disappointment, because once again, I was wrong.

'I need someone to run my website for me.'

It was so unexpected, I laughed. 'Your website?'

'Yes. I'm a writer, it helps me keep in contact with my readers.' He looked slightly embarrassed. 'You've probably never heard of me. I write under the name T.R. Bridges.'

Never heard of him! He was up there with Stephen King. When I came to see the apartment, he'd said he scribbled for a living. *Scribbled!* 'I've read all your books,' I said.

'Good, well that's a help. So, what do you think?'

'I've never run a website before.' I hadn't but I could learn. I grinned at him, saw the answering smile on his face. This could work. 'I could learn though.'

'I'd pay you the same as you get as a nurse and include your accommodation, of course.'

'It's a deal.'

* * *

A few days later, when I mentioned going to visit my mother, Theo insisted on taking me.

'I can drive you there, when you want to come home ring me and I'll pick you up.' He held a hand up to stop any argument I might have made. 'Honestly, I'd be happier. Your body is still processing all the drugs that woman gave you, and I'd just be worried if you went by bus.'

Well, it was kinder to give in, wasn't it?

It had been almost a week since I'd seen Mother. She was sitting in her chair in her room, facing the TV. She didn't turn to look at me as I opened the door, nor look at me as I bent to kiss her cheek.

'I've lots to tell you,' I said, dragging over a spare chair. Did she understand a word I said? I had no idea but putting all that had happened into words helped clear my thoughts.

Mother didn't react, not even when I explained how close I'd come to death. Not a glimmer of distress. 'I've been staying with my landlord ever since. He seems to enjoy fussing over me.' I explained about his dead daughter. 'He says I remind him of her. In fact, he often calls me Lizzie.' When it happened the first time, he'd apologised and I told him not to worry, a rose by any other name yadda yadda. He laughed, but I noticed it happened again, and now, he calls me Lizzie more often than Lissa. 'I don't pull him up on it, Mum. If I remind him of his long-dead daughter, if caring for me affords him comfort, and gives his life purpose, isn't that good?'

And if he looked upon me as a daughter...

I'd already sussed out that he had no other relatives. Who else would he leave his big detached Bathford house to when he died, except his new daughter? My perceived similarity to her made him vulnerable to being manipulated; I knew it wouldn't be hard to persuade him to ensure I was comfortably taken care of when he kicked this earthly bucket.

As soon as I was certain he'd done so, that end could be persuaded to come sooner.

It could. But there was one huge problem. I'd become genuinely fond of the man. If I reminded him of his dead daughter, he never reminded me of my long-dead father – and that was in his favour.

Anyway, as I'd said to the police, I didn't want to be a serial killer.

So, I'd leave Theo alone.

At least for the moment.

ACKNOWLEDGMENTS

My writing journey has been full of ups and downs, but the one constant has been the people who have helped and encouraged me along that journey.

I'm lucky to be currently published by the wonderfully dynamic Boldwood Books whose team are not only enthusiastic and supportive but endlessly patient. A special thanks goes to my editor, Emily Ruston, who offers unfailing guidance, encouragement and support.

I love being a writer – and being part of such a wonderful community. Many of my fellow authors help to keep me sane – especially Leslie Bratspis, Jenny O'Brien, Anita Waller, Judith Baker, Keri Beevis, Pam Lecky. And if they don't succeed, there are the reviewers and bloggers who do – so many wonderful people but I'd like to give a special mention to just a few: Lynda Checkley, Beverley Ann Hopper, Allison Valentine, Donna Morfett, and Sarah Westfield.

Jason Brooks wanted to see his name in a book – I hope I did you justice, Jason.

Real world meet-ups are a little more fun than the virtual world – I'm lucky to be a member of the Bath and Bristol Crime Book Club and would like to take this opportunity to say a big hi and thanks for the fun. In our regular meetings we might not solve every writing-related conundrum, but it isn't from lack of trying.

A special thanks, as always, to my family and friends.

ABOUT THE AUTHOR

Valerie Keogh is the internationally bestselling author of several psychological thrillers and crime series. She originally comes from Dublin but now lives in Wiltshire and worked as a nurse for many years.

Sign up to Valerie Keogh's mailing list here for news, competitions and updates on future books.

Follow Valerie on social media:

facebook.com/valeriekeoghnovels
x.com/ValerieKeogh1
instagram.com/valeriekeogh2
bookbub.com/authors/valerie-keogh

ALSO BY VALERIE KEOGH

The Lodger

The Widow

The Trophy Wife

The Librarian

The Nurse

The Lawyer

The Housekeeper

THE

Murder

LIST

THE MURDER LIST IS A NEWSLETTER DEDICATED TO ALL THINGS CRIME AND THRILLER FICTION!

SIGN UP TO MAKE SURE YOU'RE ON OUR HIT LIST FOR GRIPPING PAGE-TURNERS AND HEARTSTOPPING READS.

SIGN UP TO OUR NEWSLETTER

BIT.LY/THEMURDERLISTNEWS

Boldwood

Boldwood Books is an award-winning fiction publishing company seeking out the best stories from around the world.

Find out more at www.boldwoodbooks.com

Join our reader community for brilliant books, competitions and offers!

Follow us
@BoldwoodBooks
@TheBoldBookClub

Sign up to our weekly deals newsletter

https://bit.ly/BoldwoodBNewsletter

Made in United States
Troutdale, OR
12/05/2023

15376979R00166